Britta
Matt's

Everything dissolved for her in that instant. She
wanted to run, yet she wanted to stay forever.
Nothing made sense, and she wasn't aware
that she was crying until Matt dropped to his
haunches in front of her and touched her cheek.

"Tears? What's this all about?" he whispered.

"I don't know," she choked. "This...I...I don't
know anything anymore." She stood up and
hurried away from Matt.

"Where are you going?" Matt asked.

She turned and saw that he was inches from her.
All she wanted was to reach out, to touch him,
to feel that connection. To be a part of someone.
But she couldn't. She'd painted herself into a
corner with her charade, and now she had fallen
in love with this man.

"Please stay," she heard him say. "Let me prove
how much I want you, more than I ever wanted
anyone or anything in my entire life."

Dear Reader,

Every month Harlequin American Romance brings you four powerful men, and four admirable women who know what they want—and go all out to get it. Check out this month's sparkling selection of love stories, which you won't be able to resist.

First, our AMERICAN BABY promotion continues with Kara Lennox's *Baby by the Book*. In this heartwarming story, a sexy bachelor comes to the rescue when a pretty single mother goes into labor. The more time he spends with mother and child, the more he finds himself wanting the role of dad....

Also available this month is *Between Honor and Duty* by Charlotte Maclay, the latest installment in her MEN OF STATION SIX series. Will a firefighter's determination to care for his friend's widow and adorable brood spark a vow to love, honor and cherish? Next, JUST FOR KIDS, Mary Anne Wilson's miniseries continues with an office romance between *The C.E.O. & the Secret Heiress*. And in *Born of the Bluegrass* by Darlene Scalera, a woman is reunited with the man she never stopped loving—the father of her secret child.

Enjoy this month's offerings, and be sure to return each and every month to Harlequin American Romance!

Wishing you happy reading,

Melissa Jeglinski
Associate Senior Editor
Harlequin American Romance

THE C.E.O. &
THE SECRET HEIRESS

Mary Anne Wilson

HARLEQUIN®

TORONTO • NEW YORK • LONDON
AMSTERDAM • PARIS • SYDNEY • HAMBURG
STOCKHOLM • ATHENS • TOKYO • MILAN • MADRID
PRAGUE • WARSAW • BUDAPEST • AUCKLAND

To Joanine Dedrick
The best niece ever, and my favorite clown!
Love you lots.

ISBN 0-373-16895-0

THE C.E.O. & THE SECRET HEIRESS

Copyright © 2001 by Mary Anne Wilson.

This edition published by arrangement with Harlequin Books S.A.

Visit us at www.eHarlequin.com

Printed in U.S.A.

ABOUT THE AUTHOR

Mary Anne Wilson is a Canadian transplanted to Southern California, where she lives with her husband, three children and an assortment of animals. She knew she wanted to write romances when she found herself "rewriting" the great stories in literature, such as *A Tale of Two Cities,* to give them "happy endings." Over a ten-year career she's published thirty romances, had her books on bestseller lists, been nominated for reviewer's choice awards and received a Career Achievement Award in Romantic Suspense. She's looking forward to her next thirty books.

Books by Mary Anne Wilson

HARLEQUIN AMERICAN ROMANCE

*Just for Kids

INTEROFFICE MEMO

To: All LynTech Corporation Staff
From: Matthew Terrell, C.E.O.
Re: New Hire B. J. Smythe

Please join me in welcoming artist B. J. Smythe to the LynTech staff. Ms. Smythe has clearly demonstrated her abilities to help redesign the newly located Just For Kids day-care center. But, as a concerned C.E.O., I will gladly keep a *very* close eye on Ms. Smythe to ensure she is working up to potential. Since I am the one who initially hired Ms. Smythe, I feel personally responsible for her success here at LynTech and, as such, will also hold weekly (or daily!) meetings with the beautiful auburn-hired artist over lunch, dinner... *or breakfast.* I am willing to do whatever it takes to show Ms. Smythe the ropes and help her feel more at home. If you have any questions for Ms. Smythe, please feel free to go through me, as I plan to be by her side every step of the way....

Chapter One

France, December 9

"You are a work of art," the groom-to-be said, and the words were definitely not a compliment for the bride-to-be. "You think the world revolves around you. Well, news flash, Brittany. It doesn't!"

Brittany Lewis stared at Sean Briggs, the son of a top businessman in Paris, a man her father, Robert Lewis, had introduced her to six months ago. Sean—darkly handsome, gentle, fun, and the man she'd thought she loved until a few hours ago. Now, he looked like what he was, a stranger, a very angry stranger in a monochromatic gray suit and shirt, a stranger that she'd wish away in the blink of an eye if she had the power to do it.

Another wish would have been to go back in time and stop this fiasco before it began. But she couldn't do that, anymore than she could cancel out any of her past mistakes. So she was doing the next best thing—canceling the engagement three weeks before the planned New Year's Eve wedding in the old chapel on the grounds of the chateau just south of Paris.

"I *can't* do this," Brittany said, her tense voice echoing slightly in her father's study on the ground floor of the chateau. It had been her favorite room until that moment. With its rich wood and leather, the scent of books all around, memories of sitting in here when she was little, reading while her father worked.

"What do you want me to do, go ahead and marry you, then destroy everyone's life when it doesn't work? Because it's not going to work."

Sean came closer to where she stood by the inlaid wood desk near the French doors. He was only two inches taller than her own five foot, ten inches, but she felt very small right then. He took a breath, making an obvious effort to talk rationally. "Can't we rethink this and try to work it out some way?"

She knew the repercussions of her decision were going to explode all around her, and for a fleeting moment it was tempting to think of stopping it before it did. But she knew that things would only be worse if she let it go on. And it would hurt her father even more than this all would now. How could she have thought she loved Sean, that she loved him enough to marry him, to do the "forever" thing with him? "I don't see how we can work this out," she said, her voice sounding small and uncertain in her own ears.

But Sean wasn't going to be put off. He came closer to her. "Brittany, love, this is a wedding. It'll be fun, and we can deal with other things when they come up. It's all in place, all arranged. And any arrangement can be worked out."

Brittany felt fire stain her cheeks. An arrangement? And here she'd been worried about realizing that she loved Sean, but wasn't "in" love with him, while he'd been looking at their wedding as an "arrangement?" *Arrangement?*

"Sweetheart, what did you think the prenup was all about? There's a lot of money involved in this, the Lewis and the Briggs money. But just because we're practical doesn't mean that we can't or won't have fun, and a really good time.''

She stared at him. ''Fun?''

He was even closer, his voice getting more and more intimate all the time. In his gray-on-gray shirt and suit, he looked even darker and even more like a stranger, a stranger she'd almost married. He didn't touch her, but his gaze flicked provocatively over her, skimming over her loose cotton shirt, her jeans, all the way to her bare feet before it lifted to her face framed by her flaming hair drawn up into a simple ponytail. ''You're lovely to look at, even in these clothes. You're intelligent, well connected, sexy as hell, and we can make this work.''

His words sank deeply into her. No wonder she didn't love him. He didn't even make a pretense of loving her. And she suddenly felt more bold, more justified in what she was doing. There wasn't anger, just relief, and all she wanted right then was to have him gone. Her first broken engagement had been wrenching, filled with tears and pain, easing only with a trip to Switzerland for almost six months to forget her foolishness. Her second engagement had been easier to walk away from, after a flashing moment when she'd realized what a mistake she'd been making. Her then-fiancé had been almost as relieved as she'd been with the cancellation, and she'd gone off to enroll in art school in Vienna. But this was horrendous. Number three was not the charm, and Sean wasn't giving up gracefully or any other way.

''We can't make this work,'' she said, trying very hard to keep her voice even.

''Tell you what, this is prenuptial nerves, and I think I know what to do. We'll go away for a few days, someplace remote and private, and you can let me show you how good things can be. If we're together, I know you'll feel better.'' His voice dropped. ''Much, much better.''

She swallowed sickness at the idea of being alone with Sean. ''No,'' she said, shaking her head as she backed away and twisted the ring off her finger, a five-carat creation of diamonds and sapphires that felt like a millstone to her at that moment.

''Come on, Brit, everything's in place.'' His tone was starting to edge with exasperation now. He wasn't used to not being able to talk a woman into anything he wanted. ''It's too late. Everything's in place. All the invitations have gone out, the parties have begun and my mother's got her gown on order from Dior.''

''I'm sorry about your mother's gown, and everything else,'' she said as she held out the ring to him. ''It's over. I'll explain everything to the others. I'll take care of it.''

His expression hardened with each passing second. ''I guess you have plenty of experience doing that very thing,'' he muttered.

''I said I'm sorry.'' She opened her hand, offering him the ring on her palm. ''Just take this.''

He reached for the ring, snatching it out of her hand, but he didn't keep it. Instead he stared at her, then very deliberately dropped it in a leather trash container by her father's desk. ''That's where it belongs,'' he muttered, then turned on his heels, crossed the room and left, slamming the heavy wooden door behind him.

The sound cracked loudly in the study, followed by total silence for a long moment before the door opened again. Bracing herself, she looked at the door, afraid Sean was back for a second round, but her father was there. ''I just passed Sean in the hallway.''

''He's leaving.''

He stepped inside, a tall, slender man with a shock of

white hair, wearing a dark suit he'd put on for what was supposed to have been an engagement dinner. "I take it it's over?"

He'd always been able to read her mind, or maybe he just knew her too well. "Oh, Dad, I'm so sorry."

"What was it this time?" he asked, closing the door quietly behind him as he came into the study. "What was the sign that came to you that told you not to get married?"

She turned from him, moving to the French doors and staring out into the early evening, across the stone terrace to the rolling hills of the centuries-old vineyard on the property. "I had a dream last night, and I couldn't shake it. I knew this was all wrong."

"A dream," he said from behind her somewhere. "That's a new reason. I laughed at the first excuse, the 'he eats steak and animal products' one, considering you're a vegetarian and all. Not compatible at all, of course. Then the second time, there was the 'it came to me in a blinding flash when I was getting fitted for my bridal gown' reason. That was more dramatic, and who could ignore a blinding flash?"

"Dad," she muttered, staring hard at the distant hills. "Daniel not only thought I was ridiculous for being a vegetarian, he raised beef, for heaven's sake. At first I liked him too much to let it bother me, but then, well… And William, well, I just knew suddenly that it was wrong."

He was right behind her now. "What a mess," he said in a low voice.

"I wouldn't exactly call this a mess," she said quickly, but knew it was exactly that…a mess.

"Three broken engagements in four years," he murmured. "A third wedding gown put in storage. I don't know what you'd call it, but I'd say this is becoming a full-time job cleaning up the fallout, a real father-child thing, I guess."

"I'm twenty-seven years old, and hardly a child," she muttered.

"You could have fooled me."

It had been just him and her for years, ever since she was nine and her mother had "gone away for the weekend." The story of the small plane crashing in upstate New York, had made the news for days. He'd always been so supportive, so steadfast in being there for her no matter what she did. But this very real tone of disapproval shook her and she wasn't all that steady to begin with at the moment. She turned, and he was sitting on the corner of the desk, his arms folded on his chest, his dark eyes studying her intently. "What did you want me to do, Dad, marry Sean and be miserable? To look at him in five years and wonder how I could have ever thought I loved him? I'm just thankful that I came to my senses before that happened."

"What did you want to do?" he asked, answering her question with another question.

She bit her lip. "I wanted what you and Mom had, to be really in love, to know it and to have it forever."

His expression tightened and, even after all these years, she could see a touch of pain in his eyes. "We were lucky, very lucky," he said in a low voice. "The thing is, what are you going to do now? Another repeat of what just happened?"

"No, I'm no good at finding love. I know when to admit defeat."

"Maybe that's your problem. You're looking for it. Maybe it has to find you."

"Semantics," she muttered.

"So what direction is your life going to take now that you've sworn off love?"

"Direction?" She had never thought about directions for life, just living it. "What do you mean?"

He raked his fingers through his thick hair. "Well, as you pointed out, you're twenty-seven years old. Sane, at least in most things. Intelligent, or you should be after all your forays into higher education. Talented, if you applied yourself, and you're my daughter. The genes have to be there somewhere."

"Dad, I—"

"Shhh, just listen to me for a minute." He stood and came closer to her. "I've made a decision. You either have to get direction for your life or I'm out of it. I probably should have done this before, but..." He sighed. "Better late than never, I guess."

"What are you talking about?"

"Being an indulgent father, as if I could make up for your mother not being here for you. Giving you what you wanted, when you wanted it. Going along with everything you did or wanted. That's over. I knew this thing with Sean wasn't going to work. I could tell. So, I made some plans. You can take them or leave them. But know if you leave them, you're going to have to make it on your own."

"This is crazy. I'm just breaking an engagement, not doing drugs or embezzling from the company."

"No, you're just drifting. You've got a smattering of knowledge about a lot of things, but you don't have any knowledge about accomplishment or challenges."

She pulled out the high-backed leather chair at the desk and dropped down into it. She tugged her legs up to her chest and wrapped her arms around them, then rested her chin on her knees and looked up at her father. "Where's this all going? You want me to get a degree in something? How about art? I could get a degree in that if you want. I can go to the university in the city, get into D'Angelo's classes, take private lessons. I've got all the time in the world. How about three or four years? Is that what you want?''

"No." He pressed his hands flat on the desk and leaned toward her. "Just six months, Brittany, six months to try it my way, and if it doesn't work, you can take classes in art for years if you want."

"Six months, to do what?"

"I've had a few phone conversations with Matthew Terrel at LynTech in Houston."

They'd both accepted the fact ages ago that she was hopeless at business and wouldn't step in to take over when he retired from the company he'd founded. That had been a great disappointment for him, but a truth. She didn't have a business head. She didn't care about business at all, but she cared about him, and LynTech had been very important to him ever since she'd been old enough to remember. "Terrel's the guy that's working with the other one, the one who was going to split up LynTech, then decided to stay on and develop the company?"

"Zane Holden and Matthew Terrel. Terrel is operating it at the moment, so he's the one I contacted."

"Why were you talking to him? Is there trouble at the company?"

"No, it's transitional, but it's doing fairly well," he said. "I was talking to him about clearing it for you to go back to Houston."

"What does this Terrel person have to do with me going back to Houston?"

"He's going to set you up at LynTech to work. You are going to show up at nine and go home at five for six months. You're going to make a difference. You are going to finally have more of a challenge than trying to figure out which art discipline is superior."

She lowered her feet to the stone floor and looked right at her father. "Me, at LynTech?"

"Yes. You're not going to run away this time. You're going to work."

"Dad, I know you're upset, and I don't blame you, but that's crazy. I'll destroy the company in a week."

"You're not that good," he said with the shadow of a smile as he stood back. "And I've got a feeling that Mr. Terrel won't let that happen."

"So, you want me to head to Houston, and let this man, Terrel, babysit me?"

The smile was getting a bit larger. "I wouldn't put it that way."

"Dad, you're in shock. I am, too. I mean, I know I've upset things. But to think that I should go and work at LynTech, well..." She almost shuddered. "That is not a good idea."

"All I'm asking from you is six months of work and no engagements."

She had always felt so independent, but she knew that she would never be independent of this man, of his good opinion of her, or the fact that she felt as if she'd failed him in so many ways. She knew she owed him so much. "Just go to LynTech?"

"And give yourself a break. Stay away from men, from situations. Give yourself a breather so you can really think about things. If you find out there isn't a place for you there, then we'll call it even, and you can go to any university you want and study anything you want to study."

A break? Time to breathe and think? Even if this Terrel person was looking over her shoulder she could do six months. And for some reason she wanted to see Houston again. To see the house there. She hadn't been back for over two years. "Okay, I'll do it."

She didn't know what she expected. Him to smile, hug her, say he was happy? No matter what she thought, she didn't expect him to hold out his hand to her. "We've got an agreement. Work, no complications. Agreed?"

She took his hand, and felt as if she was sealing her fate. "Agreed," she whispered.

"Terrel is expecting you at two in the afternoon, Houston time, day after tomorrow." He tapped her chin. "Don't look so bothered. Just do your best. That's all I ask." He hugged her, and, as he stood back, he said, "We'll talk in the morning and get things straight," then he was gone.

Brittany slowly sank back in the chair again. Evening was coming, shadows creeping into the room, and in that moment, she felt very, very alone.

Houston, Texas, December 11

MATTHEW TERREL trusted very few people in his world. And he wasn't going to start by trusting the man he had hung up on in his offices at LynTech. Welsh thought he was going to buy into the company on borrowed money, but that wasn't going to happen. "Trust me," the man had said three minutes ago. "I can make this work." Matt had told him to rethink his offer, hung up and walked out of the office.

He went down the empty corridor on the executive level, went through his partner Zane Holden's darkened office and right to the executive elevator. He relished the silence all around him, thankful for the lack of voices and no ringing of the telephone. Since Zane had taken off on his honeymoon right in the middle of the transition with the company, there had been no peace at LynTech, not for him, that was for sure.

Matt hit the button, stepped into the small elevator car, then pressed the button for the parking garage and leaned back against the wall. He closed his eyes, shutting out his own image in the reflective doors in front of him. He shut out a large man dressed all in black, from the collarless shirt to the trim slacks, leather boots and black briefcase in one hand. He knew that his sandy-blond hair needed a trim, that the beginning of a new beard was starting to shadow his strong jaw, and that by all rights, his dark-blue eyes should be bloodshot from lack of sleep.

He exhaled, felt the car slide downwards and didn't open his eyes until the soft chime announced the doors were going to open. He stood straight, raked his fingers through his hair, then as the doors opened, he stepped out into the cavernous parking garage. The heels of his boots struck the cement, the sound echoing off the low ceiling and thick walls as he started over to his car, one of very few left in the structure.

Peace. God, he craved it sometimes.

As a kid he'd been alone a lot, and most people thought that was why he'd gotten in such trouble back then, because he was a loner. That was only partially true. The fact was, he stayed away from his father, avoided his mother and had no brothers or sisters. He made his own way and didn't want to change that. He didn't have much that was permanent in his life. He neared the car he'd finally bought when he'd agreed to stay in Houston for a while to help Zane get the business grounded. The large black Jeep gleamed in the low light, riding high on heavy tires and with tinted windows. He'd sell it when he left.

He got within ten feet of the car, but stopped when he glanced ahead to the left. A security door in the back wall was ajar. The door shouldn't have been open at all. There had been renovations going on, changing the original conference complex into an expanded day-care center, but that door was always locked. He reached in his pocket for his cell phone, punched in the number for security, and it was answered right away. No one was supposed to be in that area after five, and they'd send someone to check it out within ten minutes.

He told them to hurry, then shoved the phone back in his pocket, and started for the door himself. He knew what damage could be done in ten minutes, heaven knew he'd done enough damage in ten minutes when he was a kid. He approached the door, never a fan of confrontation, but more than able to take care of himself. He'd never developed a love for fighting, the way a lot of his old friends had, the friends who had ended up dead or in prison. But he could take care of himself.

He reached the door, pulled it farther back, hesitated as he looked into the broad hallway that lead to the center of the complex and saw nothing but shadows. He listened, then stepped inside. He knew the area by heart, a hallway with rooms off it, leading to a large central space with more private rooms off it, another hallway that led to the front of the building and the reception area. It was all being redone for the day-care center, with painting and restructuring. Right now it was in shadows. He felt for the wall switch, flicked it, but nothing happened.

He waited, then continued through the hallway, a faint glow coming from somewhere ahead. He went toward it. The smell of paint was heavy in the still air. He went farther, strange shapes materializing before him, something that looked for all the world like a tree of dark shadows. He was about to step into the large central area, nearing the tree-looking thing, when he sensed movement to his left. He spun around, and the next thing he knew someone was running into him, hands striking his middle and he was being pitched backwards.

Things he'd never forgotten from his misspent youth

came back in a rush, and he grabbed at his attacker, catching at flailing hands, jerking the person back with him. He twisted and as they hit the floor together, he was on top with his body weight pinning his attacker under him.

"Fire, fire!" someone was screaming at the same time he realized that the hands he'd captured were fine-boned, and the body under his was slight, although tall, and the scent of flowers and something else were infinitely female. Soft, warm, breathing as rapid as his, and a woman's voice still screaming over and over again, "Fire!"

The woman was twisting without stopping, and as his hold grew slack from shock, her hands were free and striking out at him. He let go completely, scrambling back to get out of reach of the stinging slaps on his face, arms and chest.

With a man it would have been different. He would have decked him. But a woman? He might have been a hoodlum when he was younger, but he'd never hit a woman and never would. So his only recourse was to try to grab at her hands again, to capture them to stop the blows. Despite the fact that he was battling a blurred shadow, he got the suggestion of wild curls, slenderness and real strength.

He grabbed for her hands, but before he could make contact, he was blindsided by someone on his left, the impact sending him reeling to his right, his head and shoulder striking an ungiving wall. He ignored the jarring impact, spun around, scrambling to his feet and took a punch to his middle.

As he lurched backward, he heard what sounded like a kid's voice screaming at him. "Hey, you jerk, you let her go!" And the owner of the voice was running at him again. "You stop hurting her!"

Kids and women, Matt thought at the same time he managed to catch the kid by his shoulders and hold on for dear life while he managed to evade most of the punches and kicks coming at him. Then the woman was there too, grabbing at him, jerking hard on his arm, still yelling, and the madness of the moment seemed to be suffocating him.

The screams echoed all around him until his own screams were mixed with them. "Stop it!" he yelled at the top of his lungs, then pushed the kid away from him. He felt the wall behind him, relieved that he wouldn't be attacked from the rear. "That's enough," he yelled, "That's enough! Stop. I give up."

There was a sudden silence as Matt managed to make out the shape of the child to his right, then the woman, not more than three feet in front of him. Even in the shadows, he could see her standing with both hands up, but not in surrender. She looked ready to deliver a karate chop as she spoke at a thankfully reasonable level in a husky, very female voice, "You'd better not move. Not one move."

"I'm not planning on it," Matt muttered.

The kid moved and Matt turned to protect himself, but instead of another blow being delivered, the kid turned on the overhead lights. The flash of brightness blinded Matt for a moment. Then he finally saw his attackers.

Chapter Two

Matt saw the kid first, maybe eight or nine years old wearing baggy jeans, a hooded sweatshirt and grabbing a faded Yankees baseball cap from the floor. He put it on backwards over thick black hair that curled at the ends, and he watched Matt carefully with dark-brown eyes in a tanned face. Both hands came up in front of him, and both were balled into fists.

Then Matt saw the woman.

His first impression was a tangle of wild auburn curls around a stunningly beautiful face dominated by eyes that he could have sworn were a deep green. She was tall and slender with improbably long legs defined by tight jeans worn with suede boots and topped by a loose navy sweater. If she hadn't looked so earnest and so unsettlingly beautiful, he would have laughed at her ''karate'' attack stance.

''Don't…don't you move at all,'' she said, both hands up, long fingers pressed tightly together, no doubt ready to ''chop'' if they had to. She never looked away from Matt as she spoke to the boy. ''Go and get help. Get security at the front desk.''

But the kid didn't go anywhere. Instead, he came a bit closer, his dark-brown eyes narrowed on Matt and his hands still in tight fists. ''What you up to, mister?'' he asked.

"You're ripping the people off or what? You stealing stuff from this place, or you gonna hurt the lady?"

He had to be from the day care upstairs, but he didn't look like the kids that had been coming in and out since Matt had been here. "No, I'm not ripping people off," he said as he realized there was a tree in the room, right in the middle, an almost cartoon-like thing, with holes in it and branches that were chained to the ceiling with what looked like platforms on them. A real tree house, he thought as he looked back at the boy, then down at the floor and saw his briefcase.

"Sure," the kid said with heavy sarcasm.

His briefcase had landed upside down against the wall by his feet. "Well, I'm not, and I'm not stealing and I'm not going to hurt—" He reached for the briefcase as he talked, but the kid moved faster than he did, kicking at the case, and sending it flying ten feet across the floor. It ended up near the strange-looking tree. "No, you don't, mister!"

"Oh, come on. That's my briefcase...what's left of it," he said, eyeing the heavy scuff mark on the side of the case.

"Can you prove it?" the kid asked.

He looked at the boy, then the woman. They hardly looked like a gang, but they were ganging up on him. "I don't know what's going on here, but *I'm* supposed to be here. The question is," he said as the woman moved a bit closer and he could see that her eyes really were a deep, almost emerald green, "why are you two here?"

EVEN AS BRITTANY braced herself to do whatever it took to fend off this mountain of a man in front of her, she knew it wasn't right. With the bright lights on, there was no furtive criminal in front of her, but a large man, dressed all in black, wearing clothes that weren't cheap, and frowning at her and the kid as if they were aliens.

"We...we should get Security." She glanced at the boy she hadn't even known was in the complex until he joined in the attack. "Go and get help, please."

"Yes, get Security," the man said quickly in a deep voice.

"We don't need no police in here," the boy said as he glared at the man. "I can take care of him." He moved a bit closer, his fists raised. "No problem."

She would have laughed if the kid hadn't seemed so serious and the man hadn't seemed so angry. "No, you go and get help. I...I'll..." She stumbled over her bravado as she looked back at the man. He was huge.

Dark eyes were on her, angry eyes in a sharply chiseled face. Sandy-blond hair, worn longer than was fashionable, was mussed, only adding to a strangely edgy feeling that the man seemed to radiate. Big? Shoot, he was a mountain and probably outweighed her by eighty or a hundred pounds. She remembered the feel of him against her, over her, controlling her and she inched back a bit, aware of how impossible it would be to control him.

All she'd seen was a flash, someone there, then there was impact, her body tangling with his, strength everywhere, and she'd had a flash of terror that she was being attacked, or even kidnapped. Her father had told her often enough when she was growing up that she had to take precautions against some nutcase thinking he could make money by kidnapping her. And she'd been told when you are attacked never to stop fighting. But it all seemed foolish now.

If the man hadn't been off balance in the first place, she never would have been able to upset him, let alone keep him from doing whatever he wanted to do. But the longer she looked at him, she knew that nothing made sense. He was obviously color-challenged, but his clothes were expensive, as expensive as the black boots he wore with them. And the briefcase on the floor wouldn't be carried by a thug.

"Security can figure this out," she said, her voice lower now.

"No," the kid said immediately.

But the man just shrugged his massive shoulders, leaned back against the wall and crossed his arms on his chest. After one glance at his watch, another less-than-cheap thing about him, the dark eyes were on her. "That's fine by me."

She wished she was controlling this, but knew she wasn't. She knew she'd never controlled anything about this encounter. "Okay," she said, and turned to the boy, but he wasn't there. She looked back at the front doors, but there was no one in sight. He had gone to get help, and she hadn't even heard him move.

She exhaled with relief that help was coming, that the kid had done as she'd originally asked, but that was short-lived when the stranger murmured, "He took off."

"He's getting Security."

"Not in this lifetime," the man said in a deep voice as he narrowed his eyes on her.

"Where did he go?"

"I didn't see him go, but trust me, he's long gone."

"No," she said quickly, looking back over her shoulder at the empty area around them. "He's gone for help."

"He's your kid?"

"No. I don't even know him," she admitted as she looked back at the stranger. "But he'll get help."

"You trust that kid?"

She hadn't thought of it in those terms, but she'd never been cynical, either. "I think he'll come back."

"He could, but speaking from personal experience and not being the trusting sort, why would he come back if he'd just been caught where he shouldn't be and had attacked someone he shouldn't have attacked?" His eyes flicked over her, making her stomach tighten. "My guess is, it's just you and me now."

Brittany took a step back, and knew she didn't want it to be "just you and me," with any man, especially not with this giant of a man who was looking at her with an intensity that made her thought processes amazingly scrambled.

She knew she should get out of there. She should run like hell. She looked for her purse, and saw it, right behind the stranger, the heel of his boot either pressing it against the wall or stepping on it. She couldn't tell. And she wasn't going closer to get a better look, either.

"Hey, what's going on here?" someone yelled from behind them.

She turned and saw a security guard rushing into the conference area. "See, I told you he was getting help," she said to the stranger.

He looked past her. "Not unless he's wearing overalls now."

She turned back and saw the guard coming toward them, followed by a tiny, dark-haired woman in pink overalls, but no sign of the kid. The guard stopped when he saw the two of them, but the woman didn't stop until she was right by them. She looked from Brittany to the stranger, then settled on the man. "I was in the security room when they said you called in. I came to see what was happening."

"That's what I was trying to figure out myself." The man stood a bit straighter and Brittany was vaguely aware that her purse fell to one side.

"Where's the boy?" Brittany asked as she turned back to the guard.

The middle-aged man in the gray uniform shrugged. "Boy? What boy?"

Brittany looked past him. "A boy, maybe eight or nine

years old, in baggy clothes, a baseball cap?'' She looked back at the guard. ''He went to get you.''

''No, ma'am, never saw a kid.'' He motioned to the stranger. ''Mr. Terrel here called Security and Mrs. Blake was there when the call came, and then we heard the commotion.''

Mr. Terrel? Brittany turned to those dark eyes still holding steady on her. Matthew Terrel? A C.E.O.? He wasn't like any C.E.O. she'd met in her life. No three-piece suit or pinstriped shirt. Shoot, and she'd attacked him, the man she was supposed to meet, the man who was going to ''watch out for her'' for her father. Shoot and double shoot.

''I thought there was a break-in, and I had visions of graffiti all over the place.'' The pink-overalled woman looked around as she spoke. ''I couldn't bear it if this was spoiled. That tree's perfect and everything's going so well.''

''Amy, don't worry. I think everything's okay. I saw the back door was open, called Security then came in to check.'' Matthew Terrel looked back at Brittany, and she was startled to see what might have been the shadow of a smile in his dark eyes. He couldn't be starting to enjoy this. ''I barely got inside before I was attacked. Some kid who must have been staying late at the day care got me, right after she did.'' He motioned toward Brittany and she barely hid a flinch when his hand almost struck her shoulder. ''She came out of the shadows screaming something about a fire.''

''You hit me first,'' she said, then realized how truly ridiculous that sounded. Matthew Terrel attacking someone? That was the wrong road to go down, and she knew that it was time to stop the madness. ''I'd tried to turn on the lights and couldn't find a switch that worked, then I ran into someone and he…he grabbed me, and it scared me, and I was just protecting myself.''

"But screaming *fire?*" he asked, and, yes, she knew that he was on the verge of smiling now.

"I was told to yell *fire,* because people ignore other things or don't want to get involved, but if they think they're going up in smoke, they pay attention."

The smile came to light then, a lifting of his lips and crinkling of lines at the corners of his dark eyes. "Well, I have to say, you got my attention, Miss…?"

She opened her mouth to say who she was, that she was here to meet with him, that she'd been delayed and maybe even apologize for hitting him. But before she could get anything out, the security guard who had gone to look around was back. "Nothing bothered, Mrs. Blake. Everything looks just fine."

"Thank goodness," Amy sighed. "Today has been so crazy, what with the kids and fabric swatches and toy designers."

"Is there anything else, sir?" the guard asked. He eyed Brittany, then said, "How about her?"

"I'll take care of this. Just keep an eye on the doors."

"Yes, sir," the guard said, then left.

Brittany watched the man, swearing she could catch a hint of the scents that had surrounded her when they'd fallen to the floor together. A mellow aftershave, heat and something else that oddly reminded her of when she was a kid and went to the office with her dad. That was weird. "Are you okay, Matt?" Amy asked.

"I'm fine. I was just trying to get out of here. I had an appointment that never showed, and just destroyed whatever time line I was trying to keep intact."

"Yeah, I heard about that meeting. She never showed?"

He moved as Amy spoke, lightly brushing Brittany's arm as he passed her. She moved back a step and watched him cross to the tree base to get his briefcase. He picked it up, then brushed at the expensive leather. "No. Not even a call." He came back, stopping near Amy. "Not that I expected one. Mr. Lewis said she wasn't thrilled with having to actually work, but he was sure she'd be here on time. He thought they had an understanding. But he's the father and probably wants to think the best of his only child."

Her heart sank. They were talking about her. She saw Amy grin at him, a sense of familiarity between the big man and the tiny woman. They seemed so easy together, so connected as they spoke, and a part of Brittany felt a crazy jealousy that a man and woman could be so comfortable together. Then she remembered that the guard had called her Mrs. Blake. Were they just friends, friends close enough to have an inside joke running about her? She cursed the fact that her face felt hot and she brushed at her cheek as they kept talking.

"Her idea of work is getting engaged," Amy said. "I doubt that she'll show up here."

"I hope she doesn't. The only reason I agreed to hire her on was that her father's been so decent about things. And I could tell it meant a lot to him. He's got the idea that if she just sits behind a desk, that something will kick in and she'll show what she's made of." He laughed then, a rough sound that jarred Brittany. "Poor guy, hope springs eternal, I guess. She's got to be in her twenties and he's watching out for her as if she's a teenager getting summer work."

"She acts like some spoiled teenager," Amy said.

"You've got that right, and just what I need. Babysitting a recalcitrant brat. If she shows I'll have Rita put her in an office as far away from me as she can and lock the door."

Brittany wanted nothing more than to go up to him, slap him across the face and walk out. But that would only feed into what he was saying. How she wished she had her father's way with words, knowing just the right thing to say to bring grown men to their knees. That was another trait of his that had eluded her.

"He's her father," Amy said. "Parents always hope for the best. And maybe she'll find someone else, get engaged again and this time make it to the altar, then she'll be another man's problem, and get her father off the hook."

"Sure, and pigs fly," Matt muttered, taking one last swipe at a huge scuff mark on his briefcase.

She'd had enough of their condescending ridicule and she was ready to leave. No agreement with her father was going to make her stay anywhere near this man. She moved quickly, made a grab for her purse, and would have just walked out if Matt hadn't spoken to her.

"I'm sorry. I got sidetracked."

She turned and saw thankfully that there was a buffer of space between them. "I guess so," she muttered.

"I'm Matt Terrel. Now, why were you here?"

"I came to see about a job."

"In here?"

Before she could say that she'd always thought this was the conference complex and not some crazy area with a fake tree in the middle of it where she'd been told to meet him, a smiling Amy came closer to her.

"Oh gosh, I know who you are."

But there was no embarrassment for what she'd been saying about her. "You do?"

"Of course I do." She held out her hand. "I'm Amy Blake, the person you were supposed to meet with. But I left a message for you that I had to cancel and would call and reschedule."

She glanced at Matt, who was watching her. "I thought you were doing the interview? And I never heard anything about canceling."

"Me? No, I have a totally hands-off policy when it comes to the day-care center. And I never heard about any of this."

None of this was making any more sense than their attack scene moments ago. "A day-care center?"

"Well, anyway, you're here, although I thought you'd come up to see me at the old center." Amy motioned around the room. "But this is great. You can see the new place. There's much more space, and the play tree. Lindsey's idea, actually, for the kids. There's a real kitchen, two of them and we're going to have an outside play area when we figure out the best place for it." The woman was in rapture over the place. "It used to be a conference complex, but Mr. Holden rethought his plans and decided that the conference rooms would be better on the sixth floor and the day-care center could be put down here. They've almost got the transition finished. We hope by the new year that we'll be on track for the switch."

All of that was of no interest to Brittany. Kids weren't part of her world, and she certainly wasn't going to allow Terrel to assign her to do some babysitting chores. "That's all very nice, but—"

"Oh, of course, this is where you come in," Amy said, walking to the closest plain white wall. "It's here." She motioned to the wall, then the ceiling. "Maybe even the ceilings. The woman who actually started the center wants this place to be magical, to be nourishing for the kids. And to be nearly indestructible." She came over to Brittany again. "So, what do you think? Tell me it's doable. It was my idea to hire a graphic designer for this, to get it into professional hands for the murals. Tell me you can make this all happen."

Brittany pieced together what she thought was going on, that this woman thought she was someone looking for a job doing some graphic art on the walls of this place. She loved art, always had, and in her meandering path through higher education, had had a lot of classes in both traditional art and graphics. The thought was intriguing. It was too bad she wasn't here for that job instead of a desk job under this man's eagle eye.

"It's got real possibilities," she said, turning slowly in a circle to look at the space.

"You've got ideas already?" Amy asked.

As Brittany looked around at the partially domed ceiling over the tree, and the way the branches were suspended toward both side walls, she knew she did have ideas. Ideas that tumbled over each other. "It's a babysitting thing, like preschool?" she asked.

"Day care. Both all day, and before and after school, so the kids range from babies to preteen."

It could be great. She looked back at Amy, trying to ignore the man watching her so intently. "You want art on the walls and ceiling?"

"Both, or just the walls, whatever you think would be the most stunning and appropriate. It's for the kids. Period. It doesn't have to please adults."

Pleasing adults. That phrase brought her dad into the picture. She could do this. She knew she could, and her father hadn't said just what she had to do here. But as she glanced back and caught Matt's eye, she knew that he'd never let her do this. He'd never turn her loose with paint and bare walls. Never. She looked away from him, glancing at a short hallway that she knew led out to the reception area.

"I could do this," she said, as much for herself as for them. "I'd like to try." And as she spoke, she knew this was the only way she'd get a chance without her father stepping in and calling in more favors. "I really would like to try," she said, looking back at Amy and trying to ignore the man in black. "I've got some ideas."

"Okay, but the last person who came in wanted to do wild animals all over the walls, and..." She motioned to the ceiling. "He wanted to do panthers on the ceiling as if they were coming out of the trees. I don't mind telling you it gave me the chills. Can you imagine what it would do to a child trying to nap and seeing that?"

Ideas were coming to her fast and furious. "I wasn't thinking of wild animals."

"What do you see this all becoming?" Amy asked.

She told her with growing enthusiasm the images she was getting. "If it's for the kids, I see the kids on the walls, circles of them, dancing, playing. The real kids. You know, the ones who are regulars here. They'd be in the art, part of it, and ringing the walls, as if playing 'Ring Around the Rosey' in a play yard." She looked up. "And the ceiling, it's the sky, just a simple sky, a pale blue, maybe a rainbow on the far side, and clouds, puffy balls of white cotton suspended by fishing line from the ceiling. All about the kids. As if it was their world."

She knew she'd gotten carried away, talking quickly, trying to make them see what she could see in her mind, and she was high on excitement. And pleasure that she could do this. That was the best part of all. She saw it, and she could make it happen. She'd never experienced anything like that before. She looked at Amy who was staring overhead.

"Oh, my, that's wonderful," Amy said softly, then glanced at Brittany. "I can see it, too. And it's perfect. The center's called Just for Kids and it truly would be. I love it."

"You've done a lot of this sort of work?" Matt asked, cutting into her euphoria, and drawing her attention to where he stood with his arms folded on his chest. He wouldn't let her do anything. As soon as he knew she was Brittany Lewis, he'd laugh her right out of here, and it would be

over. And, when he found out who she was, that was the
nicest outcome she could imagine.

"No, I haven't, not really," she said honestly.

Amy touched her on the arm. "If you've got the talent
to make it happen, I don't see what lack of experience has
to do with anything. Maybe you're just finding your gift in
art. This could be it."

It could be it. She wanted it to be it. "I can do it."

"Maybe we could see your portfolio, Miss—" Amy
smiled at her. "I still don't know your name."

She stared at Amy, but sensed Matt moving, coming
closer to her, stirring the air, and she never said the words,
"I'm Brittany Lewis, the spoiled-rotten daughter of Robert
Lewis."

No, she wasn't going to admit that, not here, not now,
and she wasn't going to let this go, either. She could do it,
please her father in the long run, and best of all, if it worked
the way she thought it could, she'd prove that she was a
viable, worthwhile person, instead of the brat Matt and Amy
expected to appear with that name.

She felt an odd fluttering in her middle, and avoided the
name thing. "My portfolio, it…" She couldn't say it was
at a chateau south of Paris. "I'm sorry, I forgot to bring it."

"If you can do what you say you can do, I'd love to have
you give us a proposal and I can look at your portfolio then.
I need something to send to my boss. Something she can
see so she knows where this is going. As far as I'm concerned, you're the only one in the running for the job at this
moment."

"That's great," she said, feeling as if she'd just jumped
over an incredible hurdle in her life. She'd been told she
had art talent, but qualifications had always gone with the
praise: if she could learn to apply herself…if she bothered
to use it…if she ever decided what she wanted to do with

it. Right then, she knew what she wanted to do. "When do you need it all?"

"As soon as possible. We're in a bit of a time crunch, but if it's a problem for you—"

"No, I'll have something for you by tomorrow. Do I bring it here?"

"No, the workmen will be all over the place. Bring it up to the sixth floor. You'll see colored doors with Just for Kids written on them. I'll be in there." There was a beeping sound, then Amy took a pager out of the pocket of her overalls. She glanced down at it to read the printout on the small LED screen. "Taylor's awake." She looked at Brittany. "My daughter. I need to get upstairs or she'll pitch a fit."

"Amy?" Matt said to get Amy's attention before she took off. "I know how much this center means to Lindsey and Zane, but we're still doing business here."

"Of course. And we're within budget, aren't we?"

"That's not it. It's about that kid who was in here. You can't let them run around without supervision. That little hoodlum that attacked me was probably the one who opened the door, and he was looking for trouble. He needs to be kept under lock and key."

Amy shook her head. "He can't be one of our kids. First of all, they're always supervised, and secondly, the after-school kids are long gone. But I'll check and if he's one of ours, it won't happen again."

Matt nodded, then Amy turned to Brittany. "I can't wait for tomorrow." That smile came again. "And I still don't know who you are."

Brittany stared at Amy, and was startled when Matt spoke up. "You do have a name, don't you?"

Brittany looked at Matt. "Of course I have a name," she said and remembered something her father had told her many times over the years. "If you want something, you use whatever you need to make it happen." She wanted this to happen, and she would do whatever it took to prove she wasn't a spoiled brat. She'd do it and he wouldn't have to know who she was for now.

"B. J. Smythe," she said, putting together an old nickname with her mother's maiden name. "And it's Smythe, S-M-Y-T-H-E. Not Smith," she added for good measure.

Chapter Three

"B. J. Smythe not Smith," Matt said, and she blushed slightly, high color touching her delicate cheekbones. "I'll remember that," he murmured, and knew that he wouldn't have any trouble remembering this woman on any level.

"Great to meet you, B.J.," Amy said, then hurried toward the doors. She called, "Tomorrow," over her shoulder, and was gone to get to her daughter.

"Shoot, that's just great," Matt heard B.J. mutter as she watched Amy leave.

"Excuse me?"

She shook her head and turned back to him. "Sorry. I just needed to talk to her some more, to get details."

"Well, she's long gone. When the children are involved, she's single-minded, and when it's her daughter, well..." It was his turn to shrug. "She's got tunnel vision."

"She sounds dedicated."

"She really is. Actually, I hope that kid is one of hers so she can reign him in."

"You don't like kids?"

He shrugged at a question that came out of nowhere as far as he was concerned. "I don't even think about them, until something like this happens."

"I can't say I've thought much about them, either, but I think you're hardly being fair to that boy."

That really came out of nowhere. "What?"

The suggestion of a frown tugged a fine line between her eyes. "You're calling him a hoodlum, but you don't know why that door was open or why he was here. You also know that he thought you were the hoodlum, and he thought he was protecting me from…" Those green eyes skimmed over him. "…a huge man dressed all in black sneaking around in the dark."

"The light switch didn't work, and I wasn't sneaking anywhere." He stopped, wondering why he was the one justifying his actions in this situation. "The boy's the problem, a problem waiting to happen and we probably won't have to wait much longer."

"There you go again. You don't even know him."

He had to admit that she was good at keeping him on the defensive. "Well, he didn't come back, no matter how much you trusted he would. And I've seen that type before, the way I've seen too many Brittany Lewis types."

Those green eyes narrowed. "Oh, so you know Brittany Lewis that well, do you?"

"No, and I don't want to," he admitted with a grimace. "But I know the type."

She shook her head as if she was exasperated with him. "That's a really bad habit you have there, Mr. Terrel."

"It's Matt, and what are you talking about?"

"Okay, *Matt*. You're forming opinions, no, making judgments, without knowing all the facts."

They'd started as adversaries when she'd attacked him, and it just kept going. "That's what you're doing, isn't it?" he asked, moving a bit closer to her.

He was used to people reacting to his size and presence.

It was a given that he was intimidating, but she didn't back down as he got closer. "What are *you* talking about?"

"You don't know me. You don't know how I do things, how I form opinions. But you've got your opinion of me and you're passing judgment on me. So, answer me this, who's worse, you or me?"

"The question is, who's *wrong*, you or me?" she countered without missing a beat.

"You, definitely you. You're wrong, dead wrong about me."

"So, you can't admit to being wrong, either."

He had always liked a skirmish, and this was starting to intrigue him. The first time she'd ended up under him. Not a bad start, and he wondered how this would end. "Oh, and *you* can admit to being wrong?" he asked, not bothering to stop the smile that was starting to grow at this exchange.

She stared at him hard, then turned away. For a moment he felt disappointed that she was going to give up after all, that he'd read her wrong. But she made a pretext of looking at the ridiculous tree and spoke in a low voice. "Of course I can admit I'm wrong, if or when I'm wrong," she said in an even voice. Then she turned and there was something in her expression, and it had nothing to do with humor. She thought she was going in for the kill. "Which, of course, isn't that often."

He shook his head slowly as he went close enough to her to see that her lashes were incredibly lush, and her lips were their natural color, owing nothing to any lipstick. Damn it, this was getting to be fun. That was something he hadn't even considered with a woman before. Sex, conversation, even possibly mutual interests. But fun? That was a new thing for him, and he found it very endearing. "Oh, I get it. This is an aberration, you being wrong?"

"No, it's not, because I'm not. And that being said, I've

only got until tomorrow to get my ideas down for Mrs. Blake and nail this job. I just wish…''

Her voice trailed off, and he found himself interested in what she would wish for. "So, you're a person who wishes? The next thing I know, you'll say you believe in Santa Claus.''

"And you don't." It was a statement, not a question. "That's too bad.''

"It's not smart to sit around waiting for someone to drop presents in your lap,'' he muttered, annoyed that her words had made him sound like Scrooge. "So, what were you wishing for?''

"More time with Mrs. Blake. I have such a vague idea of this place, and I want to get this job.''

"Amy's easy, don't worry. And it has to go by me, anyway.''

She tilted her head slightly to one side and those lashes lowered a fraction of an inch as she studied him for a long moment. "And you must have a full working knowledge of this place, what it's going to be, what the vision is for it?''

He didn't know where she was going, but he went along willingly. "I don't know if I'd get visionary. Imagination isn't my strong suit, but I've seen all the projections, the ideas and their budget.''

She came a bit closer, and he could feel whatever control he'd thought he'd had in this encounter evaporating. She was less than two feet from him, bringing with her a soft fragrance that he remembered from their collision, a subtly seductive fragrance that he could almost name. Almost. But not quite. "Okay, you have this knowledge about the day-care center, and I don't know much, except it's for the kids.''

He waited, feeling something coming, knowing it was coming, but not about to ask her for a map. He knew on

some level that if he asked her directly, she'd gain ever
more control. So, he just waited.

Finally she spoke and upset his balance again. "Do you
have a car here?"

He nodded, waiting.

"Do you drive?"

"Since I was twelve."

At least that took her back a bit, her green eyes widening
slightly. "What?"

"I took a car for a joyride when I was twelve, went ten
miles before I was stopped. That was the beginning of my
life of crime."

He had no idea why he'd just said what he said. It was
the truth, but it wasn't something he ever told anyone about.
Not even Zane. But before he could backtrack, he was faced
with her smile, an expression that quite literally lit up the
world at that moment. It was all he could do to concentrate
on what she was saying now. "Oh, sure, and I just bet you
did time in Sing-Sing, too."

God, she was beautiful when she smiled, and that angered
him just a bit. He was very happy for women to exist on
the fringes of his world. That was comfortable for him, and
nonintrusive. He'd never welcomed distractions, especially
not with a possible employee, and he really did have a lot
of work to do. He still had control. And that control was
the fact that he could walk away whenever he wanted. He
spoke quickly, looking at his watch as an excuse not to look
at B.J. for a moment. "No, I missed Sing-Sing on the tour,
but I really am running late. My timetable's shot to hell."

"The car?"

He looked back at her, the smile was gone, but its shadow
lingered in her eyes. "Excuse me?"

"The car. Your car?"

"I told you I have a car, but what does that have to do with anything?"

"Well, I don't have a car. I took a taxi to get here, and I'm short on time, and I need to know more about this place." She hesitated. "So, simply put, the solution is for you to give me a ride, and we can talk on the way."

He knew that if he drove away from here with her, nothing would be simple. "I don't know." He hesitated. "I don't even know where you live."

"Where do you live?" she countered.

"Do you ever answer a question directly?"

"I like to get all the facts before I speak," she said, that smile playing around her lips again.

"Okay," he murmured. "I live in a loft in a converted warehouse near the industrial district. I've barely moved in, but it's got lots of space."

"Well, that was more information than I needed," she said. "I just wanted to know what area of the city you lived in. South, north, in the middle, east or west?"

"Okay, to be exact, west of the middle of the city in the area that they're trying to redevelop. Now, where do you live?"

"Around that area."

"Where exactly?"

She hesitated, the first time he'd seen her stop to think of an answer before she answered him. "A town house complex—yes, the Fortress—no, the Forestry. No, shoot, the Forest Lane complex." She almost seemed flustered and color brushed her cheeks. "I'm sorry, I haven't lived there very long. Do you know where that is?"

He knew. He passed by there most days. A park-like area of town houses being refurbished for upscale tenants. And it was close enough to his place to be "on the way," if he took a slightly circuitous route. "Yes, I know where it is."

"Then can I have a ride?"

He looked at her, his response as strong as it had been at first. It wasn't diminishing. It had to be hormones, or maybe the fact that he'd been alone for quite a while now, he reasoned. Or lust. Maybe that was what this was all about. This woman was made to be lusted after, that was for sure. He could deal with that. Lust was a fiery explosion that faded almost as quickly as it came. He knew that from his own experiences in the past. Gone and forgotten. And he could deal with it easily.

"Okay, I'm parked in the parking garage."

"Great," she murmured and headed into the back hallway. When he got to the door, she was there, pushing it open and stepping out of the building.

He reached for the nearest light switch, flipped it, but it didn't do anything. He'd have to go back to find a switch that worked, and he wasn't going to take the time. Leaving the lights on, he went out after her, letting the door slam tightly behind him.

She'd stopped a few feet from the exit, looking back at him questioningly, and his whole body tightened. Yes, lust. Pure and simple. "Over there," he said, pointing to his car. "The black Jeep."

Brittany turned and walked quickly toward the car he'd pointed out before she lost her nerve or came to her senses. Her first lie about her name had come with amazing ease, but lying about where she lived was unsettling. She'd had to think fast, to remember where an old friend had lived in that area. Thank goodness, the complex was still there. But she still didn't have a clue what she'd do when they got there. Fooling Matthew Terrel wasn't a simple process.

She'd take his ride, learn whatever she could about the center. When he'd asked her about liking kids, she could have easily said she was totally ignorant of them. She'd never even thought about having any. There hadn't even been a center the last time she'd been at LynTech. But with Matt's information and her imagination, she knew she could do this. She approached his car; it fitted its owner perfectly. It was a huge sports utility vehicle with a perfect shine, chrome rims on huge tires, and darkly tinted windows. Strong and mysterious looking.

Matt hit the remote, the door locks clicked open, then he was reaching past her to grip the handle and open the door. Despite being fairly tall, Brittany had to step up and pull on a leather strap to get into the gray leather of the passenger seat. While she settled, she watched Matt stride around the front to get in behind the wheel, and she found herself looking at him, blocking out that response he immediately brought. She wasn't going to look at him as a man. He was a means to an end. Pure and simple.

She looked away from him as he started the car, and she remembered what he'd said about Brittany Lewis just minutes ago. She let his snide remarks settle in her mind, and grabbed at the anger that had come with them. She stared hard out the window at the almost empty structure. The car moved and Matt spoke as they approached the exit ramp.

"Do you want to get started?" he asked.

"Excuse me?" she said as they left the garage.

"I thought you wanted to talk?"

"Yes, of course. I was wondering about that tree." She said the first thing that came to her mind. "What's the idea behind it?"

"Sort of a jungle gym, I guess. Tunnels in the trunk to climb in, and the platforms for play and napping. Part of the fantasy theme that Lindsey, the director, wanted. Personally, it would scare me to death if I was four years old waking from a nap and finding myself in there."

She made the mistake of turning to look at him. If she'd thought he was disturbing before, in the close confines of the car he was downright dangerous. The low lights from the dash cut angles and planes of shadows on his face, and the sexiness was magnified. She turned back quickly, staring straight ahead. She would not make the mistake she'd made so many times in her life. That way she had of meeting someone, seeing something in him that blinded her, then, somewhere down the road, realizing that he was simply a stranger. Matt Terrel was a stranger.

"With the right backdrop, the tree could be magical," she murmured.

"And that's where you come in, turning a nightmare into a…" He paused. "What would you call it?"

"Just what you did, a fantasy, and one that revolves around the children. Or the children around it." She braced herself, then looked back at Matt. She was thankful that he was turned away from her, looking to his left up the street at the stream of traffic. "The children dancing around it, laughing, enjoying the magic."

He exhaled, still staring to his left. "Sounds good to me. Lots of kids' stuff that reeks of make-believe."

She could see the way his jaw was working, and she had no idea where that cynicism came from, any more than she had any idea why he had seemed so negative about the boy involved in their "incident." "That sounds cynical to me."

He turned to her as they waited for an opening in the traffic that filled the street done up in Christmas finery. "Cynical? No, just realistic," he murmured.

"There's a big difference between cynical and realistic."

"Oh?" His eyes flicked to hers, narrowed in the softness of the lights. "And you're going to enlighten me? Go ahead."

"Well, a realist looks at that tree and figures it's a toy, a plaything and isn't expected to look like a real tree and accepts that. A cynic looks at the tree and figures it would scare any four-year-old and wants to tear it down.''

''I never said I wanted to tear it down,'' he said as he managed to finally merge into traffic.

''Would you?''

''That's not an option. It cost an arm and a leg, so it's staying.''

''Money's the bottom line?''

''Isn't it always?''

''Cynical, cynical, cynical,'' she murmured.

A Santa clone walked right in front of the Jeep to weave his way across the street, and Matt braked to a stop. ''No, if I was that cynical, I would have taken out Santa Claus,'' he muttered.

''No one would take out Santa,'' she said. ''Not even a world-class cynic.''

Matt laughed then, a sound that both startled and disturbed Brittany. It was soft and rich, wrapping itself around her in the close confines of the black car, an enticing pleasure that she wanted to push away. ''I guess I'm not world-class,'' he said, starting to drive again, but so slowly that they could have walked faster. ''Just cynic enough to look at LynTech realistically and try to make it viable.

''There's viable and there's viable. Right now LynTech has more money leaks than a sieve, and it has subsidiaries that aren't exactly stable.'' He eased into the next lane behind a car decorated with flashing Christmas lights around its rear window. ''If we can get some cash flow from new investors, we might survive. If not, it's a lost cause.''

She knew LynTech hadn't been in top form when it changed hands. It had been a source of real pain for her father. After he'd spent years building the company, it had started to fail and he didn't have the time or the energy left to pull it back up. And she hadn't been there to help. Her sense of business would have sunk the company completely. "Can I ask you something?"

"I have no idea how many years it's going to take to get out of this traffic," Matt said.

The traffic was incredible, people out shopping or going off to dinner. "Why did you and what's-his-name, Holden, walk into Lyntech and take it over, if it was on the brink of corporate suicide?"

He finally made it to the corner and turned onto the main street in front of LynTech. "Corporate suicide? What did you do, take a class to learn sound bites for the business world?"

"I'm just asking a question."

He shrugged as he fingered the leather-covered steering wheel. "We got involved because we figured if someone was at the helm who wasn't attached to the company, someone who could make solid, unemotional decisions, it could be viable."

She'd heard enough about Matt and Zane Holden during the change of power. Her father's reluctance to hand the corporation over to them had been there, but he hadn't had a choice. He'd had to get out, otherwise there would have been an ugly takeover from some other sources. "Slice and dice" her dad had called the two of them, "but bright." He'd chosen the ones to take it, and Matt and Zane Holden had been that choice.

"Didn't you acquire LynTech with the intent to disassemble it, sell off the parts, pocket the money and get out of town?"

The traffic had stopped again, and horns were being sounded when Matt looked at her. "You claim to be an artist, and talk about magic and fantasy, then in the next breath, you're talking like some corporate shark. What are you, an artistic business person?''

He was so far off the mark that she could have almost laughed. ''I'm just an artist.''

''And I'm just impressed. Most people at LynTech thought we were horrible, especially after kindly Mr. Lewis and the way he coddled them. They couldn't understand our actions, still can't, in some measure. But you do.''

She'd absorbed it, but had had little interest in it until she saw how it had affected her father. Now she knew the slice-and-dice concept forward and backward, along with her father's hopes for the company after he'd learned that Matt and Holden were staying on. His relief had been immense when he'd found out they weren't disassembling it at all.

''I understand what you're doing,'' she admitted as they moved slowly toward the front doors of the company. Familiar doors to her, doors that she'd actually seen put up when the building had been redesigned ten years earlier. ''The question is, what are you and Mr. Holden doing with LynTech now?''

''Trying to fix it.''

''And is it working?''

''Well, cynic that I am, I wouldn't be sticking around to throw money down a black hole, would I?''

''And money is the name of the game.''

That brought that laugh, sudden and deep, a rich sound that felt as if it was slipping around her. ''You got it,'' he said as the traffic inched down the street.

She had never met anyone who could laugh and make her feel like laughing, too. She looked away from him again, and out at the city streets. ''So, you're in it for the long haul?''

''Zane is, but I'm just here until everything's in place.''

''Then what?'' she asked.

"Another challenge," he said. "There are millions of them out there, it's just a matter of finding them. But first, I need to get past this, and that means I've got a night of work ahead of me, if we ever get out of here."

"Do you want to park and walk?" she asked.

He laughed again, soft and sensual. She stared very hard up the street, concentrating on the way the Christmas lights danced on the polished finishes of the cars ahead. "Just lock the car and walk away?"

"Why not? It's like a parking lot out here."

He motioned ahead. "Once we get past the bus stop, it should move better."

She glanced up farther and saw the bus stop with a single bench and an overhead protection roof decorated with Christmas garlands. Two people were on the wooden bench, and as they got a bit closer, she recognized one of them as the boy who had come to her rescue in the center. "That's him," she said, sitting forward to get a better look at the boy, slouched down on the bench, staring at the ground, his hat on backwards.

"That's who?"

"The boy from tonight," she said pointing to him.

The woman sitting by him was thin and dark, with a deep scowl on her face as she spoke to the boy. "I guess that's his mother with him." Not a loving mother, that was for sure.

"Poor woman," Matt muttered.

As they passed by, Brittany was shocked to see the woman slap the boy on his shoulder, and he moved to get away from the blow. He looked at her, his face twisted with anger, but he didn't move again. "She hit him," Brittany said. "Stop the car!"

"Stay out of it," he said as he kept going. She reached for the door handle, but Matt caught her other arm. "No.

Don't do it. You don't know what's going on.'' He looked back over his shoulder. ''And he's okay. He probably did something that got her crazy.''

They were past him now, and she sank back in the seat, jerking her arm away from Matt's touch. ''How could you just let her do that?''

He slowed the car, pulled out of traffic and stopped. He turned to her, one hand on the steering wheel and one resting on the console. ''Okay, what do you suggest we do to stop her?''

She sank back in the seat, resting one arm on the door frame and pressing her other hand to her eyes. ''I don't know. Call the police.''

''And they'd come, take a report, then send them home together where she could really do some damage. She'd be angry and embarrassed and take it out on him.''

She lowered her hand and looked at Matt and hated him for his perfect logic. ''Do you think so?''

''I know so. I grew up around that kind of stuff, and you wouldn't help him if you stepped in right now.''

He moved a bit closer to her as people rushed by outside, carrying bright Christmas parcels and going to their homes. ''B.J., the kid is in a situation you can't change. No one can change it. Leave it alone.''

She swallowed hard. ''Just like that?''

He moved slightly, his hand lifting, and this time he touched her cheek, the contact of his fingers lighter than a feather's kiss, but riveting. ''Just like that,'' he said in a low voice. ''Walk away. You'll never see him again.''

''You can do that?'' she asked.

''I've done it all my life, and I've survived.'' He smiled slightly, a shadow at his lips, and it made her heart lurch. ''I'd like you to survive, B. J. Smythe not Smith.''

She'd known him an hour tops, and as he repeated her lie back to her with that smile, she felt her heart sink. It was no secret that he'd like to do away with Brittany Lewis.

Chapter Four

Matt didn't know why he was doing this, touching her, and experiencing this overwhelming need to fix whatever was "broken." He wasn't a rescuer of people. Companies, yes. People, no. He gave them a wide berth, and that's what he should have been doing with B.J. right then. This whole thing felt awkward and alien to him. And when she moved quickly, turning away from him and breaking that contact, he let her do it.

"I'll survive," she said, pushing toward the car door. "I just hope that kid can."

"He will. He's tough," he said, turning from her to look over his left shoulder at the traffic. It had thinned some and he slipped easily out into the road.

"You sound so damn sure," she said.

He didn't look back at her. He didn't want to start that craziness all over again. "I am. He's a survivor." He negotiated a lane change and sped up to a normal speed finally. "Now, ask me whatever it is you need to know about the center."

"If he isn't going to the center, could he?"

"I meant a change of subjects," he said.

"I want to know."

He gripped the steering wheel, smoothing the leather with

his hands and wondered why he could still almost feel the silky heat of her skin on his fingertips. "If someone in his family works for LynTech, he can."

"And if no one in his family works there?"

"Then he can't, at least until it opens in the new facility where we were. Then it's going to go public and be available to people working in the neighborhood."

"For a price?"

"It needs to get some capital to help keep it going. That's a given."

"I know, money is the bottom line, even with the kids."

"If it was up to Lindsey, she'd let all kids in for free, even a kid like that."

"There you go again. He might be a good kid, just impulsive. A lot of people are impulsive. He's not about to hot-wire some car and go for a joyride."

"Give him time."

"What is it with you pigeon-holing people you don't even know?"

He glanced at her and was a bit taken back to see a real degree of anger in her face, even with the lights of Christmas touching the sweep of her throat as her chin lifted a bit. This was crazy. He was tired of defending himself to her. "All things being equal, I should be at my place working, and if I hadn't been kept late waiting for…" His words trailed off and he looked back at the evening streets. "I'm not going down that road."

"You can say it. If Brittany Lewis hadn't kept you waiting you'd be doing something exciting like balancing figures."

He narrowed his eyes on the road, thinking that after meeting B.J. anything would be anticlimactic. "Now I have to figure out how to tell her father she never showed. He's not going to be a happy camper."

"Maybe she got held up somewhere?"

"You're probably right," he conceded, rerouting his thoughts to something less complicated. Something very simple. "She probably got held up trying to figure out which color lipstick looks best with wedding gowns," he said, turning toward the middle of the city.

"Why did you bring up wedding gowns?"

"I guess it's not big news when she dumps another fiancé," he murmured. "But being a no-show for a job that her father knocked himself out to set up for her seems pretty self-absorbed and petty. She's probably never worked a day in her life, then her dad gives her a chance to do something productive, and she bolts. She's probably on her way to some exotic place to lie around in the sun until the urge to work goes away. And her father's going to feel betrayed and angry and—"

"Her father told you all of this?" she asked, cutting off his rambling dissertation.

"Not verbatim, but it's obvious. He's just trying to do something to salvage the situation. He's her father, for heaven's sake. How's he supposed to feel? She's put him through the wringer, and the poor guy just wants things to be okay."

She was silent for a moment before saying, "You...you never know. Maybe she just got delayed."

"Doing what?"

"I don't know, but I can't imagine she'd come all this way and not be busy doing something. Paris isn't just a 'hop over the pond,' no matter what Europeans say about it."

She glanced at him and found him studying her with a tight frown. "How did you know she was in Paris?"

She shrugged, looking away from him. "I must have read it somewhere, or you probably mentioned something about Paris. And...and, it just figures that she'd be on her way. I mean, what would be the point of her making her father even angrier? She has to care about him.''

"That's up for grabs, but no matter what's going on, she isn't here, and with any luck she won't show up. That would make things simpler all the way around," he said as they drove on. "There's so much going on, and I don't have time to babysit.''

"And you, with your take on kids, you'd be some babysitter," she muttered.

He shot her a look, but she was still staring out the windows, her hands pressed flat to the purse on her lap. "It wouldn't be my idea of fun," he said, turning away from her to look out at the early-evening streets. Then he heard himself admitting a truth he hadn't expected to say to her. "You have this knack for getting me way off the topic and I'm not sure how you do it."

"My father never figured it out, either," she said. "He gets so annoyed when I—" She cut off her own words, then said, "Sorry, I'm doing it again."

"I wasn't complaining," he murmured, and meant it. She kept him on his toes.

"I think it's because I was brought up to be 'seen and not heard.' Look pretty and be quiet. Make a good impression, but don't ask questions."

He glanced at her. "You're an only child?"

"An only child brought up by my dad."

"And you never gave him any trouble?"

"I wouldn't say that. I'm no saint."

"Well, join the crowd," he murmured.

"You weren't kidding about joyriding at twelve?"

"I did it from time to time." Matt concentrated on his driving, instead of on words that were there, words that he'd never said to anyone before. Not even Zane. Yet he was on the verge of telling a woman who was almost a perfect stranger about himself as a twelve-year-old. He stopped himself before he went down that path. Enough was enough. ''And we're off the subject again.''

Gratefully, she let the subject of saints and sinners go. ''You're right. Let's see,'' she murmured as if trying to think of something to ask him. ''So, the center, yes. Are you committed to making it work or are you in a wait-and-see position, and you'll cut your losses if it fails to perform?''

He was taken aback again to hear words of ''corporate speak'' coming from this woman. ''I guess that about sums it up.''

''I should have gone up to take a look at the original center to see how it's decorated.''

He drove off when the light changed. ''It's done in Mother Goose sort of stuff.'' He tried to think, but was having a bit of a hard time focusing when she shifted, sighing softly, and he knew she was looking right at him now. He grasped for what he could remember about the center. ''The Big Bad Wolf, Three Little Kittens. Lindsey did most of the decorating herself. She did everything with the original program. And Mr. Lewis was behind her a hundred percent. I think it might have been his idea to begin with, maybe a way of making up for the shortcomings of his own parenting.''

This time there wasn't a sigh, but a rush of air, and he knew what she was going to say before a word was uttered. So he cut her off at the pass. ''Okay, okay,'' he said with a chuckle. ''I'm sorry. I'm jumping to conclusions.''

''Amen,'' she breathed.

He flashed her a look, half expecting a smile, but there wasn't any humor there. The soft light exposed the cut of her high cheekbones, the fullness of her bottom lip and the anger in her expression. Despite that, her image stirred him.

And he realized that he actually owed Brittany Lewis for not showing up, for making him late, for setting up the circumstance for him to meet B.J. But that didn't mean he had to like the woman.

They were getting close to where B.J. lived, and he turned to concentrate on where he was going. "I suppose you want me to give Brittany Lewis the benefit of the doubt?"

"It wouldn't hurt."

"Even if she never shows up?"

"I'd even bet that she'll show up."

"Oh, you do, do you?"

"Yes, and I'll even bet that she'll be sincere and willing to work."

"Now, that's a sucker bet," he said. "She'll never show up and even if she does, she'll be more worried about color coordinating her wardrobe with her office than doing any work."

"Do you want to make a bet?" she asked.

"How long do I have to wait tomorrow for her to show?"

"What time do you go into the office?"

"Usually around seven, but I've got some off-site meetings and won't be in until ten."

"Okay, ten it is."

"Why are you so sure of this?" he asked, his fleeting glance finding her looking at him intently.

"Is it a bet?" she asked, matching a question for a question.

"That depends. What's at stake?"

She shifted again, and the air stirred slightly in the car, carrying that flowery scent with it to brush his skin. Then she spoke and shocked him, something she'd seemed able to do with ease ever since they'd collided in the empty rooms of the center. "For you, an apology to Brittany Lewis."

He slowed, but for no other reason than shock as he looked at her. "What?"

"An apology, as in, 'I'm sorry I thought what I did of you,' or something like that. You can write your own lines."

"Thanks for that," he murmured, and saw the street ahead of them where the town house complex was.

"Agreed?"

He had no idea how this whole conversation had ended in a bet that he knew he'd win. "First, tell me what do I get if I'm right and she never shows up?"

"What do you want? You name it."

He knew what he wanted from her, but how could he tell this woman that he'd like her? "You admitting I was right, but this can't just be her walking through the door." He upped the stakes. "She has to actually do something productive at LynTech."

"Then the ten o'clock deadline doesn't work, does it?"

"Okay, why don't we extend it for…oh…let's see… December 23rd at—" He glanced at the dash clock, shocked that it had only been an hour and a half since this had all started. "Seven-thirty," he said. "Give her—and you— plenty of time."

"You've got a deal," she said without hesitating. Then sat forward. "Let me out here," she said abruptly, motioning to a small shopping center.

"The complex is just around the corner, isn't it?"

"I need to shop," she said as she motioned to a small market at one end of the complex.

He pulled into the parking lot and stopped by the grocery store. "I'll wait," he offered.

"No, thanks, I'm fine. I can walk. Thanks for the ride." She opened the door, scrambling out, then she was looking back in at him. "I think Brittany Lewis will surprise you."

He shrugged. "Maybe," he said, and thought B. J. Smythe was the one who was surprising him. All he wanted right then was to figure out how to prolong this contact, but he didn't have a chance. B.J. flashed him a smile, a stunning expression that literally made his breath catch in his chest.

"See you tomorrow," she said, then the door closed and she was walking away.

He was tempted to watch her, just to watch her move, the way her hips swayed, her long legs, the way her hair brushed her shoulders. But he didn't. He put the car in reverse and drove back out onto the street. Odd how the night seemed interminable now. Not long ago it had been packed with things for him to do, mostly work. But right then he couldn't think of any of the things he had to do. Just the things he *wished* he could do.

BRITTANY MOVED into the store, going as far away from Matt Terrel and her stupidity as quickly as she could. A bet? What in the world had possessed her to do that? Probably the same thing that possessed her when she asked him for a ride. How could Brittany Lewis show up tomorrow, and not jeopardize the job she really wanted? She knew if she told him the truth, he'd put her in that office his secretary would find for her and banish her to the farthest regions of the place. As far away from him as he could get her.

But Brittany Lewis had to show up. Her father had to know she was there doing what she'd promised she'd do. And Matthew Terrel had to know she was there. Then she realized something. She never had to see Matt as Brittany. He'd said his secretary was taking care of everything. He wouldn't be in until ten the next morning.

She turned, looked out the glass door at the fading taillights of Matt's car and waited until it disappeared to the south. If he wouldn't be there before ten, Brittany Lewis would be there at nine. She'd meet with the assistant, then leave again. With a good excuse. Maybe Brittany Lewis would need a new wardrobe to match her new office after all. She didn't realize that she'd laughed out loud until someone spoke behind her.

"Can I help you, Miss?"

She turned to see a bulky gray-haired man behind a long glass counter. He was staring at her, and her laughter died. "Is there a local cab company?"

"Diamond." He motioned over his left shoulder at a small ad board, one of many that lined the walls of the store. "That's them."

She saw the ad for Diamond Cabs, read the number, then looked back at the man. "Thanks," she said and went back outside.

There was no sign of Matt, and she paused for a moment, a bit shocked when she realized how her life had shifted in the past hour. Crazy. She felt a bit insane at the speed of the changes in it, but there was an exhilaration, too, partly due to her desire to get this job on her own, with her own talent and work, and partly because she knew that she was going to face Matthew Terrel as Brittany Lewis in one week, and get an apology from him.

She called the cab company on her cell phone to get a ride to her family home south of the city. While she waited for it to arrive, she put in a call to her father. It rang four times before it went to his service. She left a quick message, just saying she had arrived in Houston safely, and she'd call him tomorrow evening with details about her job with LynTech.

As she hung up, she realized how relieved she was that she hadn't had to talk to him directly. It had been hard enough twisting the truth with Matt, but she'd never get away with it with her father. So, the less he knew, the better.

December 12

BY THE TIME BRITTANY returned to LynTech the next morning at nine o'clock, she'd slept sporadically, finished a rough idea for the wall murals for the center and dressed to look like Brittany Lewis. A beige silk shirt, perfectly tailored slacks in taupe linen, leather sandals and her curls swept back with diamond combs and falling to her shoulders. She looked somewhat like a "spoiled brat" she thought, with gold added at her wrist and ears. It would be perfect for her meeting with Matt's assistant.

She parked her sports car down the street in a public garage, gathered up her small leather tote bag, her purse and her portfolio, then walked up the block along the Christmasy street. The drive had taken forever last night with Matt, but now she seemed to get to LynTech in the blink of an eye. She took a breath, then stepped into LynTech, crossed the lobby filled with the scent of pine from a towering Christmas tree, to head for the elevators near the back. She first went up to the executive level and was thankful that she'd remembered there was a ladies' restroom immediately to her right in the corridor.

She stepped inside the sitting area done in lavenders and pale turquoise, spotted a small couch and crossed to it. She slipped her tote and the envelope behind the overstuffed pillows, stood back, glanced at herself in the mirrors that lined the walls, then with a flip of her curls, slipped back out into the corridor.

A gray-haired man in a navy uniform was coming down the hall and stopped when he saw her. "Can I help you, Miss?"

"I'm Brittany Lewis. I have an appointment with Mr. Terrel," she said quickly, then motioned to the offices her father had used for so many years. "Is that his office?"

"No, ma'am, that's Mr. Holden's office," he said, then motioned in the opposite direction. "Mr. Terrel's down there, the third door on the right."

"Thanks," she murmured, then passed him to head to Matt's office. The thick carpet in the monotoned corridor muffled her footsteps. She stopped by the double doors labeled simply M. Terrel. She pushed back one of the doors, and, as she stepped into the reception area, her heart started to pound.

"Please let him not be here," she prayed as she looked around the large space, starkly modern in design, with glass and black marble in sleek lines and very little of it. There were a few shelves, a couple of plants, a tiny Christmas tree, all silver and blue, sitting in front of low windows and a huge reception desk. A woman sat behind it, working at a computer, and she looked up as Brittany went farther into the room.

"May I help you?" she asked as she turned toward Brittany.

"Miss Lewis to see Mr. Terrel."

The woman looked at her for just a fraction of a second too long, before she fell into her "professional" face with a nice smile. "Oh, Miss Lewis, I'm sorry. Mr. Terrel isn't in yet."

Brittany was surprised at the degree of relief she felt at not having to face Matt. She smiled, hoping that the expression didn't look too forced. "Oh, I'm the one who's sorry," she said with determined politeness. "I was supposed to be here yesterday, but got held up in London. The Season's in full swing and the parties and shopping...." She rolled her eyes expressively. "Well, you know how it can be." She waved her free hand. "But I made it, finally."

The woman was a master at looking polite. "Yes, indeed, you made it," she said, not giving away any of the disgust she probably felt. "I'm Rita Boyd, Mr. Terrel's personal assistant, and since Mr. Terrel won't be in for a while, I could get you started, if you like?"

She probably thought that Brittany would reject that out of hand, that she'd demand to speak to Mr. Terrel. "Rita, that sounds lovely. You know how men are? I think that we women can get things straightened out much more quickly without them around. Just show me what you can and I'll take it from there."

Rita came around to where Brittany stood in front of the desk. "That sounds lovely," she said, echoing Brittany's own words from a moment ago. "Shall we go to your office?"

"My office? That sounds important, doesn't it?"

"Very," the woman murmured as she turned away from Brittany and crossed to the outer door. "Mr. Terrel specifically said that he wanted a very nice office for you to…work in."

Rita was good. She was very good. She hadn't choked on that lie, had almost made it sound like a compliment. Brittany followed her out into the corridor then headed back toward the elevators. "He thought you'd be more comfortable in an office with a southern exposure, and the only one available is one floor down."

And as far from him as it could possibly get, Brittany thought. "A southern exposure, perfect," she said as they got in the elevator and headed down. "Oh, do you know what the color scheme is?" she asked as the elevator stopped at the next floor.

The doors slid open, but Rita didn't move as she looked at Brittany. "I'm sorry?"

"My new office, the color scheme? It has one, doesn't it?"

"Well, yes, I suppose you could say that. Beige carpeting, off-white walls, wood-toned desk."

"Well, we can fix that, can't we?" Brittany asked as she stepped out of the elevator. She looked back at Rita, motionless in the elevator. "This is the floor, isn't it?"

"Floor?" Rita shook her head slightly, trying very hard to slip that smile back on her face. "Oh, yes, the floor. Yes, it is," she said and moved out quickly, passed Brittany and headed to the left in the hallway.

"How long have you been with LynTech?" Brittany asked, hurrying to catch up.

"Six years in January," Rita said as she stopped at a single door with no plaque on it.

"You knew my father?"

"Not personally. I was in the secretarial pool then, but everyone spoke well of him. He really seemed to care about the company." She opened the door and looked at Brittany. "And it's very nice to see you here to carry on his tradition."

Brittany marveled at Rita's ability to say something like that with a straight face. "I haven't had much experience," she said, uneasy with the idea of carrying on any tradition.

"We all need to start somewhere," Rita said evenly as she crossed to open the beige curtains on windows across the less-than-spacious room.

The light of morning exposed a bleached-wood desk, a cloth-covered chair behind it with empty bookcases on the wall to the right and short filing cabinets to the left. The desk held a single business lamp, an idle computer under a dust cover and a phone.

"I've always loved this view," Rita was saying as she turned back to Brittany who had stayed in the doorway.

Brittany looked around, then grimaced slightly for effect. "You know, since Mr. Terrel isn't here, maybe you could give him a message for me?'' Even though it sounded ridiculous in her own ears, she finished in a rush, ''I really need to take care of something very important. I need a whole new wardrobe. I put it off until I saw the setting, but nothing I have would work in this place.'' She shook her head, not daring to look right at the woman. She wouldn't have been able to finish the charade if she had. ''Nothing would work. I think it just demands earth colors, rich and deep. I just don't have a thing to wear here and that's so important, the right tone, the right…aura.''

Rita stared at her, the smile completely gone now. ''Excuse me?''

''I need to coordinate my look so I feel right in here.'' She motioned around the small office. ''I mean, I want to do this properly and I'll stand out like a sore thumb if I wear my current wardrobe.'' She faked a slight shudder. ''Appearance is everything, don't you think?''

''Oh, yes, of course,'' Rita said in a small voice, then cleared her throat. ''When should I tell Mr. Terrel that you'll be…coordinated and able to start work?''

''I'm not sure. Why don't I contact you when I have a better idea of what's involved?''

''Of course,'' Rita said. ''Just call me and let me know and I'll keep Mr. Terrel informed.''

''That works for me,'' Brittany said, then looked at the emptiness again. ''I wonder if I should just redo the office to match what I have?'' Before Rita could choke on that, she shook her head. ''No, no, maybe later. Clothes, that's what I need to see about now.'' She turned, and, as she went back out into the corridor, she tossed over her shoulder, ''Thank you for everything. I'll be in touch.''

Rita didn't follow her as she hurried back to the elevator, quickly got in, went back up to the executive level and stepped out. The guard was nowhere in sight. She went back into the restroom, retrieved her things, then went into a private stall and transformed herself from Brittany Lewis to B. J. Smythe.

The elegant clothes were gone in favor of jeans, a loose white sweater and leather boots. She took out the clips, tugged her hair into a ponytail, then pushed her other clothes into the tote and took a deep breath. Now she had to get to the sixth floor and to Amy. She was more nervous about showing Amy her work than she had been about what she'd just done. Almost.

She peeked out into the corridor, saw it was empty, then slipped out. But when she heard the soft "ding" of one of the elevators approaching that floor, she ran to the stairwell door and pushed it open. She stepped into the stairwell, turned and was ready to push the door shut when the doors to the elevator silently slid open and Matt stepped out. She looked at her watch. It was just past nine o'clock. He'd almost caught her. But he hadn't, and she watched him for a minute.

His clothes were dark again, but a rich charcoal tone, from the silky, collarless shirt that clung to his broad shoulders to the dark slacks defining muscled legs and the boots. The same boots, from what she could tell. The effect only emphasized his size and the way he moved as he started down the hallway to his office. Smooth, easy, as if he owned the world. He probably thought he did, at least the world he touched. Poor man, she thought. He's going to have to apologize. And she just wished that she could be there when Rita told him about her encounter with Brittany Lewis.

Chapter Five

Matt strode toward his office an hour earlier than he'd expected to arrive, inhaled and hesitated for a moment when he caught a whiff of something in the air. Flowers? He looked around, but there were no fresh flowers anywhere in sight. It was elusive and as he moved again, the scent was gone. Whatever it stirred was gone with it. He pushed the door to his office open, but Rita wasn't there. Neither was anyone else. He crossed to his private area, went into the stark office and tossed his briefcase onto the desk.

"You're here," Rita said, and he turned as she came into the room after him.

"I told you I wasn't going to be here until ten." He looked at his wristwatch. "I'm early for a change."

"I'd say you're about fifteen minutes too late," she said, coming over to the desk as he went around to drop down in the high-back, leather chair.

"What emergency happened and what's the fall out?" he asked, more than used to the emergencies at LynTech being ugly and time consuming.

"Brittany Lewis."

He sat forward, pressing his hands to the desk top. "What?"

"She was here. You just missed her."

His luck was holding. "So, what happened?"

"She came and said she'd been held up shopping in London."

The image of B.J. telling him Brittany would have a good reason for being late made him laugh out loud. "Shopping?"

"That's her story and she's sticking to it," Rita said. He knew there was more and wasn't disappointed when she kept talking. "Then I showed her the office I found for her, and she promptly told me she'd be gone a few days finding a new wardrobe to go with the office. It's all about image, you know."

The laughter exploded in the room, and Matt could barely catch his breath. The bet he made with B.J. would be the easiest he'd ever won. "Image?" he asked.

"You got it. She's a pistol, as far removed from her dad as any kid could be. Oh, she's pretty enough, elegant, sort of, distinctive, but my goodness, she's self-centered and shallow." Rita shook her head. "If I hadn't met her, I'd never have believed it."

"Oh, I believe it," he murmured, the laughter dying when he remembered the earnestness of her father's wish for her to "accomplish" something. That wasn't going to happen and he'd probably have to be the one to tell Mr. Lewis.

"So, boss, when she shows up again, what do I do with her?"

He sat back in his chair. "Do whatever you want with her, but keep her out of my way."

"Okay," she said. "Although, we might never hear from her again."

"We couldn't be that lucky, could we?"

"No, boss, I'm afraid not." She looked at the wall clock. "You've got a ten-fifteen. Do you want to do it here or in the new conference area?"

"Here. And Rita?"

"Yes?"

"If Brittany Lewis ever shows up here again, tell her that I'm in a meeting, out of the office, out of town, or out of the state. Take your choice."

She held up her hand. "I get the idea." With that she turned and left, closing the door behind her.

"New clothes to match the office?" he muttered and his rough laughter echoed in the room.

BRITTANY FOUND AMY in the current day-care center, a much smaller space on the sixth floor, but with a real warmth to it that she felt as soon as she went through the door. Kids were everywhere, in groups for story reading, laying on mats in a side alcove, coloring on low tables that looked like mushrooms. And as Matt had told her, murals of Mother Goose tales brought the walls to life. She liked it. She liked it very much.

Amy saw her as soon as she came in and hurried over to her. A toddler, a little girl in a pink top and jeans, was cuddled in her arms. Huge brown eyes watched Brittany as the child hugged Amy. "Oh, I was hoping you'd make it." She looked at the envelope in Brittany's hand. "You have something?"

"It's rough, but I think it's something that you'll like."

Amy kissed the little girl on the forehead and crouched to put her on the floor. "Taylor, honey, mommy has to talk to this nice lady. Eileen's reading the Magic Jug story. Don't you want to hear what happens to the little boy in it?"

Amy's daughter glanced at Brittany, then at her mother. "No."

Amy touched her cheek. "How about a cookie and some juice?"

Taylor shook her head. "No."

"Okay, how about you listen to the story, then when I'm finished, just you and me will go downstairs to the big room and you can twirl?"

She hesitated, then finally agreed. "Uh-huh, twirl."

"Good girl," Amy said, then urged her daughter toward the reading group. "Mommy won't be long."

Taylor walked slowly to the group, plunked down on the carpet by the lady reading the story, but never took her eyes off of Amy.

"Okay, let's talk in the office," she said, motioning to a hallway framed by the mural of the Big Bad Wolf. "We can have some peace and quiet."

Brittany followed Amy down a hallway and into a cluttered room with file cabinets, boxes stacked here and there, toys in piles and a desk almost hidden under stacks of paperwork. Amy moved the things on the desk around, then motioned Brittany to put her papers on the cleared space. "I'm anxious to see this after what you told me last night. And to be honest, everything else that's been submitted has been…ordinary. At least it seems that way to me."

Brittany hoped hers didn't seem that way to Amy. She quickly took the sketches and notes out of the folder and laid them on the desk. She felt her heart start to race a bit at the sight of sketches that had seemed great in the middle of the night, but right then, looked almost "ordinary" to her.

Amy studied them silently for a long time, and Brittany spoke up nervously. "They're rough, you know, just ideas. But I think concentrating on the kids themselves is the main thing." She looked at her idea for the entrance area to the center. Kids holding hands, heads lifted upward, smiling and dancing. "I really would like to use the kids at the center, get their photos and use them to personalize the faces of the children. Link them to the place in a personal way."

Amy studied the ideas for the ceiling, sketches of the solar system in different stages, all revolving around the tree and a special star labelled *Just for Kids*. It had seemed great in the depths of the night, but as Amy hesitated, Brittany felt her heart skip. She couldn't read the woman's expression, just the intensity in it. She literally held her breath until Amy looked at her.

"B.J., these are terrific. They're just what I had in mind. I'll have to run them past some others here, but I want you to do it."

She blinked, the shock of the approval overwhelming to her. "Are you sure?"

"Absolutely." She lifted the main sketch and smiled. "I can imagine the faces on these, a place that's really for them. Lindsey is going to love it."

"I hope so," she said.

"Trust me, she will. Then we need to get it past the powers that be."

"The powers that be?"

"Mr. Terrel and Mr. Holden. They have final approval on anything in this redevelopment process."

She knew right then that she'd done the right thing not admitting to being Brittany Lewis. This wouldn't be happening if Matt knew that B.J. and Brittany were one in the same. And she wouldn't be feeling this euphoria at Amy's approval. "How...how long do you think it will be before there's a decision?" she asked.

"I'll get a hold of Matt...Mr. Terrel as soon as possible and—"

"Get a hold of me?" a deep, familiar voice said from behind them. "What for?"

Brittany turned, and all she could do was stare at the man while Amy spoke. In this room, his presence was almost overwhelming. He'd seemed big last night and earlier this morning, but right then, he filled every space around her. Dark as the night in his clothing choice, his hair sun-streaked against the darkness. And his eyes, dark too, intense, but crinkled with a bit of humor at the corners. Her breath caught in her chest, and she wasn't sure if it was from his sudden appearance or the fear that he'd take one look at the sketches and reject them out of hand.

She caught bits and pieces of Amy's words as the woman handed page after page to Matt. "Fantastic...perfect for what I was thinking...faces of the children...magic..."

She was staring at Matt and didn't care. His whole attention was on the sketches...her sketches. His dark eyes narrowed, then they were turned on her, and it jolted her. He took a step toward her with the main sketch she'd made in one hand.

"This is what you've done since last night?" he asked.

She nodded, her throat tight. "Yes."

His smile came from nowhere. "I'm impressed."

She felt giddy with relief, and just barely fought the need to grab at the edge of the desk for support. "Really?"

"I've told you that I don't know a lot about kids, except that I was one myself a while back, quite a while back, but this is good stuff." He glanced at Amy. "Since time is of the essence, I think we can make a decision about this between the two of us?"

She nodded. "I agree."

He looked back at Brittany. "The job is yours, if you can start right away and have something to show by the night before Christmas Eve. We're having a reception for families and investors, and we need to show what's happening at LynTech and what will happen. The center's not going to be completely done by then, but this..." He held up the paper. "...I want them to see at least a bit of it. I know it's the holidays and all, and everyone's made plans."

"I don't have any plans," she said quickly.

"No family pulls that are going to put you in a bind?"

"None. My family isn't local. I'll have all the time I need. I can do it."

He studied her for a long moment. "The money?"

She stared at him, his words not making sense, then she realized what he was saying. "Oh, yes, sure. I forgot."

"Maybe you aren't as savvy about business as I thought," he murmured with a crooked smile.

"Okay, how much?" she asked, trying not to fall into the snare of that smile. It was too damn appealing at the moment.

He named a figure and she realized that she had no idea if that was good pay or not. She had nothing to compare it to. "Okay, fine," she said.

He held his hand out to her, and smiled. "Welcome to LynTech."

B.J. took his hand, Matt knew he was in way too far with this woman. He knew right then that if he touched her very often, something would definitely happen between them. A bad idea, he told himself. An employee. A complication. Something he'd warned Zane about, taking his focus off LynTech at the most crucial time. Bad idea, a very bad idea. But so damn appealing.

He looked into those green eyes and found himself leaning closer, not expecting that soft parting of her lips or the slight tremble in her handshake. God, she was seductive. "By the way, I'm going to win our bet, so start thinking about your apology to me," he heard himself saying.

She blinked, lush lashes shadowing her green eyes for a moment. "Now, why would I do that?"

He had a flashing question of his own. How and when had a woman who was almost a stranger to him begun to fill spaces in his world that he hadn't known existed until right then? When had he lost that sense of teasing with another person? Even Zane and he had become sober in each other's company. The jokes were few and far between these days. But with B.J., the teasing came back so naturally. As naturally as the slight flush that came to her cheeks. "You're going to lose."

He felt her draw back from his touch and realized that the air around them was cold now that the heat of her hand was gone. "I wouldn't be too sure of that," she said in a softly husky voice.

"What are you two talking about?" Amy asked, and he realized he'd all but forgotten she was in the small office with them.

He spoke without looking away from B.J. "Miss Smythe seems to think that the Lewis heir is going to turn out to be a real businesswoman, that she has an insatiable appetite for productive work and is anxious to take on the family mantle of corporate responsibility." God, teasing her was so easy and so pleasurable.

He heard Amy's laughter. "Nice fairy tale," she said.

"I just think that everyone is too ready to form an opinion before all the facts are in," B.J. said. "And after all, the woman is the daughter of one of the most respected and influential businessmen around Houston."

"The same man who sold his shares instead of handing them over to his daughter," he said.

The humor that had been sparkling in her eyes died as he spoke. "How do you know he didn't want to hand them over to her and she wouldn't take them?"

"He didn't."

"She didn't."

"It doesn't wash," he murmured, wondering where the fun had gone.

"Why?"

"Reason number one: She's made a career out of finding men who want to marry her, then never getting married. Reason number two: Her father called to set this whole job up. She didn't call. Reason number three: she never showed yesterday. Reason number four: she showed up today."

"See, I told you so," B.J. said, the smile coming back and playing at the corners of her full lips.

"Then she promptly left."

"You drove her off?" Amy asked from behind him.

"No, I didn't drive her off," he said. "I never even met her. She met with Rita, and she said she couldn't possibly start work without a new wardrobe that fit with her office."

He expected B.J. to get flustered or to get defensive, or to even laugh out loud at the ridiculous scenario, but she didn't do any of that. She just cocked her head to one side, slanted him a look and said, "She showed up and she's taking this so seriously that she's worried about her image. I'd say she's on the right track."

"And she left to go shopping!"

"She showed up. You didn't expect her even to do that. She can surprise you again. And she might."

"Don't bet on it," he said.

"But I have," she murmured, then looked at Amy. "Can I get those photos of the children as quickly as possible?"

"Sure," Amy said. "You can have them now. I've got pictures we took for the parents' Christmas gifts. I took extras so that if they ruined one making the ornament for their parents, I'd be covered." She headed for the door. "I'll be right back."

As soon as Amy left the room, Matt felt a strange sensation of intimacy that came from nowhere. It was time for him to leave. "I have to get to work, but if you need anything, just ask Amy, okay?"

"Thanks, I will."

He hesitated, then couldn't resist. "Start writing your apology."

She grinned at him, a sudden expression that had the same effect as the sun breaking out on a gloomy day. "You get started on your apology to Brittany Lewis, and you have to do it yourself, no ghostwriting by your assistant."

"I'll do it personally—but I won't lose," he said and left the room.

Brittany released a breath she hadn't realized she'd been holding until Matt was gone. She'd never been around anyone in her life that kept her on edge the way he did. There was nothing simple or easy about him.

She heard Matt say something that was muffled by distance, then Amy was there with an envelope. "Here are the pictures," she said handing it to Brittany. "I'm so excited about this. When Lindsey gets back, she'll be thrilled."

"When will Lindsey be back?"

"She's on her honeymoon and won't be back until after the new year."

"We should have it partially worked out by then," Brittany said. "Thanks for the pictures. I'll just need to get some supplies, then I'll be back later today. I'll need a key for the center if I'm going to get to work."

"I'll leave word at the front desk that you're to be let into the center and I'll try to get you a key."

"Thanks," B.J. said. "I'll get started right away. Do you think there'll be a problem with me working at night around here?"

"I don't think so. Mr. Terrel is here till all hours. But I'll let Security know when I call down to have them let you in."

"Thanks," Brittany said, then hurried out, making her way through the kids who seemed to be everywhere now. She slipped out the front doors and closed the barrier behind her. The noise diminished, and she took the time to inhale deeply before she headed for the elevators.

She'd done something she'd never even thought of doing before. She'd been hired for work on her own. It was nothing her father had arranged, or anything that anyone else had done for her. It was hers, all hers. She hugged her arms around herself, crushing the tote to her chest as she went along to the elevators. It felt good. And it would feel even better when she looked right at Matt Terrel and told him who she was...after she'd succeeded at the job.

IT WAS THREE IN THE afternoon before Brittany got back to LynTech and had the security guard help her carry in her supplies that she'd bought. He stacked the boxes in the deserted rooms on the bottom floor and left. Brittany stood very still. There was emptiness everywhere, even on the walls, but that wasn't going to last long.

She found the envelope Amy had given her, slipped the pictures out on the floor, then sat down cross-legged and started sorting through them. They were candid shots filled with laughing and smiling children, and she methodically began to put them in some sort of order. There was Amy's little girl, grinning at the camera with great delight. A little boy with a cap of blond hair, huge blue eyes filled with mischief. Another showed two older boys, maybe eight or nine, around the age of the mysterious boy who had come to her rescue. They definitely would look great framing two of the smaller children.

She sorted and sorted, then got out a box of tacks and tacked each picture to the wall. She staggered them, putting them at the approximate height of each child. She had turned to reach for more of the pictures when she realized she wasn't alone. There was a sense of someone there, and she spun around, expecting the security guard, or maybe even Matt or Amy, but it wasn't any of them.

The boy was there. He stood not more than five feet from her, and she hadn't even heard him come in. He was in baggy clothes, frayed jeans, a faded T-shirt, a baseball hat turned backwards and oversize tennis shoes with the toes almost gone. "I had no idea you were here. You scared me to death," she said, pressing one hand to her chest.

"Sorry, lady," he said, moving back a bit, and she was sure he was going to take off. "I didn't know no one was in here."

With the baggy clothes, she'd thought he was bigger, but she had a feeling he was pretty small, maybe even younger than she'd thought. "Aren't you supposed to be upstairs?"

"Me? What for?"

"You're from the day-care center, aren't you?"

He shook his head. "No, I don't go there."

"Then how did you get in here?"

He glanced around nervously. "Listen, I don't want no trouble. I was just looking around. No one's ever in here after them men leave."

"What's your name?"

"What's yours?"

"Brit...B.J."

"Anthony. And I gotta go," he said, starting to turn to leave.

"Can you wait a minute? I wanted to talk to you," she said, and he stopped, looking back at her.

"Say what?"

"About what happened last night."

He held up both small hands, and she could see that they were touched with grease and dirt, as if he'd been digging around outside. "I didn't know that dude was one of the big guys. I thought he was gonna hurt you."

"I know, and I wanted to thank you for helping me. He could have intended to hurt me. You didn't know that he was okay. I owe you."

He shrugged. "No way."

"Yes, I do."

He'd come a bit closer, and she could see the deep brown of his eyes, almost black. "Who was he, anyway?"

"His name is Matt and he's the boss here. He just hired me, actually." She motioned to the supplies scattered all over and to the pictures on the wall. "I'm going to put drawings on the walls."

He looked past her. "You're getting paid for it?"

"Yes, I am."

"How much?" he asked bluntly, startling her.

She blinked, then found herself telling him the amount Matt had quoted to her.

His eyes widened and he let out a low whistle. "That much?"

She didn't have a clue if it was a lot or a little, but he was obviously impressed. "Yeah, just to make some drawings for them."

"That's a scam," he said. "I don't mean nothing bad about you, but that's a lot of money for drawing stuff."

"I guess it is."

He came even closer. "So, what're you gonna draw?"

She turned, motioning to the pictures on the wall and told him her ideas. Surprisingly, he listened quietly, taking it in, and when she was finished he was silent for a long moment. Then he looked at her. "Can you really do that?"

"Do what?"

"Draw faces that look like the kids?"

"Yes, I can."

"Cool."

"Cool," she echoed.

Then he shocked her again. "Do you need help?"

"Help?"

"Cleaning up? Picking stuff up? I can do that real good."

"Anthony, how old are you?"

"What's that gotta do with it?"

"I'm just wondering."

"I'm nine. How old are you?"

She laughed at that. "Twenty-seven."

"You're old enough to do the drawing, and I'm old enough to do the picking up."

"Don't you have other things to do? It's almost Christmas and your mom and dad must have plans."

"Don't got a mom and dad. Just Esther, and she's glad to not have me anywhere around." He turned those brown eyes on her. "Christmas don't mean nothing."

She remembered when she was nine and how magical Christmas was. How magical it still could be. But Anthony looked so matter-of-fact, so sober. "Where are your mom and dad?"

"My mom's dead, got killed, and my dad just left. That's why I'm with Esther. She's okay, but she don't want kids around much. That's why I come on over around here and stay away from her."

"Where is she?"

"Down the street."

"She works around here?"

"She's a maid at the hotel down near the lights. And there's always after school. I can't stay at the apartment cuz Bert's there and he doesn't want no kids around, and when she's working I can't get her in trouble."

In that garbled explanation, she found the truth. His mom died. His dad deserted him. Esther, whoever she was, didn't want him, and someone named Bert wouldn't let him stay at an apartment during the day. And he came to work with

Esther, but had to keep out of sight. It was so far out of her realm of experience that she had to forcibly push it into her mind and let it solidify. "So, you come on in here and hang out?"

"You got it."

"How do you even get in here?"

The openness was gone, and he backed up a bit from her. "Just do."

"It's okay. I'm not going to tell anyone. I was just wondering. I didn't hear you come in."

"You were too busy looking at the pictures and the stuff."

That was true. "So, you're on your own for the day?"

"Most of the time."

"Can't your... Esther get you into day care?"

He grimaced at that. "No, I'm too old and it costs money."

Her father had always mentioned that he'd thought the day-care program should expand to help kids that needed it the most, the latchkey kids, like Anthony. If she got it right, that's what Lindsey and Amy were aiming at. Maybe the center could help Anthony now. "You want to work?"

He nodded. "I'd do real good for you."

"Okay, you've got a job."

He grinned at her, the first really childish expression she'd seen on his face. "You mean it?"

"I mean it."

"Cool."

There was a sound behind the entryway, then the door clicked and Anthony moved quickly. Brittany had an impression of him going behind her as she turned to the doors. They opened and Matt came in.

"I was wondering if you were still here."

He paused, glanced behind her, then came closer. "Did I interrupt a strategy session?"

She frowned. "What?"

He motioned to Anthony who had all but hidden behind her. "You and the kid. Are you planning your next attack?"

"We were talking."

He frowned, looking past her right shoulder. "Kid, aren't you supposed to be upstairs or something instead of down here bugging the lady?"

She felt Anthony stir, then he stepped out from behind her, and she glanced to her right. His hands were in fists at his sides. Instinctively, she touched his shoulder, not about to be part of another scene like that the night before. She felt him jerk slightly at her touch, but he never looked away from Matt.

"He's not bugging me," she said quickly, wondering why the man and the boy were so instantly adversarial. A little kid and a man the size of a small mountain. It didn't make sense.

Anthony moved slightly, away from her touch. "My name's Anthony, mister," he muttered.

"My name's Mr. Terrel, kid, and why aren't you upstairs in the center?" Matt asked again.

It was ridiculous. They were almost circling each other now. "He's not from the center."

Matt looked at her. "Then what's he doing in here?"

She went closer to Matt, partially shielding Anthony from him. "He's visiting me."

"You said you didn't know him."

"I didn't know him then, but I do now."

Matt turned from her, looking to her right, then left, then glancing around the room. "Where in the hell did he get to now?"

She turned, looked behind her, then back at Matt. "You scared him away."

"What?"

"He's on his own, killing time while the woman who takes care of him works at a hotel down the street."

"And going to get into trouble, if he hasn't already done damage around here."

"He won't. He's just bored and probably a bit scared."

"How do you know that?"

"How do *you* know that he's going to do damage?"

He hesitated, then his eyes narrowed. "I know the type."

"Oh, sure, you know all types, the Brittany Lewis type, rich, spoiled and indulged, and the Anthony type, a little hoodlum waiting to destroy LynTech brick by brick."

He studied her intently and for a moment she thought whatever chance she had of proving herself to this man was gone. She was certain he was just going to tell her to get out and keep going. But, unexpectedly, he came a bit closer, inclining his head to one side. "How do we always wind up doing this?"

"What?" she asked in a small voice.

"Arguing about strangers."

"We aren't arguing," she said, but knew he was right. "We're…discussing things."

"And keeping you on subject is damn near impossible," he murmured.

"Why did you come down here? Were you checking up on me, making sure that I wasn't housing any juvenile delinquents?"

He shook his head. "Let's start over, okay?"

She'd wished she could restart things so many times in her life when she couldn't, that she readily agreed with Matt. "Hello, Mr. Terrel. What brings you down here?"

He smiled, an explosive expression when she was so

close to him. "The name is Matt, and I came down to bring you this."

She quickly looked down at his hand, and saw a key lying in the palm. "What for?"

"Amy said that you thought you'd be working late a lot to get this going, and it seemed like a good idea to give you your own key to this area. There's always a guard on duty at the main entrance to let you in and out of the building."

She took the key, annoyed that her hand was slightly unsteady. She drew back, ignoring his body heat caught in the metal, and closed her fingers tightly around it. "Thanks," she murmured, drawing her hand back to her middle. "That'll be a big help."

He looked at all of her things scattered around the area, and the pictures tacked to the wall, then back at her. "I also came to tell you that Amy gave me some copies of your sketches and ideas, and I faxed them to Lindsey and Zane even though they're on their honeymoon."

She felt her breath catch in her chest. Even though Amy and Matt had agreed to let her do the work, she knew that the final answers came from Zane Holden and Lindsey, his wife. "And?" she asked.

"They were very impressed and said it's exactly what they wanted."

"Yes!" she said, spinning away from Matt and turning around and around several times euphorically. The room passed in a blur, but she could envision the life and color that would be there when she finished. "Wow, this is so great!"

She came to a stop facing Matt, and was startled by the intensity of his expression. It almost took her breath away, and she felt mortified that she'd acted so impulsively. Not businesslike, and not something that he liked obviously.

"Oh, I'm sorry," she gasped, hugging her arms around herself.

Without warning, he reached out, touching her chin with the tip of his finger, cutting off any other words from her. The contact was like fire on her skin, searing that spot, the way it had in the car the night before. "Don't apologize," he said, his finger lingering on her for a long moment before he drew back and put some distance between them.

"I tend to get carried away." Boy, that was the truth, and she had three broken engagements to attest to it. She cringed at the memory. "My father always says that I get too excited before I really think something through."

"That's called being a human being," he murmured. He reached out to her again, this time cupping her chin with the warmth strength of his hand. "So is the fact that I think I'd like to..." His gaze dropped to her lips, and she was stunned to realize he wanted to kiss her. And even more stunned at her disappointment when he finished his thought. "I'd like to take you to dinner."

"What?" she asked, and could hear the slight breathlessness in her own voice.

"Dinner. Food." He drew back, the connection broken again, and this time she barely covered a shiver at the loss of contact. "It seems that I've been eating alone a lot lately, and I'd like some conversation with good food. We might not agree, but it's never boring."

"Oh, I don't think that—"

"You're not married, are you?" he asked.

"Me? No, I'm not."

"Engaged?"

"No."

"Involved?"

"No."

"Then let's have dinner."

"No." She couldn't. Not when she wanted to so badly, or when the idea of really being alone with him again was so appealing. Or when she knew that he'd never ask Brittany Lewis out to dinner.

"That's it?"

"I'm not doing that, I mean, dating or getting involved with anyone," she said, her words as awkward as she felt at that moment.

"I'm not either," he told her. "I don't want to. I don't have the time or the inclination to get involved. It was a dinner invitation, not an invitation for the night."

She took a step back as she felt the fire in her face. Stupid, stupid, stupid, she told herself. Dinner. That was it. But she wasn't doing it again, jumping in, expecting something that wasn't there. She'd made so many mistakes with men, been too impulsive, too ready to go with her feelings. Big mistake. "Thanks, but no, I...I really need to work. Time, it's not a luxury I've got at the moment."

She didn't know what she expected, maybe, "Are you sure?" or "Can't you take a break?" But it wasn't for Matt to give up easily, to say, "Yeah, I've got work, too. You have a good evening and get plenty of work done," then turn and head back for the entrance.

Before she could say anything else, he was gone. Then there was nothing. Emptiness. "Well, you could have asked me again," she muttered, but was thankful he hadn't. She knew what she would have done if he'd persisted.

Chapter Six

Matt closed the door and headed for the elevators. He got on and realized that the hand that had touched B.J. was clenched in a fist. He opened it, pressed it to his side and exhaled roughly as the floor numbers flashed by. He usually understood everything he did. He had a reason for it. Logic behind it. But he'd touched her and he had no reason to. Oh, he knew *why* he'd done it. He'd wanted to do it from the moment he'd felt her softness when he'd touched her in the car last night, when he'd noticed the sweep of her throat, the way her chin lifted slightly when she was gearing up for a confrontation. But why he'd allowed it to happen still didn't make sense.

The doors opened and he strode down the corridor to his office. He passed Rita's empty desk and headed for his own private area. He looked down at the work stacked on his desk and ignored it, sinking down in his leather chair. He turned to the view, the duskiness of evening over Houston below, and leaned back.

The phone rang, but before Matt could swivel around and answer it, it stopped. He sat back, then heard someone in the outer office just before the door opened. Rita was there, peeking into the office. "I wasn't sure if you were here or not."

"I'll be here for a while."

"I came back for my purse and caught a phone call." She pointed to the phone on his desk. "Mr. Lewis is on hold. I told him you might not be here, so do you want to talk or should I tell him he missed you?"

"I'll take it," he said. "But how do I tell him that she's color coordinating her office and wardrobe?"

She smiled ruefully. "Somehow I don't think he'll be surprised, but then again, maybe he just doesn't need to know. After all, she did show up."

He nodded. "You're right. He's lived with her all her life. I'm sure he knows a lot more than we do."

"Oh, Mr. Holden faxed in some extra ideas for the center. He asked that we get them to Miss Smythe. Do you want me to run them down in the morning?"

He shook his head. "No, I'll do it. Just leave them on your desk."

"You got it, boss. Now, I need to get going. Stan got the boys from the center a while ago, but I was supposed to meet them at the pizza place..." She looked at her watch. "Ten minutes ago. Bye."

She was gone, and Matt braced himself before reaching for the phone. "Hello, Robert?"

"Yes, Matthew, sorry to bother you, but I wanted to thank you for all you've done for Brittany."

All he'd done? "Excuse me?"

"She called last night and said that you'd been very accommodating, and she seems anxious to work." He laughed to himself. "A miracle. You've worked a miracle, Matthew."

Matt closed his eyes tightly and forced himself to cut back his immediate response. Instead, he took a breath, then said, "Well, it's up to her, isn't it?"

"Yes, yes it is." He heard the man sigh. "Life is so short,

and I'm hoping that Brittany will realize that there's more to life than living it. I know she's been inundated with LynTech since its inception, and I always thought…'' He sighed again. "You know, she's very much like me.''

He almost choked on that. "Excuse me?''

"Oh, she looks like her mother, just beautiful, but she's very determined to do things her way. Stubborn, I guess. Impetuous, definitely. But I also believe that she's got the ability to make a difference in the world.''

"Well, Robert, if she's anything like you, she'll definitely make a difference.''

"That's what I'm hoping for.'' He heard the older man exhale softly. "What is that saying? Life is what slips past us while we mourn the past or lust after the future.''

Matt thought for the umpteenth time since he'd been in contact with Robert Lewis, that he liked the man. Straightforward, no game-playing, even in business. At first he'd thought the man had been likeable but weak where the hard decisions for the company were concerned. Too compliant. Too involved. Making things too personal.

But lately he'd started to believe that *weak* hadn't been the right word. Now he was thinking that the man was quietly wise. Even in whom he chose to turn the company over to. Maybe, on some level, he'd known that Zane would do an about-face and keep LynTech. Maybe not. But it seemed that way.

"I guess now is all there is, but if you ever think of coming out of retirement, we could use a good advisor.''

Robert Lewis laughed suddenly. "Oh, I might end up working for Brittany, if she does as well as I think she will.''

Not unless you're going to go into fashion designing, Matt thought, but said, "You never know.''

"I need to go, but thanks again. I think this might be just what Brittany's been looking for all along.''

Maybe she'll find fiancé number four here, he thought with a smile, a smile he kept out of his tone of voice. "You never know," he repeated.

Matt hung up and sat back again. "Life is what slips past us." And that thought conjured up the image of B.J. downstairs, alone. And him up here, alone. Life just slipping past. Matt sat there for a very long time just staring at the city as it darkened. Finally, he stood, ignoring the work, and turned off the lights. Night was here, with deep shadows, and the loneliness in the room was almost suffocating. Odd, he hadn't thought of loneliness for a very long time. Being alone was fine by him. But right then he *felt* alone, and he didn't like it. He grabbed his briefcase and left the office. He looked at the elevator doors and almost headed towards them.

Instead he bypassed the elevators to go to Zane's office and use the private executive elevator. He had work to do and things to take care of. He'd spend Friday night alone, doing work that would stretch well into the weekend, then there was the chance he'd have to fly to New York to meet with possible investors. None of that included B.J., and none of it would include the wild fantasies that she could engender in him.

December 17

BRITTANY SPENT her weekend working at the Houston estate, sketching and doing layouts. During the next week she worked all day and into the evening at LynTech. Every day that week, Anthony had shown up at three o'clock in the afternoon and stayed until six. And every day Matt had been nowhere to be seen. She knew he was in the building off and on. He'd had papers brought down to her that Lindsey

Holden had faxed. She knew from Amy that he'd made a hurried flight to New York to meet with investors.

Whatever was going on, he never came down to where she was working, and it was a relief. She had to concentrate and that was nearly impossible when Matt was around. Work had to be her total focus if she wanted to succeed.

Late in the afternoon on Wednesday, Anthony was at her side watching while she sketched one of the children on the wall. "That's way cool," he said softly.

She looked at him, his huge brown eyes intent on her work, his faded baseball cap backwards, and wearing jeans that looked four sizes too big for him. "You like it?"

"It's real…like a person," he said.

"It's…" She picked up the corner of the picture she was working from and read the back of it. "Simon. He's Simon, and he's four."

"Just a baby," Anthony said, moving back a bit. "They're all babies."

"No, not all of them. A lady named Rita has two boys that are about your age."

"Which one's her?"

"The lady who works for Matt?"

"The skinny one?"

"Well, I wouldn't put it that way."

"Why're her kids in that baby place?"

One thing she'd learned about Anthony over the past few days was, he was a man. He told her that over and over again. He was a man. He did whatever he had to do, and he took care of himself. He didn't know that the scared look that flashed in his eyes from time to time was readable to people around him. That look when he had to leave, and a look that was starting to really get to her.

She'd seldom thought about kids in her life, but this little boy was a real little human being. And despite what Matt said, he wasn't a bad kid. Just lonely and scared and alone. Despite the fact Anthony didn't say much about Esther, Brittany knew that she didn't care about the child. Esther had hit him at the bus stop, an image Brittany hadn't been able to shake since it had happened.

Now she explained to Anthony, "They're being taken care of, and their mom wants them close to her."

He moved away from her, crossing to where she stacked her supplies on a drop cloth against the wall she'd been working on. "They're babies," he muttered.

She looked at him as he crouched to reach for the case that held her charcoal supplies. "It's almost time for you to go," she said, looking at the clock. Ten minutes to six. "Esther's going to be looking for you."

He turned, his bottom lip out a bit. "No way. She don't worry about me."

"Of course she does," she said automatically.

"She says that she's stuck with me, that I'd better not give her no problems."

He said the words so matter-of-factly, but they hurt just hearing them. "She's probably just saying that."

"You don't know nothing. Esther said if she didn't get no check for me, she'd let them put me in jail."

"She gets money for having you?" A foster parent?

"Sure, they pay her to keep me. You don't think she'd do that if she didn't get no money, do you?"

She looked down at the charcoal pencil she'd been holding, at her fingers smudged with black. "Then she's not related to you?"

"I don't think so. She knew my dad way back, and she says she's like a cousin or something like that."

She looked at the glowing face of the boy she was sketching, the picture almost alive with his grin of pleasure, then she looked at Anthony. His face was impassive, his eyes wide, but not with wonder. He was just looking at the world the way it was. "How long have you been with Esther?"

"Three months."

"And you've been coming here every day after school and just…?"

"Hanging." He shrugged. "It's better than being with Bert. He yells all the time, even at Esther and she's his girlfriend. I don't think he even likes her."

She wanted to go over and just hug Anthony, but she knew that was definitely out. She wasn't sure what he'd do, but she knew he wouldn't endure it. So, she went closer and just smiled at him. "I can't see how he can't like you."

He cocked his head to one side. "You serious?"

"Absolutely. You're smart, and you're a good worker and you're handsome, and…" She smiled. "You know how to hang."

Suddenly he grinned at her, and he was a little boy. An endearing little boy. "Yeah, I guess I do." Then the smile was gone as he looked at the clock. "I gotta go."

"Anthony, tomorrow you'll be here, but what about Saturday. What are you going to be doing?"

"Hanging," he said, but with no smile this time.

"Where?"

"Don't know. Esther works some, and Bert's there." He shrugged. "Don't know."

"How about here? I'll be working. In fact, I'll be working every day until Christmas. So, if you've got time, you want to hang here?"

He nodded quickly. "Yeah."

"Noon?"

"Yeah, good," he said and looked at the clock again. "Gotta go."

Anthony moved before she could do anything, running into the back hallway, then she heard the door open. For a minute she heard someone yelling, yelling words that she couldn't quite catch, but the tone was scary before the door slammed. She hurried to the back, pushed open the door and stepped out into the parking garage just in time to see the same woman who had hit Anthony that first night. But this time she was grabbing him by his arm and jerking him toward her.

She wasn't tall, but heavy, with dark features and a round face that looked bleak, her hair pulled tightly back into a knot. In a blue coat and heavy black shoes, she looked formidable, and angry.

"You disappear, and you know we have to leave!" the woman was shouting, her voice echoing all around them in the almost-empty garage. "I tell you and I tell you, but you don't listen." She was shaking him hard now, and Brittany hurried toward the two of them. "You're no good, that's for sure, just like your dad. You're—"

Brittany was almost there, ready to grab the woman to make her stop, when someone called out from behind her. "Hey, what's going on?" Matt. His voice rising above Esther's.

"Just taking care of the kid," Esther said, looking past Brittany with an annoyed frown. "Ain't none of your business."

"My building, my business," Matt said as he came up beside Brittany. He looked like a shadow in a black silk shirt, snug black slacks and leather boots. He seemed to have come from nowhere, but he was very real, and Esther was paying attention to him. She'd stopped shaking Anthony, at least for the moment. "I heard the commotion as I was getting out of the elevator."

Matt wasn't yelling, but actually speaking in an easy voice, as if he was interested, but not judgmental. It amazed

Brittany that he could be so calm when all she wanted to do was slap the woman and snatch Anthony away from her.

"I've been looking all over for him, then some old drunk in the alley says that he's probably in here. So I had to get in with that delivery guy to check and find him."

"Annoying, isn't it, after a hard day at work?"

Anthony was staring hard at the ground, not moving at all. "You bet. It's real annoying. And he don't belong here."

She shook him sharply, and all that kept Brittany from going after her was Matt's sudden grip on her shoulder. She twisted toward him, but he never let go, and looking away from the woman in front of him. "He's here because he's helping Miss Smythe. I didn't realize that you hadn't been told about him helping here." His dark eyes turned on her, their expression unreadable. "Isn't he, Miss Smythe?"

Matt pressed B.J.'s shoulder slightly, hoping against hope that she would make this as easy as possible. But she seemed incapable of saying anything else, so he took over. "He's working for you from, oh, three to six, isn't he?" She was staring at him, and he moved quickly, skimming his hand across the back of her shoulders, hugging her to his side. The sensation of delicate bones, heat and softness was there, and he tried to block out the feeling. He stared at her. "Isn't he?" he repeated.

Then she finally spoke and didn't disappoint him. "It could be earlier, but usually...that would be it."

He looked back at the woman with the boy. "I'm Matthew Terrel," he said, holding out his free hand to her.

"I'm Esther, Esther Ray." She let go of Anthony to shake his extended hand. The boy was free, but apparently knew better than to move away from her. He stood still, then looked up at Matt, his face set in an expression Matt had seen before…on kids that he'd grown up with…probably on his own. "Did you say the kid's working for you?"

"We're expanding our day-care center, and he's helping pick things up." He looked right at Anthony, hoping that the boy was as smart as he thought he had to be to survive having a mother like this. "Right, Anthony?"

He barely nodded and spoke in a low voice. "Yeah, right, mister."

Matt looked back at Esther. "Of course, he can only do this if it's okay with you."

"How much pay is there for it?" she asked.

Matt felt B.J. tensing again, and he squeezed her shoulder lightly. "Five dollars an hour."

That made Esther smile. "Good. And you'll be paying me, not him, then he won't spend it all on garbage?"

"Of course, we'll make sure that we do that. We'll get your address and phone number from Anthony and get in touch with you directly," Matt said.

"Good, that's good. But what about Saturdays?"

Matt knew he'd be here and B.J. probably would be, too. From what he'd heard, she put in long, long hours working on the new place. "He can come in on Saturdays if he wants to."

"He wants to," she said.

"Good."

"Time to leave," Esther said, taking Anthony by the sleeve, but easier this time. "How do we get out of here?" she asked the boy.

He shrugged and Matt stepped in again. "Go out the exit by the car ramp." He pointed across the garage to the security area. "The guard will let you out."

"Thanks, mister," she said, and tugged Anthony to get him to go with her.

He watched the two of them cross the cavernous area, go

up the ramp, and they were barely out of sight when B.J. twisted out of his hold. She was going after the boy and the woman, and he made a grab to stop her. He caught her by her upper arm. "Oh, no, you don't," he muttered.

to the top. They were barely out of sight when B.J. stood, opened her mouth, as if to scream, then clamped it shut. "I couldn't stand to listen to her crying," she whispered in a rush.

Chapter Seven

B.J. spun around, jerking free of Matt. She had color in her cheeks and her eyes blazed with anger. "What are you doing?" she gasped.

"Hey, I'm not the enemy here," he said as he held up both hands, palms toward her.

"Well, you just stood there and let her leave with Anthony."

He'd thought she'd understood when he was talking to the woman, but he knew she hadn't. She was furious with him, as if he should have struck the woman dead and taken off with the kid. "What was I supposed to do?"

"Stop her. Make her leave Anthony here and go away." She was starting to shake, and he watched her hug her arms around herself. "You know she hit him before, and she's going to hit him again. He doesn't deserve what she's doing to him."

"She's his mother—"

"No," she said quickly, cutting him off. "No. She's somebody being paid to look after him, a distant cousin or something, and she hates him." She exhaled in a rush, the anger replaced by an extra brightness in her eyes. "God, he told me that she hated him, and I thought it was a kid's exaggeration. But she hit him, and she was shaking him and yelling at him.''

"She *has* hit him, and she will again.''

"Then how could you let her leave with him?''

"How couldn't I? If I'd threatened her, she'd still leave with the kid, and God knows what she'd do to him when they were alone.''

She looked pale all of a sudden. "Oh, God,'' she whispered.

Matt came closer and touched her shoulder. "Are you all right?''

She closed her eyes tightly, the shaking getting more pronounced. "We can't just…just ignore it, pretend that it isn't happening. We just drove by the other night, and now… we…we're just letting her take him.''

"Of course we can't ignore it,'' he said softly and he shifted his hands, lifting them to frame her face. "But we need to think about things. He's okay for now. He's going to make her money, and that's all that matters to her at the moment. He seems smart, at least smart enough to keep his mouth shut.''

"But he's just a kid. He's only nine years old.''

"Hey, I grew up around kids who were living through what Anthony is right now. For now he's okay.'' He studied her intently, and contemplated the impact the scene had had on her. "What I don't understand is why you're so upset about this, about a kid you barely know.''

"I just…'' Her tongue touched her soft pink lips. "He's so little and I…I never…''

She shivered sharply, and Matt acted instinctively, pulling her to him, holding her in his arms, trying to do something to stop the trembling. And she didn't fight him. She almost fell against him, burying her face in his shoulder and her arms slipped around his waist.

He closed his eyes tightly as he inhaled her sweet warmth, letting the softness of her body against his filter into his being, and at that moment he felt a stunning sense of connection that he'd never experienced before in his life. For one whole week he'd pretended that B.J. didn't exist. For one whole week he'd done his work and ignored her presence at LynTech. He thought he'd managed to push her out of his thoughts and to stop whatever had been starting between them.

He'd been able to do that for what seemed forever. There'd been women, but never anything like this. Never this all-consuming awareness. Never this feeling that, although separated for a week, they'd been apart for less than a heartbeat. It shook him and confused him. But all he wanted right then was to touch her, to protect her and support her. And to figure out why just being close to her seemed to shut off a sense of loneliness.

He felt her heart beating against him, the trembling breaths she took, and he found himself holding her more tightly. "He'll be okay," he whispered. "We'll work something out."

She shifted back a bit, but stayed in his arms as she tipped her face up to look into his eyes. "How do you know that?"

He didn't know anything at that moment, except that he wanted to kiss her. Her lips were softly parted, the heat of her rapid breathing brushing his face, her body against his. Kiss? He wanted more than that, but right then, touching her lips with his seemed the most important thing in his world.

Brittany felt lost in a jumble of sensations. Fear for Anthony and a sense of being anchored with Matt—his arms around her, his heat and strength everywhere, and then he was looking down at her. His eyes were as dark as the night and every bit as seductive. He'd seduced Esther into easing off on Anthony, and now he was seducing her into feeling as if he could right all the wrongs in this world.

When his head lowered and his lips touched hers, it seemed like the most natural thing in the world. The contact was stunning, something that robbed her of all reason, of all common sense. He was the center of the world, and his touch ruled that world. His hands on her, circling her, his body hard and solid against hers, and the heat…it was everywhere, around her and inside her, igniting an ache of need that reached into her soul.

She trembled, slipping her arms around his neck as she yearned toward him. His heart beat against her, her fingers tangled in his thick hair and his mouth ravaged hers. She'd been kissed before, but never had that kiss connected her in such an irrevocable way with another human being. Never had she had a sense that if she just let go, she'd be lost in another person.

She'd heard of the earth moving and rockets going off, but suddenly there were bells and sirens and whistles, and the cacophony echoed all around her. It wasn't until Matt jerked back, his hands holding her away from him, that she realized that the noises weren't just in her head. His eyes held the fire that seared her, the awareness of what was happening echoed in his gaze, then he was letting her go, he was fumbling in his slack pockets.

She looked down, then jerked her eyes up as she saw evidence of his arousal. God, what had happened? She felt panic running through her. The sounds ripped painfully through the air. Then Matt pulled something from his pocket, and the noise stopped. The silence was overwhelming, broken only by their mutual ragged breathing. Matt was holding something up, a leather fob on a gold ring that held two keys and a car remote.

Matt smiled at her, a decidedly unsteady expression.

"The alarm," he said in a voice tinged with a degree of hoarseness.

An alarm. She stared at the small black piece of plastic with three blue buttons on it. An alarm. Thank God. She backed up, turning slightly to smooth at her clothes, unable to look at Matt again. An alarm stopped everything. Too bad she didn't have a built-in craziness alarm. She closed her eyes tightly. She was still doing it. Jumping in with both feet. Not looking. Not thinking. She'd almost done it again. Just because the man had been a hero of sorts, talking Esther into easing up on Anthony, because he'd said things would be okay, because he'd touched her.

She took a shaky breath, and she forced herself to look back at Matt. He hadn't moved, his face intense with a frown. And she didn't know what to say. If she'd been Brittany, she would have laughed at it, said that things happened, that maybe they should look into it further. But B. J. Smythe couldn't do that. She felt angry at herself, and afraid of just how easy it had been to forget everything when it came to Matt.

"I'm sorry," she heard herself say. "I was scared. I've never..." She bit her bottom lip hard, the slight pain helping her focus as another shiver shook her body. "I'm sorry."

He narrowed his eyes on her. "Don't be. Things happen," he murmured. Then he shrugged, his broad shoulders testing the fine material of his shirt. "No harm, no foul."

Trite words. But she nodded. "Exactly."

He stayed where he was. "What now?"

She thought he was asking about the kiss, about them. But there was no them. "I don't know."

"Well, for now, Anthony can work here and at least he'll be safe for a few hours a day."

She touched her tongue to her lips, thankful that there was no taste of him there. "I don't know what else to do."

"It's a start," he murmured as he moved toward her, and he literally held her breath until he went past her without touching her again. She turned and saw him cross to retrieve a briefcase leaning against the closed doors of the private elevator that went up into her father's old offices. He picked it up, then turned to her. "I almost forgot about this."

"Thank you for what you did," she said quickly.

"It wasn't anything." He came toward her. "Are you ready to leave?"

She shook her head, knowing that he was going to offer her a ride. And driving in the car with him again was out of the question. "I've got more to do."

"I could wait."

"Oh, no, no," she said quickly. "You go ahead. You must have a lot to do, too."

He hesitated, then said, "Okay, but don't work too late."

Polite, easy words, as if the kiss had never happened. "I won't," she said and turned to head for the security door that hadn't closed completely. She was thankful it wasn't working correctly, closing tightly when it was let go. An error that saved her having to go up the executive elevator to come back down to the bottom level. She never looked back as she stepped inside, closed the door tightly, then almost collapsed back against the metal barrier. She closed her eyes for a long moment, took several deep breaths, then stood straight. Blocking the kiss from her mind, she went over to the wall, picked up her sketching material and got back to work.

December 18

MATT SAT ALONE in his office after Rita left and stared at the paperwork spread on the desk in front of him, but it was a blur. He couldn't forget about B.J. even after twenty-four hours. He couldn't forget how he'd been on his way to dinner then heard the yelling as he got off the elevator, or the way he'd thrown himself into the middle of the battle. Or the way he'd kissed B.J. The way the car alarm had sounded, and B.J. had turned from him as if the kiss hadn't happened.

She'd been upset, afraid, scared for the boy. And she was obviously an emotional person. He'd never met anyone whose eyes were so readable, so devastatingly able to expose the soul. Or a woman who could draw such a raw immediate response from him. He'd never experienced that before either, nor had he had a woman apologize for letting him kiss her.

He looked down at the papers again. Work had always been a way of sorting things out, of stopping any foolish impulses he had, but it wasn't working. He got up, paced back and forth in front of the curtainless windows of his office, stopping long enough to stare out at the gathering night. And thoughts of B.J. wouldn't leave him alone. No any more than the idea that he could still taste her in his mouth even after all this time.

He pressed both hands to the cool glass of the window and leaned forward. "We're going to build LynTech, not tear it down," Zane had said. And that meant getting the money to make it happen. But he couldn't even focus on the meetings he had on Saturday with the New York investors. He couldn't make himself sort through his options or get his thoughts straight. God, he wished Zane was here, then he could step back and let him do the thinking. But Zane wasn't here. He was. And it was up to him.

"Damn it," he muttered, turned and put the papers he'd been trying to finish in his briefcase and closed it with snap. He gave up. That was it. He was out of here. He'd go back to his place and at least he wouldn't be thinking of

B.J. down in the center working. He picked up the briefcase, headed out of the office and went down, past the elevators to Zane's office. He'd take the executive elevator again. He'd take it for the same reasons he'd taken it for the past week. He'd avoid meeting anyone. And this time when he got to the garage, he wouldn't find a flame-haired woman ready to do battle for a street kid.

As the elevator slid down he didn't realize how apprehensive he was about what he'd find in the parking garage until the doors slid open and he found the place deserted. His car was the only one still parked there. No kid, no screaming woman and no B.J. He didn't know if he was relieved or disappointed. Either way, he got into his Jeep and headed for the exit ramp.

The traffic was lighter, and he easily slid into the nearest lane and drove off down the street. Then he looked up and realized that despite the fact that he wasn't a man who believed in chance or luck, a man who truly believed that Fate was what you made it, his own fate was totally out of his hands. There, under the overhang of the entry to a public parking structure, was B.J.

B.J. in ridiculously tight jeans, a big white jacket and her flame-colored hair a splash of brilliant color and loose curls. B.J. talking to one of the parking-garage attendants. No, they weren't talking. She was obviously upset, the man was angry, and before he realized what he was doing, he was going to her rescue again.

BRITTANY STARED at the kid in the navy uniform. "What in the heck are you talking about? I brought my car here this morning, in one piece, and now you're telling me that it's totaled out?"

The kid, who couldn't be more than twenty, had been calm at first, but when she'd gotten upset, he'd gotten defensive and now he was staring at her. His arms were crossed on his chest, and she could tell he was ready to do battle. "Lady, things happen and your car is not totaled. It's got a gouge on the front fender and the driver's door. And the fender's hitting the tire, and you can't drive it. But we'll take care of everything. I told you, we've got insurance."

She'd felt upset since yesterday, and this wasn't helping. A new Porsche that her father had had delivered for her was a thing of the past, obviously. But it wasn't the car that mattered, not really. It was Anthony coming in for work, acting as if nothing had happened with Esther and Matt the night before. And it was still Matt, a man who didn't have a clue who he'd kissed. "So, I don't have a car," she said, trying to control her anger.

"We'll call a cab for you, and you can get a rental car, and we'll pay for it until your car's fixed."

He was being reasonable, she knew that, but she couldn't quite quell the horrible feeling of upset that she was experiencing. The car was minor. Her actions weren't. "I'm sorry," she said.

He immediately mellowed. "Hey, that's okay. That's a killer car you got there. I know it's upsetting, but we'll take care of everything."

She heard a car stop behind her, and the kid looked past her, waved at the driver to wait, then looked back at her. "I'll go call a cab for you, okay?"

She nodded. "Sure, that's fine. Just fine."

He actually smiled at her. "I'll be right back." He looked past her again. "Just park it there, mister, and I'll be right back to get the car."

Brittany turned and was stunned to see Matt not more than two feet from her. Matt in a pale-gray shirt, the throat open, and gunmetal-gray slacks, Matt talking to her, asking something about her getting into trouble again.

The question came with a slight smile, and she found herself staring at his mouth. She had to force herself to look up into his eyes, crinkled slightly at the corners.

"Trouble?" she finally asked. "Oh, no, not really. It seems that my car's been in a fender bender in the parking garage."

Before Matt could say anything, the attendant was back, talking quickly. "The cab will be here in fifteen minutes."

"Thanks," she said, glancing away from Matt and to the attendant.

"While you're waiting," he was saying as he held a clipboard with one hand and a pen with the other. "We can get the information for the insurance company." He looked at her expectantly. "Name?" he asked, pen poised to write.

Matt was right there, watching her, listening, and obviously not about to leave. There was no way she could do this now. "Why don't you just give me the papers and I'll fill them in at home? I can drop them by tomorrow."

"Well, I guess you could." He hesitated. "But we have time before your cab gets here to get it all taken care of."

"I'm tired. I'd rather take them home with me."

"Okay, sure," he said, taking the papers off the clipboard and handing them to her. "Just get them back as soon as you can?"

"I will. I'll bring them in tomorrow."

"Why don't you forget about the cab and I'll drive you home?" Matt said.

She glanced at him, her nerves totally overextended as it was. Riding with him would wreak havoc with her, not to mention she didn't want him finding out where she really lived. "Thanks, but I don't want to put you out again. I can wait for the cab."

The attendant spoke up. "Sure hate to see that happen to that car of yours," he was saying. "I mean, a car like—"

She cut him off, sure he was going to go into rapture about her Porsche. And how could she explain a brand-new Porsche to Matt? "Just fix it and we'll be okay."

"Oh, you bet. It'll be good as new, no problem. We'll make sure that we take it to a specialist in those—"

"Good," she said quickly. "Great."

"You sure wouldn't take it to just anyone."

"I appreciate that," she said, and felt as if she was truly caught between a rock and a hard place. The kid wasn't going to shut up and Matt wasn't going to leave. And if the two of them stayed right where they were, all bets were off.

So, she'd leave. "Forget the cab," she said to the attendant. "I'll take care of it myself." Then she looked at Matt. "I don't need rescuing this time."

She would have left right then, but she wasn't lucky enough to make that clean an escape.

"Ma'am," the kid said before she could even turn to get away. "I need a name and phone number at least."

She went closer to him. "Have you got a piece of paper?" she asked.

He held out the clipboard to her and she saw it had a sheet of plain paper on it. "You can use this."

"Thanks," she said, and shifted her purse and the insurance papers to under her right arm, then took the clipboard and the pen the kid offered her. Quickly she wrote out her name as B.J. Lewis, put her phone number and insurance company with it, then handed it back to him. "There you go. Now I'm leaving. I'll be in tomorrow."

"Thanks, Miss—" He started to look down at the clipboard for her name, and she spoke up quickly.

"B.J. Just call me B.J."

He pushed the paper in his pocket, then smiled at her. "Okay, B.J., we'll get that baby of yours all fixed up."

"Good night," she said to the kid, then with a glance at Matt, she turned to walk away.

But she'd only taken a few steps when she knew she wasn't alone. Matt was there, right beside her. "What are you doing?"

"I'm going to walk a bit to cool off, then I'll find a cab and go home," she said without looking at him as she paused at the curb. The air was heavy with humidity, yet almost cold. It was an odd combination that she remembered from her childhood in this city.

"Aerobics?"

She looked at him then, so close she could see the pulse beating at the hollow of his throat exposed by the open neck of the shirt. "Excuse me?"

"Exercise. I was wondering if this is part of your exercise program?"

She felt moisture on her skin, then realized that it was beginning to rain, a gently cool mist that seemed to halo Matt and shimmer from the Christmas lights strung around the light poles. "Not any more than having my car messed up was part of my plan. But I thought I'd walk for a bit, enjoy the Christmas decorations, maybe get something to eat, then go home and do some work." She looked up and down the street, then turned to her left and started walking. "See you," she said over her shoulder without looking back.

He was still there, she could feel him next to her, not touching her, but so close she knew if she swung her arm, she'd hit him. Her nerves were raw now, and as the mists turned to light rain she stopped in the middle of the sidewalk and spun around, almost bumping into Matt. "What?"

He studied her intently for what seemed like forever before he finally said something. "It's raining," he said, as if she wasn't feeling the drops on her face.

"I know."

"Let me give you a ride."

She looked up at him, the moisture starting to sheen his skin and glistening on his sandy hair. Damn it, why did he have to ask her something so patently logical? Something that she could refuse, but would look ridiculous if she did so? "There have to be cabs around here," she said as a final defensive effort.

He turned, looked up and down the street, then back to her. "Not one in sight. But I've got a car close by. No charge. I'm going your way."

Why did he have to smile when he asked her, too? It was a conspiracy, her being tired and worn down by nerves, and this damn rain. Even Mother Nature was in on this, and that was only emphasized further when the rain started coming down faster, harder. She tugged her jacket more tightly around her as someone called out from behind Matt, "Hey, mister?"

Matt glanced back over his shoulder as she looked around him to see the parking attendant standing on the sidewalk waving in their direction. "What?" Matt called.

"You want your car parked, or what?"

Matt looked back at her. "Well?"

"Okay, okay," she muttered, and went around him, heading back through the rain to where the Jeep stood.

She got there just ahead of Matt and quickly got into the Jeep. She ran a hand over her slightly damp hair, pushing the clinging curls off her face, then Matt was there, getting behind the wheel. He closed his door, shutting them in together, then looked at her. "That was more work than it should have been," he murmured.

"What was?" she asked.

"Getting you to take a free ride in the rain," he said,

then reached toward her, gripping the back of her seat as he backed out of the driveway into traffic.

She ran her hand over her jeans, feeling the dampness there, then on her purse and where the moisture had touched the insurance papers. She laid the papers on the console, then placed her purse on the floor by her feet.

He flipped on the windshield wipers, then glanced at her. "You said you're hungry."

"Starving," she said before she thought.

"Good, then we'll stop and have dinner somewhere," he said, not a question, but a statement.

She looked at him, at his profile etched by the soft light from the dash and oncoming car lights mingled with the overhead city streetlights. "Oh, no, you don't have to do that."

That was when he turned to her, his eyes shadowed, but their gaze rocking her slightly, the same way his voice did as it dropped to a seductively lower level. "One thing you should know about me is, I never do anything I don't want to do. Never have, never will. So, B. J. Smythe, where do you want to eat?"

Chapter Eight

Brittany sank back in the seat with an exasperated sigh. A meal. Food. Maybe an hour of time, tops. She'd do it. She'd eat and go home. Then she realized that home for her in his mind was the town house complex. Another hurdle she had to pass. Lying to Matt wasn't an easy job. In fact, it was downright exhausting. "I'm a vegetarian," she said, hoping that with any luck he'd say that he was a steak man and he'd drop her at a salad bar. But the only luck she had right then was bad luck.

"Okay, vegetables it is," was all he said as they drove. A silence fell between them as he made his way along the rain-slicked streets.

Brittany looked out the window and watched the city pass, saw pedestrians scrambling for doorways or going into shops. Rain glittered all around, picking up the Christmas lights, making the city look almost ethereal. Despite the rain, the traffic kept moving, not like the first drive they'd taken together.

She saw a group of children running, laughing in the rain, being herded into a toy store by two women. And she thought of Anthony, her stomach knotting as she remembered Esther.

"I was wondering something?" Matt said, breaking the silence with his deep, slightly rough voice.

She tried to push her thoughts of Anthony away. She spoke quickly, anything to shut out the images of Esther hitting him. "Vegetarians don't eat animal products. But I can eat around any menu," she said in a nervous rush of words. "There are vegetarians, then there are *real* vegetarians. Some people say they're vegetarians, but they eat chicken and fish. That's not vegetarian. That's an I-don't-eat-red-meat person. Then there's vegetarians that won't eat animal flesh. But they still—"

"B.J.?" he said, cutting her off.

She looked at him, thankful that the evening light and the rain blurred the sharp images, even in the car. "Yes?"

"That's all very interesting, but I was actually wondering what B.J. stands for?"

She felt her face flame, and knew that she'd been babbling from nerves. "I'm sorry." And she was sorry that saying Brittany Jayne wasn't an option. "They're just initials."

"No names connected to them, like Barbara Joan or Betty Joy?"

She didn't get a chance to answer before the car phone rang. "Just a minute," he said to Brittany, reaching for the phone. "Terrel here."

He listened, not speaking, then, saying, "I'll look right away," he hung up.

He slowed and turned right down a side street. "Sorry, I need to get information right away, and it's at my place." He cast her a shadowed glance. "I live nearby and this won't take a minute."

Matt turned into a small industrial area, with streets lined with warehouses and small manufacturing businesses. They were all closed up tight and Christmas decorations were scarce. The rain didn't wash this area with magic, but it made it look dreary and gray. "You live around here?"

"A few blocks away," he said, turning onto another street that looked like the last one.

"I know you said you lived in a converted warehouse, but I didn't think you meant a *warehouse*."

"The operative word is *converted*," he said and turned onto yet another street. "They're trying to refurbish the area, but I'm not sure it's going to work." The next thing she knew, he was pulling into a driveway by a hulking building with concrete walls, stones imbedded in the cement, and high barred windows on the lower floor. A dark awning protected the entryway, and the only nod to Christmas was the security lights on either side of the door illuminating potted plants. One was red, one was green. "Home sweet home," he said as he stopped the car in a parking space at the side of the building, a carport of sorts, with a roof for shelter but no walls.

"I'd tell you to stay here while I go up to get the papers, but I'm not sure it's safe."

"It's your home, isn't it?"

"I only moved in a week or so ago. Until then I was living out of a hotel room. Lindsey—Zane's wife—used to rent it, and I took it over when she moved out." He got out, then looked back in at her. "Come on and stay underneath the overhang. You'll be dry enough."

She got out and followed Matt to the front entrance. Matt unlocked a heavy security door and let them into a foyer. There was a door on either side wall, and in front of them across a scarred wooden floor, was an old-fashioned caged freight elevator.

Matt crossed, lifted the chain-link barrier that acted as a door for the lift, then stepped in and motioned her in with him. "Come on. It works."

She followed him into the car and he lowered the barrier. He hit a button on the side wall, then the elevator started upward. The gears ground, the chains clanked, but the elevator did indeed work. They lurched to a stop at the second floor.

Matt lifted the gate, and Brittany stepped out into a hallway with two doors off it. Matt let down the gate, then crossed to the door directly opposite the cage and unlocked it. "The loft," he murmured as he motioned her to go ahead of him. She brushed past him into his home.

As he flicked on the lights, she was faced with a cavernous space with beams and pipes crisscrossing overhead, painted white to blend into the high ceiling. Walls were only partial barriers rising maybe six feet off the hardwood floors and topped by wooden shelving. And the furnishings were definitely masculine, all navy linen and grays, with clean lines, low profiles, plants the only decorations. There were plants everywhere, creating screens, draped on top of the partial walls, and lining multi-paned windows across the space.

"I'll be right back," Matt said, striding across the room. She watched him go into a side space where she could make out shelving and a long work table filled with papers, files and a computer. "I just need to get some figures," he called from beyond the partial barrier.

"Okay," she said, as she looked around and realized she'd never before been in a place where she couldn't see a human touch. She wandered around a space that was neat, orderly, but without a touch of Christmas anywhere. Her family house in the city was fully decorated, thanks to the usual staff who always did an impeccable job. But here there were no decorations, no pictures, no books, nothing personal. He really had just moved in.

At least she thought there wasn't anything personal until

a huge orange tabby cat silently walked out of a side area. It stopped, turned round eyes on her, then, with a flick of his tail, turned, jumped with surprising grace onto a bleached-wood side table, then jumped again onto a high shelf attached to the wall.

He hunkered down, flicked his tail one more time, then closed his eyes. Brittany crossed to the wall and looked up at the cat. "Well, hello there, big boy," she murmured.

"Joey, his name's Joey," Matt said from behind her. "And he's spoiled rotten."

She turned. "I never would have figured you for an animal lover," she said.

He had a stack of papers in his hands. "I'm not. He's just here until Zane and Lindsey and Zane's son get back from Aspen. I'm his food source until after the new year, then he's off to their place."

"Which is?"

"A place they're buying just outside the city. It's supposed to be ready soon. Then Joey goes and I get some peace and quiet." He crossed to one of two navy sofas, dropped down and put the papers on the table to his right.

She went to the other couch and sat down facing him. "I can't believe a woman used to live here," she said without thinking.

He glanced around. "Why?"

"It's so…so sterile."

"It's a place to be. Better than a hotel room. It's fine with me as long as it's leak-proof, reasonably comfortable and conveniently located."

She looked around the room. "What about Christmas?"

"What about it?"

"Are you a 'bah humbug' sort of person, or are you going to decorate?"

"Nope." He sank back into the navy linen. "You're the

one who said I'm a cynic, and I just don't have the time to worry about things like Christmas.'' He grinned at her. ''I didn't run down Santa the other night. That's my good deed for the season.''

''But what about the fun and celebration and nostalgia and the presents?''

''Oh, so that's it? The real lure of Christmas is what you get?''

''No, what you give. It's the most fun to get the perfect present for someone. It's the best feeling when you give it to them and know that you did it just right.''

''Better to give than to receive?'' he murmured.

''Yes.'' She narrowed her eyes on him, a bit surprised that he seemed so vivid to her at that moment.

''What would you get me?'' he asked as he sat forward, resting his elbows on his knees.

''I don't know you well enough to know what you really want or what you need.''

''What about Anthony?''

That caught her off-guard, and the knot in her stomach was back. ''I wish I could get him what he needs.''

''What's that?''

''A good life with someone who loves him.''

Matt stood and came to where she was sitting, then he hunkered down in front of her, his eyes level with hers. ''You think big, don't you?''

''My dad always said to start at the top and work your way up from there.''

She'd said it without thinking, something she'd heard all of her life. ''Damn, your father sounds like a winner,'' he said with a grin that was so boyishly endearing it made her slightly lightheaded.

''He is. Very much so,'' she said.

Unexpectedly Matt rested his hand on hers clasped in her

lap, and she fought the urge to turn her hands over and entwine her fingers with his. His touch was gentle and warm, and so real that it made it hard for her to breathe. "Well, look who he's got for a daughter." She could feel Matt's breath brush her face and it made her tremble slightly. "I'd say he's a real winner. Way ahead of people like Robert Lewis."

That jarred Brittany. She didn't want to hear this. Now was not the time for her to play it off, to lie to this man, or to try not to feel the pain that came from knowing he thought so badly of the person called Brittany Lewis.

"If you're finished here, I'm hungry," she said, the words sounding a bit tight in her own ears, but, she hoped, killing any more talk about the shortcomings of Brittany Lewis.

"Amen. I'm starving," he said with that grin. "I know we're going out, but I don't suppose that you're that sort of vegetarian who could take what I have in my refrigerator— two eggs, a tomato, some yogurt and a bottle of beer—and make a gourmet meal?"

"Me? Boy, do you have the wrong vegetarian," she said, actually able to smile, at least until he tightened his touch on her.

"Let me be the judge of that," he murmured and she knew it was time to go.

She stood abruptly, with no thought but to get some space between herself and this man. However, she wound up doing the opposite. She bumped into him sharply, sending him reeling backwards. "Oh, no," she gasped as she made a grab for his hand. But instead of stopping his fall as she caught him, his weight pulled them both back.

In one fell swoop, she was on top of Matt, tangled with him, and the only thought she had was to get free. She twisted her body and ended up on the floor. The coldness of hardwood was against her back and the heat of Matt's body was along her front. She was almost afraid to look up, into eyes as dark as the night, with his body on hers.

MATT FELT THE IMPACT, then everything blurred until he looked up at B.J. over him. She was fighting to get away, tangling with him, then he was over her. Every atom of his being was aware of every place her body touched his. The way her rapid breathing echoed his own, the scent of her filling him up, the softness. She filled the void around him, and in a moment of aching clarity, he knew that he wanted her. Not just physically, but in every way a man could want a woman.

But before he could figure out what to do, she pushed at him with both her hands flat on his chest, shoving him back with as much strength as she'd used to send him reeling in the first place. She was sliding sideways, then getting to her feet, and in less than a heartbeat, she was standing. He got to his feet, brushed absentmindedly at his clothes, and never took his eyes off her.

"We have to stop running into each other," he said, trying to joke, trying to break a tension that almost crackled in the room.

Women had seemed so simple, so much alike in the way they reacted. You kissed them. They kissed you back or they didn't. He could read them, usually. But reading B.J. was about as easy as reading Latin. Both were impossible for him.

She looked almost afraid, and that disturbed him. She was made to loved, not hurt. Made to be held and cherished. Damn it, he was waxing poetic and all she was doing was staring at him.

"That's a joke," he finally murmured because he couldn't think of anything else to say. Words weren't coming easily to him at the moment.

"Yes, of course," she said. "I knew that."

"Good, then quit running into me." He rubbed his shoulder where she'd made contact with him. "I was expecting Anthony to come running at me from the other side."

That softened her expression a bit, her sense of fear seeming to diminish. She ran her fingers through her loose curls, then pulled her hair straight back from her face for a moment. Her beauty at that moment was stunning, the bone structure, the green eyes, the lips. He jerked his mind back as she shook her hair around her shoulders. "He's a fighter, isn't he?"

"He was going to do battle for you, that's for sure," he said, knowing that any male of the species would do battle for this woman. "Now, food." He held up a hand. "We'll go out. We'll do it calmly and quietly. Okay?"

"Yes, okay," she murmured as she looked at him again.

He motioned to the doors, and she silently crossed to the exit with him following her. He flicked off the lights, stepped out and turned after locking the door to see the lift just stopping. A middle-aged man with six earrings in one ear lifted the cage front. His thinning gray hair was caught back in a ponytail, and he was wearing paint-stained jeans with an equally stained T-shirt imprinted with the words Reality is for those with no imagination. A backpack was slung over one shoulder, and he had what looked like a tackle box in his other hand.

"Hello, there," the man said and motioned vaguely with the tackle box in the direction of the other door. "I live in there." He came toward them, put down the tackle box and held out a paint-stained hand. "I'm George Armstrong."

Matt held his hand out to the man. "Matthew Terrel," he said, a bit surprised that the man's grip was so strong. "I just moved in."

He eyed Matt. "Oh, Matthew Terrel. The one with LynTech?"

"How do you know me?"

"Everyone that's had that place has been with the company," he said, nodding to the loft behind them. "And I've seen your name on the company reports. Makes sense that you're one and the same."

"You read company reports?"

"I've got a few shares in the company and like to keep an eye on things. We need to talk when you're free."

"About what?"

"I think you're taking LynTech in the wrong direction. I thought you and Holden had turned things around, opting for growth instead of disassembly, but after what I heard this morning, I don't mind telling you, I'm a bit worried."

He felt B.J. move a bit closer as he asked, "What are you talking about?"

"You trying to get Quintin Gallagher onboard."

Matt had just met with Gallagher three days ago in New York when he'd gone to meet the investors, but he'd thought the stockholders wouldn't hear about it for a while. "What about Gallagher?"

"He's old-school, slash-and-burn, trample-the-little-guy for-the-greater-good-of-the-money-machine." He smiled a bit wryly. "Okay, I like money as much as the next guy, but there's limits on what I'll do to make it. And Gallagher goes over those limits. All you have to do is just look into Gallagher's background, and you'll see what I mean. The word is you're bringing him in to help with the company's direction, its growth. Not a good idea."

This made no sense, arguing the merits of Gallagher coming onboard at LynTech with an aging hippie who owned a "few" shares of the company. Nor did it make sense when

B.J. stepped a bit closer and spoke up. "Where did you get your information on Gallagher?"

"He's been around about as long as I have, and his name's come up quite a bit. He's a player, and he doesn't keep a low profile."

"Then you know that he's an effective businessman, a man who can manage growth well and who has helped quite a few companies ward off bankruptcy. And his business ethics are impeccable."

George looked as impressed with B.J. as Matt was at the moment, and maybe just as confused. "You sound as if you know the guy."

"Do *you* know the guy?" B.J. countered without missing a beat.

"No, of course I don't, but…"

B.J. moved closer still, and Matt felt her arm brush his shirtsleeve. "First of all, Mr. Armstrong, businesses like LynTech are the backbone of the American economy, and LynTech is not about to bring anyone in who's got the wrong mentality. So, maybe they're asking Gallagher to join them to direct their growth as opposed to fighting their wars."

George stared at her, and for a moment Matt thought he'd attack. But he didn't. Instead, he smiled at her. "Boy, remind me to get you on my side if I ever go to war."

"I'm an artist, I don't fight wars," she murmured.

"Another artist in the house? Cool," he said, and Matt was waiting for him to declare it "groovy," too. He was beaming at B.J. now. "A kindred spirit."

Matt felt as off balance as he ever had during a business discussion. A very weird, confusing discussion with a fiery-haired woman and an aging hippie. Both of them sounded like corporate types, and they weren't even close. Then George turned to him, and that balance tipped even further off-kilter. "I just bet this wife of yours keeps you on your toes."

"Oh, no, we're not…I mean, I'm not his wife," B.J. said quickly.

George looked from Matt to B.J., then back at Matt. "Whatever. It's totally cool with me," he said. "Now, I've enjoyed this discussion, and as a stockholder, I'll be bringing this up again about Gallagher, but for now, I have things to do." He lifted the tackle box. "Brushes to clean. Later, you two," he said and headed for the other door.

Matt glanced at B.J. and found her watching George intently. Then, without looking at him, she turned and walked into the lift. He went after her, pulled down the door and hit the Down button. Matt turned to B.J. "Where did all that come from?"

She stared straight ahead, her purse held to her middle. "I guess he thought, seeing us both, that we were living there," she said in a low voice. "It's a natural assumption, I suppose."

"I was talking about all that LynTech, Gallagher stuff."

She shrugged. "He started it, I didn't."

"No, but you finished it."

"I just pointed out his lack of intimate knowledge about Gallagher," she murmured.

"That you did."

She glanced at him then, long lashes shadowing her eyes enough to make them almost unreadable. The woman was a puzzle to him, and the longer he knew her, the more that puzzle grew. He didn't have any answers and she certainly wasn't supplying any. "LynTech is…seems to be a good company, and I hate to see it stoned by someone who…" Her voice trailed off and he saw her bite her bottom lip before she turned toward the front of the lift.

"Who's stoned?" he supplied.

He could have sworn that she started to smile at that, but she caught herself before the smile became a reality. "He's concerned about things as a stockholder, whether he's stoned or not, and that's someone you have to worry about."

"He owns a few stocks and probably got them in trade for some modern painting that he couldn't sell."

"I think there's more to him than that," she murmured.

There was more to her than he could begin to fathom. "There probably is." He watched her closely as she stared at the cage in front of her. "There is to you, too."

She looked at him again. "Excuse me?"

"This crusade for Anthony."

"He's a real person, not a company. No company is as important as people, not ever."

Another piece of the puzzle was the way she could say a few words and totally change the focus of where he thought they were going with the conversation. "That's a given."

The elevator stopped, and she glanced at him. "Not to some people," she murmured. "So, tell me, is LynTech talking to Gallagher?"

He reached for the cage gate and lifted it. "Actually, yes. He's been considering our offer for a day or two."

"What offer?" she asked as she stepped out into the entry area.

He got out, lowered the gate, then turned to B.J. "We want him onboard to help with the direction we're taking. Neither Zane nor I are long-term people in business. Get in, get it done, get out, but Gallagher has a knack of setting things up for the long haul. What I want to know is how you know anything about Gallagher or LynTech?"

She shrugged, a fluttery motion of her shoulders. "I heard it somewhere. I don't remember where. I just absorb things."

She turned away from him, and when he reached for the security door and opened it, she went past him into the night. He followed. The rain had stopped, but the night was clouded and cold. He felt as if he was forever playing "catch up" with her, both literally and figuratively.

They reached the Jeep and he barely missed running into her as she stopped suddenly. She turned, the harshness of the security lights doing little to dim her beauty. If anything the sharp shadows only more clearly defined the sweep of her throat. "You know, I'm not hungry any more. I think I'll just go home."

He hated not being able to make sense out of people around him, and to make matters worse, he had totally forgotten what he'd come here for in the first place. B.J. seemed to take up all the space around him and he decided to take care of business later. It was as though when B.J. was around, everything else seemed unimportant.

Chapter Nine

"You were starving a few minutes ago," Matt said, with what Brittany knew was unfailing logic.

"It's passed," she said, grasping at any explanation to stop this evening in its tracks.

"What?"

"You know, if you put off eating long enough, you aren't hungry anymore?"

"I never heard that. Maybe it's not that you're not hungry, but you're getting a little delirious and don't remember that you're hungry."

She looked at Matt, at the way the harsh red and green of the security lights backed him, making him more shadow than substance. She could almost imagine that she *was* delirious when she realized she wanted nothing more than to touch him, to feel his reality under her fingertips. That was suicide. She'd promised herself and her father that there would be no more of this madness. Even if the madness with Matt was of a different variety than her everyday, garden-variety madness when it came to men.

She was also a liar. A fake. As far as Matt was concerned, she was a charade. She wished that it was December 23rd so this would be over, the bet would be won and she could be Brittany Lewis to Matt. She wasn't sure how she'd tell him in the end, but she knew that she couldn't just go and eat dinner with him now.

"I'm not hungry," she said. "I need to get home."

"Are you sure?"

"Very sure," she murmured.

He unlocked the car and she got in, then closed her eyes tightly while Matt got in on the other side. She didn't open her eyes until she heard the car start and begin to move.

"Okay, let's get you home," he said.

Home? God, she was tired of this. The town houses. The rain had stopped, so she could pull off walking inside the complex, waiting for him to leave, then going to her real home and trying to calm down. She glanced at Matt, and wondered what would happen if she just opened her mouth and said, "I'm Brittany Lewis." She couldn't. She wouldn't. Not yet.

He drove through the night streets, then, just when he turned onto the main street that led out of the industrial area, the phone rang again.

Matt reached for it as he merged into the light traffic. "Terrel here."

She watched him as he listened, watched the way he frowned slightly, the way a nerve jumped in his jaw. Then he murmured into the phone, "Hang on and I'll check," as he looked at her. "Can you get my briefcase off the back seat?"

She twisted, reached for the case, then tugged it onto her lap. "What do you need?"

"Open it up," he said as he flicked on the overhead light. "See if you can find a file labeled Dunlop, probably in the top pocket."

She clicked the case open, and found the folder right where he'd said it was. "It's here."

"Look in it and see if you can find the pages on distribution, probably headed Western States, Electronics." He kept driving while he spoke to her. "Highlighted with yellow at the top, I think. Rita favors yellow."

She sorted through the thick stack of documents. "Here it is."

"Who signed it?"

She looked down at the bottom of the page and saw a dark, scrawling signature. "You did."

"Are you sure?"

"Well, it's not that legible, and the light's not that great, but it's got your name typed below the signature."

"My problem," he said back into the phone as he turned off the light again. "So, I'll take care of it. I'll get back to you by tomorrow at ten and give you the information." He hung up.

"There's a problem?"

"Yes, all mine. I blew it."

"How?" she asked, tucking the papers back in the pocket then closing the briefcase.

"I signed it blind. Rita brought in papers, said they needed my signature, gave me a brief rundown, but I didn't have the time to double-check."

She scanned the page. "This projected distribution plan isn't viable?"

He slowed the car slightly, and she felt him turn to her. "It will be, after another ten hours of me working it out, tinkering with patterns and projected stock."

She met his shadowy gaze before he looked back at the road. "Then it's not irreversible."

"No, it's not, and I don't get how you know exactly what I'm talking about. You're an artist, yet you speak the speak and walk the walk of business. You know about scorch and burn, and corporate negotiations." He glanced at her again. "You're damned smart about this stuff."

He was complimenting her, Brittany Lewis, and the irony of the situation almost made her grin. But she held that back and murmured, "I just pick up things."

"What are you, a corporate spy or something?"

"A spy?" The laughter came, an easy chuckle that felt beyond good to her at that moment. "Me? No, not hardly."

"Then who are you?"

"I'm an artist and the only child of a father who lived and breathed his business." That was the real truth. "He tried to teach me enough to do what he did, but I never wanted to do that. I wanted to do something else."

"Art?"

She knew that now. "Yes, art."

"And how did he take that?"

"The way he took everything else in life, he figured that I'd come to my senses sooner or later."

Matt laughed this time, a rich, deep sound that ran riot over her nerves. "I'd like to meet your father sometime."

That would happen, a moment in the future when she'd stand by her father, face Matthew Terrel and have Matt tell her father, "Brittany has done a good job for the company." That daydream couldn't come soon enough for her. "Maybe you will."

The phone rang again and Matt exhaled. "Another crisis," he murmured and reached for the phone. "Terrel here."

She settled back in the seat, thinking about that final confrontation, that moment when Matt would know that Brittany Lewis was a viable, important human being. And she suddenly realized that it wasn't just getting him to admit that he was wrong, that she'd win her bet, that he'd have to make a public confession that he'd been wrong about her. It was beyond that. She wanted Matt to look at her, to know that she was Brittany Lewis and not have contempt in his eyes. She shivered slightly thinking about the way he looked at her now.

His voice filtered through her thoughts, and she realized he wasn't talking business. "My assistant has taken care of everything, and I'm sure she'd be more than willing to fill you in on Brittany's progress."

Brittany felt her breath catch and she turned to stare at Matt. He was talking to her father. He was talking about her, and she shivered again, but this time it was because of the barely contained condemnation in every word he said. "Sir, I have to be honest. Your daughter's not really working. She's settling in, and getting prepared, getting things…coordinated." She could see him grimace slightly as he listened again. "I understand. Of course. All I can do is promise you that whatever happens, she'll be given every chance to succeed. It's up to her how this all turns out."

Every chance to fall flat on her face was more like it. And he'd feel so vindicated, justified, even. But that wasn't going to happen. She sat up a bit straighter, never taking her eyes off Matt.

"Yes, sir. I certainly will do that. You have my word on it." He paused, then said, "You, too. Merry Christmas."

Matt hung up the phone and exhaled in a rush. Brittany braced herself for what was to come. Matt drove for a long moment in silence, then spoke abruptly. "That was Robert Lewis. Seems good old Brittany, his princess, has been spinning lies out of whole cloth, instead of spinning gold out of straw."

He bit out every word, and it made her cringe. "What's going on?"

"She says that she's working at LynTech. That she's doing a *fabulous* job, and having the *adventure of her life*." He laughed abruptly, but there was no richness in this sound of humor, and it grated across her nerves this time. "She's out on a buying spree, and she's convinced Mr. Lewis that she's working long hours. Her only adventure is making a fool out of him.''

''Matt, everything's open to interpretation.''

That really made him laugh, a burst of sound that filled the car. ''Oh, yes, of course,'' he said. ''She's lying, manipulating and running her father a merry chase and you think she's got a problem with word usage?''

She laughed at that herself. ''Maybe she's challenged that way,'' she conceded, then scored one for her side. ''But then again, you're fairness challenged.''

''Excuse me?'' he asked, the laughter dying as he glanced at her.

''You're still doing it. Passing judgment before all the votes are in.''

''You do have time before Christmas comes and you have to render your apology, don't you?''

''Don't count your chickens.''

''She's shopping for clothes, B.J., and I suspect if she comes back to the office, it's going to be to redecorate. Or maybe she'll never come back. Maybe she found another fiancé to keep her amused for a few months.''

Brittany's humor faltered just a bit. Part of what he thought of her was too near the truth for comfort, and that part was her stupidity and impulsiveness when it came to what she thought was love. She moved back against the door, farther away from a man who could jumble her thinking and make her start to dream. ''She'll be back.''

''Hope springs eternal,'' he muttered, then motioned ahead of them. ''We're almost there.''

She looked up as they passed the strip mall he'd dropped her at the other night, and turned left at the next corner. The town house complex was there, at the end of the street, huge gates framed by stone pillars with wrought-iron fencing spreading out in either direction. They protected the multi-level condos behind them. Christmas wreaths framed all of the security lights on the fences and posts, and multicolored twinkle lights were laced through the branches of trees that lined the fences.

"Just drop me by the gates," she said. "I'll walk in."

Right then a car came up behind them, and the gates swung open. "I'll take you to your door," Matt said, swinging in through the gates onto a cobbled drive that led right, left or straight ahead into the heart of the houses. "Where do you live?"

She looked ahead at a central park-like area with a huge pine tree decorated for Christmas in the middle. She motioned in that direction. "Over there," she said, looking at a unit on the end that didn't have any lights on. "That one, right there."

Matt slipped into a parking area in front of the unit and, with the car idling, turned to her. He reached toward her and she felt her breath catch until his hand touched the back of her seat and not her. "Home sweet home?" he asked.

She shrugged. "A place to live." She reached for the door handle, but before she could get out, Matt did touch her. His hand slipped onto her shoulder and cupped the back of her neck. "Are you sure you aren't hungry yet?"

She shook her head, not daring to look right at him. Stupidity came in waves, waves that were pushing her to turn to him, to reach out and touch him. "No, thanks."

He hesitated. "I should say something, but I'm not sure how."

"Then…then maybe you shouldn't say it," she whispered.

"No, I need to." His fingers moved slowly, softly over the back of her neck. "I've found out in life that being honest pays off big-time. That people aren't mind readers and you have to say what you mean.''

''Sometimes the truth isn't necessary,'' she said and gasped softly when his fingers tangled lightly in her curls.

''Oh yes, it is. Always.'' He was silent for so long that she finally glanced at him, trying to ignore the light sensuality of his touch. ''Finally, you're looking at me,'' he whispered, and she was certain she'd done the wrong thing making that contact.

Matt had his rules for most everything in his life, one of them being that he'd never get involved with anyone connected with his work. He went into a company, did the job, lived while he was there, passed time in any way he chose, then he got out and moved on. No one got hurt on any level. But B.J. had shattered that philosophy for him from that first moment. She'd shattered it literally and figuratively. And now, she was so close, the heat of her body filtered into him.

''I'm going to be totally up-front about this,'' he said, a hoarseness invading his voice. ''I've always had a self-imposed rule to keep my personal life separate from my business life.'' He shifted, coming a bit closer. ''You are very much in danger of putting that rule at risk.''

She stared at him as he spoke, the softness of the night lights only making her more achingly desirable. ''You're right,'' she whispered. ''It's not a good idea. It's too…too confusing and…it gets things all…'' Her tongue darted out to touch her lips and it was almost his undoing.

He touched her cheek with his other hand, brushing at the curls that clung to her silky skin there. ''It makes things complicated, doesn't it?'' he breathed. He felt her tremble slightly, and the need in him was echoed in her. He could feel it, from a connection so deep that it defied explanation.

It was something he'd never felt before with a woman, or that he'd ever even known existed until then.

"Oh, no," she whispered, and he would have laughed at the frustration in her words if he hadn't felt as frustrated himself with his inability just to walk away. And if he hadn't gone closer and if his lips hadn't found hers, he might have worked up the strength, but once he tasted her, all was lost.

He touched her, tasted her and knew that he wanted more. A man who prized rationality, who prized control, lost everything. He shifted, pulled her toward him, ignoring the way the console bit into his side. All he felt was her, everywhere, saturating his senses, and the idea of being in a place he'd always wanted to find was solid in his mind.

He sank his fingers into her lush curls, tasting her, drawing that sense of her into his soul and he knew that the other kiss had been nothing, kid's play next to this contact. His lips trailed to her cheek, to her throat and he tasted the exposed curve of her neck. Her skin was like silk under his touch, his hand slipping under the collar of her jacket, finding her heat and softness. The slipping of reality was a sure thing, any thoughts of why or how this had happened totally obliterated by a need in him that grew quickly.

Suddenly a loud noise cut through the night, and Matt drew back, looked down at B.J., and the noise was there again, a sharp rapping sound. He turned to the driver's window, toward the ongoing noise and was all but blinded when a bright light flashed right in his eyes. He felt B.J. scrambling back as he focused beyond the brilliance and saw the source of the noise and the light—a cop holding a flashlight and rapping on the window with his other hand. No, not a cop, a security guard. Dark uniform, cap, and motioning to Matt to roll down the window.

"Caught in the act like some horny teenager," he thought

with chagrin as he reached for the button to lower the window.

"You got ID, mister?" the man asked without preamble.

"I'm sorry about this," Matt said.

"ID?" the man said and flashed his light past Matt. "And yours, ma'am?"

"She lives here," Matt said as he shifted to get out his wallet. "This unit."

Brittany had never known such embarrassment or such anger in her life. Embarrassment for someone seeing the way she'd all but thrown herself at Matt, and anger directed at herself for being so weak and allowing this to happen. The guard was looking at her intently, then his light trailed over her, stopping at her top, still askew. "Er...uh...so you live here, ma'am?" he said, as the light flashed off.

Quickly, Brittany tried to adjust her top, then tugged her jacket back up over her shoulders. "I'm sorry about this," she whispered, sinking back in the seat.

"I'm the one who's sorry," the security guard said. "I'm new here, and I don't know everyone yet."

"She just moved in," Matt said as he handed him his driver's license.

The man stood back and flashed his light on it, seemed to hesitate, then bent down to peer back in at Matt with the light held just a bit lower. "Mr. Matthew Terrel? Are you working at LynTech from New York?"

Matt took the license back from the man as he held it in the window. "Yes, I am."

The man stood back, snapped off his light, then said, "Have a merry Christmas," and walked away toward the entrance.

"Is there some sort of grapevine in Houston that sends out announcements about LynTech? I all but expected him to say he owned a few stocks and knew George."

Brittany took a shaky breath, looking away from Matt as he turned to her. "Your fame precedes you," she muttered as she reached for her purse. She grabbed the door handle, but hesitated getting out. "Speaking of LynTech, do you pay Anthony, or should I?"

"We'll take care of it. Have his information sent up to personnel, and I'll approve it."

"Six dollars an hour?" she asked looking back at Matt.

In the soft glow of the Christmas decorations that filtered into the car, she found him staring at her...hard. "I thought we mentioned five an hour?"

"*You* mentioned five, but I think he needs more, something for himself and not that woman and he's a hard worker, a very hard worker. And he's got so much going against him. He's had a pretty rough time, so, six dollars an hour sounds good, don't you think?"

He was silent for a long moment, then nodded. "Six, okay. I'll approve it."

"Thank you," she said and meant it, as much as she wanted to get out of there and get some space between them.

She tugged on the door handle, opened the door and scrambled out, but was shocked when Matt was there before she could do more than close the door behind her. If she moved in either direction, she'd touch him, so she stood very still.

"What now?" she asked.

He moved without warning and touched her cheek, a fleeting, feathery touch that rendered her incapable of moving at all. She wanted to run, to keep running until she had space, plenty of space between them. But she stood there, frozen, his touch the center of the world at that moment. "I was thinking of what George said, about having you on his side if he ever went to war."

"He didn't—"

"It was something like that, and I'd like to second that motion. If I'm ever in trouble, I hope to hell that you're on my side."

"You could take care of yourself," she said, moving back a fraction of an inch, just enough to break the contact between them.

"I always thought I could," he said in a low voice, then leaned toward her, and for one panic-stricken moment, she thought he was going to kiss her. Quite literally, she put up a barrier, the only one she had, her purse. And the next thing she knew, Matt laughed, a soft sound in a winter's night still holding the scent of new rain in the cold air. "Oh, come on. I'm not going to do anything out here," he said in a low voice.

He made her think stupid, foolish things one after the other, and she could almost hate him for that. Almost. As he touched her purse and lowered it slowly until he was looking at her, she knew with a certainty, that he was a man she'd never be able to hate. "I knew that," she muttered.

"Sure you did," he whispered, as his hand moved from her purse to her cheek, the touch a mere brush along her skin. "Your hair has this way of clinging to your cheek."

Even his voice was making her think foolish things, making her ache somewhere deep inside. His touch was the most dangerous thing she'd ever experienced in her life. She drew away from it, then murmured, "Thanks. I need to get inside."

"Go ahead."

"You go ahead. You don't have to wait."

He hesitated, then nodded. "Sleep well," he said before he turned and walked away.

She hugged herself, not turning to watch him get in the car. But she heard the door being shut, the sound echoing around her, then the engine roared and he drove off. That was when she turned, in time to see his car go through the open gates, and she didn't look away until the taillights disappeared into the night.

The air was downright chilly, and she was unnerved to find her hand was shaking when she took her cell phone out of her purse. She was such a fool. So stupid. Letting things with Matt get this far. So far that she had a horrible ache in her that didn't diminish as she dialed the taxi service, and put in a request for a cab to come to the front gates of the complex. She pushed the phone back in her purse and headed toward the walk-through gate by the main entrance.

"Excuse me, ma'am?"

She stopped and turned to the male voice to see the guard coming up behind her. "Oh, you scared me. I was just on my way out to wait for my taxi."

He came closer, and she could see that he was middle-aged, with graying hair under his billed cap. "Taxi?"

"I have one coming to the entrance."

"So, you don't live here, do you?"

She wished that she could stop this ridiculous unsteadiness in herself. "Excuse me?"

"I checked the unit you said you lived in, and it's been vacant for six months." He eyed her. "You look respectable enough, and you were with Mr. Terrel, but I don't understand. You obviously aren't here to rob someone or to trash a unit, so what's going on?"

She could see it now, Daughter of Well-Known Houston Businessman Arrested for— She could fill in that blank with a lot of not-so-nice things. "It's personal."

His hand rested on the holster on his hip. "That might be the case, but you're going to have to give me a reason not to take this any further."

There was no way she could tell him the truth. "The man I was with, Mr. Terrel..." She scrambled for something, anything to say. "Well, my car got in an accident, and he was there and he offered to give me a ride home."

"And you were thanking him for the ride?"

Her face flamed. "No, of course not. We…he and I, well…"

"Listen, if you wanted a place to make out, why did you pick this place?"

"It wasn't like that," she said quickly.

"You never showed me your ID back there, and I think I need to see it now."

"Of course," she said, fishing around in her purse for her driver's license, then she handed it to the man.

He took it, flashed his light to read it, then lifted the light to her face again. She squinted at the brilliance. "Brittany Lewis?"

"Yes."

The light finally lowered, and he clicked it off. "I used to work at LynTech in Security, before the takeover. You're Mr. Lewis's daughter, aren't you?"

Her heart sank. "Yes, I am."

"I liked your father. He was a good man and I hated to see him leave. He used to stop and talk to me at the security station. He knew the names of my kids and my wife. A nice man."

"Thank you," she said.

"My name's Ron Blanchard. Tell your dad that Ron says hello, okay?"

For some reason, Brittany felt tears burn at the back of her eyes. "I will," she murmured, then as she took the license back, she said quickly, "About all of this, I—"

"You never mind about this. Whatever happened, well, it's between you and Mr. Terrel. I owe your dad a lot and I think we can just forget about this."

He thought Robert Lewis's daughter was making out with

an associate in a strange parking lot, and because he liked her father, he was willing to forget all about it. She just wished she could. "Thank you, Ron. I was thinking, maybe you should come back to LynTech and check on hiring back on. They're expanding and they might need more security guards."

"I'd like to work there again, but I don't know. Without your dad there, and people like Mr. Terrel..." He cut off his words. "Oh, no offense on that, ma'am, it's just...I don't know."

"Think about it," she said.

"I will. Now, let me walk you out to get your cab."

A horn sounded and she looked through the gates at a cab idling by the curb. "Thanks, but I'm okay. There's my cab now."

She hurried to the walk-through gate and reached the cab. Then she turned and waved at the guard. "Thank you," she said, and got in the cab and gave her address to the driver.

He pulled away from the curb, and she sank back in the vinyl seat. Life had gone crazy: from Anthony's problems to her reactions to Matt to a stranger thinking she was hormonally challenged. If it hadn't been her life, she would have died laughing at the ridiculous mess it had become.

She pressed a hand to her mouth, killing the nervous laughter that was almost there. And she had the fleeting thought that she could still taste the essence of Matt on her lips. She rubbed her hand over her mouth. There was no way she'd be alone with Matt again, not until she was ready to face him as Brittany Lewis.

Chapter Ten

As the rains started again, Matt drove through the night. He thought he'd learned one thing in his life—never let your guard slip. Never. You didn't act impulsively or let insanity take over, and you didn't expose your deepest needs to anyone. He'd done that in his life and paid dearly for it. But B.J. made him crazy. She brought out things in him that he'd thought he'd grown past. Obviously he hadn't matured as much as he thought. A chuckle came when he thought about making out in a parked car. Damn it, he couldn't even remember doing that when he was a teenager.

The phone rang and he reached for it. "Terrel here."

"Matt, it's Amy."

He glanced at the clock in the car's dash, and was a bit surprised to see that it was barely nine o'clock. It seemed an eternity since he'd spotted B.J. at the parking garage. "Amy, what's up?"

"I've been trying to reach you all day about the quotes on the work for the outside area at the center."

He realized that there had been a message from Amy earlier, and he'd totally forgotten to call her. "What about them?"

"Did you get quotes yet?"

"I'm checking on them and I'll get to them as soon as I

can, but I've got something really pressing to take care of right now."

"The center's important, Matt."

"Of course it is, but I've got myself in a mess with some papers I inadvertently signed."

"I can't imagine you'd sign a paper before really looking at it," she said.

Neither could he, at least, not until a green-eyed woman had walked in and turned his mind to mush. He knew exactly when he'd signed the paper, and why he hadn't read it himself. He'd been distracted, wondering if B.J. was down at the center or not and wishing he hadn't needed to go to New York on a red-eye. "Well, I'll fix it and won't do it again."

"Oh, you probably will," she said with good nature. "Human beings are easily distracted. It's called life."

Amy was remarkable, bringing up her little girl by herself, having been widowed at a time when she should have only been starting her married life. She knew all about distractions. "I'll get some answers for you on that play area as soon as possible, I hope on Monday."

"Thanks," she said. A child started to cry in the background. "Cheer up, things could be worse," she said. "You could have a two-year-old who's spread chocolate pudding all over the floor. Talk to you Monday," she said, then hung up.

He reached to hang up the phone, and hesitated when he noticed papers lying along the console on the passenger side. He dropped the phone in its holder, reached for the papers and saw the insurance forms from the garage that the attendant had given B.J. He thought of going back to give them to her, but knew he had work to do, work that couldn't wait.

He dropped the papers on the seat and reached for his

phone again. He put in a number and waited. A kid picked up on the other end. "Hello?"

"Is Rita there?"

Without saying anything to him, the kid yelled, "Mom, phone!"

A moment later, Rita was on the line. "Hello?"

"Rita, I need you to do something for me."

"Sure, boss, as long as it doesn't mean that I have to go back downtown."

"No, you can do this on the computer, I think. Can you pull up the employee files and get me the phone number for B. J. Smythe, S-M-Y-T-H-E," he said, spelling out the last name carefully.

"Are you going to tell me what the B and the J stand for, or is this a test?"

"It's no test. Just B.J."

"Where are you going to be?"

"I'll be at the loft in five minutes. Call me there."

"Okay," she said and hung up.

He swung into his driveway and parked beside an old van. He dropped B.J.'s papers in his briefcase, then got out into the rainy night. He hurried along the building, toward the front awning, through the steadily misting rain and the cold air. He got to the entrance, and as he reached for his keys, the door swung out and almost hit him.

He stood back and saw George, dressed now in baggy dark pants, and a painfully loud red and green shirt with stylized Christmas wreaths all over it. He was carrying a bottle of wine with a red bow around the neck and wearing rope sandals.

"Oh, sorry, man, I wasn't watching," George said, then moved to one side, letting Matt back under the shelter. He lifted the wine bottle. "I'm off to party and in a bit of a hurry." He looked past Matt, then back at him. "Are you alone now?"

"Very."

"Bummer. Say, you want to come with me? Wine, women and Christmas carols, or maybe just wine and women. I'm not sure on that," he said with a grin.

"Thanks, but I have to work. That's why I'm alone."

"You've been thinking about Gallagher?"

"Not really."

"Well, if I was you, I would. Long and hard." He tapped Matt lightly on the chest with the bottle of wine. "Sure you won't come with me? You might want to take advantage of partying while you can, and we can talk about Gallagher."

"I'll pass, but you enjoy."

"I plan on it," George said, then, with a wave, went off toward an old VW.

As Matt went inside, he heard a motor roar to life, then the door clicked behind him, shutting out the rainy night. He took the lift to the second floor and as he stepped out into the upper hallway, he heard the phone in the loft ringing. By the time he got inside and made his way through the darkness to the phone, the ringing had stopped.

He hadn't had time yet to set up an answering machine, so once the caller hung up, that was it. But he was sure it was Rita, and knew she'd try back every few minutes until she got him. He went back to the entry, closed the door he'd left ajar, shutting in the darkness all around him. The place had seemed so alive when B.J. had been here, but now it felt just plain empty, he thought, almost tripping over the cat that came out of nowhere.

Catching his balance, he snapped on a small light by the phone, then looked down at the cat. "A nice hello would do just fine," he muttered. The cat meowed with disdain. "Okay, okay, food. I know that's all you ever want."

He crossed to the kitchen area and put out a can of food for Joey. Then he headed into the bedroom area and undressed before stretching out on the bed.

He'd rest for a few minutes, get some control over his thoughts, regain his focus, and wait for Rita to call him back before he got to work correcting his mistake. Just a few minutes where he didn't have to think. And if he didn't think, he wouldn't think about B.J.

He closed his eyes and exhaled. Sleep was there, and he welcomed it. Just a few minutes, then he'd get to work, was his last thought before he fell into the void. But there wasn't peace there. There wasn't forgetfulness. He fell into a place of mist and shadows, a place where he sank into craziness. He felt cool air on his skin, a stirring of someone near him, feathery touches, heat coming to him, gentle contact, and he knew that B.J. was there.

Her fiery hair tumbled around her face, shadowed gently as she stretched over him, around him, her scent filling him, and heat came from her. The only source of heat. B.J. The very thing he'd wanted earlier, to feel her touch him, to feel a skimming contact as she teased him, her touch almost not there, her lips trailing over his chest, leaving pathways of fire on him. Closer, so close, her hair tickling his skin, and his body responded instantly and totally.

His body ached for her, needed her, and he knew that if he could just keep her like this, if he could just hold on and not think, everything would be okay. He'd have her. He'd know what it was like to lie with her and possess her and the world wouldn't matter. Nothing would matter, just B.J.

He reached for her, wanting to pull her even closer, to taste her and know her. Those green eyes alive with the same fire that was in him, her mouth tasting his skin, tasting his chest, making his nipples harden. Suddenly the dream exploded in front of him as the phone rang, annihilating the fantasy in a sickening rush.

But when he woke he still felt the weight, the heat and that touch on his chest. He opened his eyes and came face-to-face with Joey sitting on his chest, licking it and purring so loudly that the sand vibrated against him. He jerked up, and the cat slid back, catching him on the side with his claws. Then he scooted back on the bed to sit on his haunches and calmly start cleaning his paw.

"You damn cat," Matt muttered as he made a grab for the still-ringing phone. "Yes?" he said into the receiver.

"I was getting ready to hang up again."

He raked his fingers through his hair and exhaled roughly, ignoring the tension in his body that hadn't diminished. "What did you find out?"

"I checked the records, but there isn't anyone on file by that name."

"Maybe I got the spelling wrong," he said and touched his side where it burned from the cat scratch.

"How many ways can you spell Smith or Smythe or whatever it is? I went through all the S's and didn't find any B.J. anything, or anyone with the first name beginning with a B.J."

He stood, taking the cordless phone into the bathroom with him as he flipped on the overhead lights and squinted at the brightness. Averting his eyes from his reflection in the mirrors over the sink, he turned on the shower and set the heat toward the cool side. "Okay, thanks for trying."

"Anything else?"

"Yes. Find out who thought it was necessary to announce that we approached Quint Gallagher. And see if you can get anything on a background check on Gallagher."

"A background check on Gallagher? Why don't you just read the papers or ask anyone who's dealt with him?"

"Humor me. See what you can find. Dig a bit, both personally and professionally." He caught the phone between his shoulder and ear and stripped off his slacks. "Use the agency if you need to."

"Whatever you say, boss," she said. "Anything else?"

"No, I'll see you on Monday," he said and hung up. He put the phone on the side of the sink, took off his pants and shorts and stopped with a glance in the mirror. Ignoring the evidence of the dream still showing on his body, he grimaced at three fine scratches just below his rib cage on his right side. "Damn cat," he muttered again and stepped into the coolness of the shower.

He leaned forward, pressing his forehead against the cold tiles and let the water run over him. The stinging in his side began to go away and the tightness in his body ebbed. Closing his eyes tightly, he almost laughed at the idea of being caught necking like a teenager, having an erotic dream with a cat, then taking a cold shower so he could think straight. But the laughter died when he remember who he was necking with, who he thought he'd been making love with in the dream, and just why he needed the shower. He stood back, reached for a body brush and started scrubbing his skin with a vengeance.

December 19

LATE ON SATURDAY afternoon, Brittany heard someone behind her in the center, and thought it was Anthony coming back from the bathroom. The workmen had only worked half a day and she and the boy had had the place to themselves for hours. But when she turned, she found Amy coming toward her. The small woman was in overalls, a white T-shirt and sandals, and she smiled as she looked around. "I can't believe how fast you are and how wonderful this all is.'' She stopped by Brittany, where she was working on more sketches for the faces of the children on the wall. Amy touched the nearest photo, then stared at the sketch right by it. ''It looks just like Justin.''

Brittany stood back, the pleasure of the woman's words easing the tension in her, a tension that had seemed to grow since last night. When she'd slept last night, she'd slept deeply, but when she woke, she'd still felt tired. Now she was starting to think she needed to leave earlier tonight. She needed rest, but didn't know if she could get it or not.

She stretched her arms over her head to ease the tightness there, then tugged at the cropped white sweater she was wearing with jeans. ''Do you think that looks like your daughter?'' she asked, pointing to the tiny girl in the chain of dancing children to the left of the entrance.

''Oh, yes,'' Amy said, going over to look closely at the sketch. ''It's perfect.'' She turned to Brittany. ''I'm very pleased. And I know Lindsey will be when she gets back.'' She peered at the picture beside her daughter's photo while she kept talking. ''She wanted to come back for the investors reception, just for the day, but it's so close to Christmas Eve and Walker's teething. It wouldn't work.''

''She's got children?''

''A boy, two years old. Actually, Walker's her husband's son, but they're so close.'' She looked back at Brittany. ''You must be terrific with kids to do this. There is such joy in their faces. It's very special.''

''Actually, I've never been good with kids.'' She moved to where she kept her supplies. ''Goodness knows, my father's given me his speech often enough, though,'' she said, reaching for a rag to wipe her hands all dusted with charcoal. ''You know, the 'grandchildren will be my legacy,' speech?'' Grandchildren, kids who could maybe do what he'd always thought she'd do, follow in his footsteps.

"Oh, I've heard that one before." Amy moved nearer the front hallway area, looking at the other sketches. "Maybe that's why I was so anxious to have my own family. Although I wasn't a kid when I had Taylor. I was twenty-seven, but it took time to find the right man." She touched one of the sketches with the tip of her fingers, and her voice dropped a bit. "It's not easy finding the love of your life."

Brittany frowned at that. "Do you suppose everyone has a 'love of their life' out there?"

Amy's fingers stilled. "I don't know. I sure hope so, but sometimes life isn't exactly what we'd want it to be."

She knew Amy was widowed, yet she felt almost envious of her. She'd found something that Brittany hadn't even come close to finding, even if she hadn't had it long. "No, it's not, is it?"

Amy was quiet for a moment, an awkward gap in the conversation, then, just when Brittany tried to think of something neutral to say, Amy spoke up as she looked at another sketch without a picture by it. "Is this the boy who's been helping you in here?"

"Yes, that's Anthony."

"He's so young to be working. Kids should have childhoods, you know, the wonder of the world and discovery without worrying about making money."

That's what she'd had, a real childhood, even without a mother. No problems, no trouble, just the magic of being a child. Anthony wasn't getting very much of a childhood at all, and that familiar ache for him was there again. "He's on his own a lot, and it seemed like a good way to keep him safe for a few hours each day when he's not supervised. Matt agreed to pay him for helping."

"He isn't here today?" Amy asked as she turned back to Brittany.

"He's in the bathroom." She glanced at her watch. "But he has to leave soon."

"I was thinking that maybe he should be in the day care instead of working here."

"In an ideal world, he'd have parents that cared and he'd be protected, maybe in some after-school program or with a mother to take care of him at home. But his world isn't perfect, and for now, he can only be here."

"That's sad," Amy said, then sighed sharply. "I need to go. Oh, I almost forgot, Rita, Matt's assistant, asked me to let you know that they don't have you in the computers yet in personnel yet, and you need to get up there with your employment information. Also, she needs to see you about something."

Going to personnel was out of the question. She'd "forget" about that until she faced Matt. And facing Rita as B.J. was even more out of the question. "I forgot completely to go to personnel," she said. "I've been so busy."

"You sure have. I can't believe how much you've already got in place. Do you think you'll have some of the final painting done by the reception? The investors should see it."

"I hope I can get a bit of it done, at least enough to give a hint at what the finished product should be like."

"That would be great. See you Monday," Amy said, and left.

As the door closed behind Amy, Brittany crossed to pick up a glass of water then went back to face the area she was currently working on and sank down on the carpet. She sat cross-legged while she sipped water and scanned the sketches, envisioning the colors she'd use for the kids' clothing and trying to figure out what background she'd use. But no matter how hard she tried to concentrate, she kept getting flashes of last night.

Matt in the car, Matt touching her and the craziness that was almost her undoing. She was so close to making the same mistake she'd made so often, and to doing exactly what she'd promised her father wouldn't happen. All Matt had to do was touch her and her mind became scrambled.

She took a drink of her water and stared hard at the sketch she'd done of Anthony before he got there today. He hadn't noticed it yet, and she wasn't sure she'd caught his essence. That flash of joy that she'd barely glanced in him, his smiles so few and far between. He deserved so much better. Matt had protected him from Esther in his own way, buying the woman off with the promise of Anthony getting money. That made her stomach knot. Matt the defender? Matt the hero? Damn it, that was so appealing, she thought as she took another drink of cool water.

"I ain't going to no day-care center."

The glass in her hand jerked, sloshing most of the water out onto the carpet and down her front as Anthony spoke from right behind her. She jerked around and he was there, within feet of her. "You scared me to death," she said, swiping at the water on her sweater and jeans. "I never knew anyone who moved around so quietly."

"You told that lady I was going to day care, didn't you?"

"You shouldn't eavesdrop," she said as she stood and felt the carpet squish under her feet from the spilled water. "But if you'd listened, you'd know I didn't say that."

"I wasn't eavesdropping on you. I heard that Amy lady telling the skinny one that you thought I should go to day care."

"What?"

"Her and the skinny woman, they was talking about me, and she was saying that she was gonna make me go to day care, that it wasn't right, that you said it wasn't right about me working here, that I was too young to do it."

She got to her feet to face the boy. "Where did you hear them talking?"

"Around."

"You've been in the bathroom, and she's been gone for a while."

He looked down, scuffing at the wet carpet with the toe of his worn-out tennis shoe. "I heard her."

"Okay, then tell me how you heard her talking to someone else? There hasn't been anyone in here but you and me, then Amy. No other woman."

He stared hard at the carpet.

"Anthony, if we're going to be friends, you have to tell me the truth. You can't make up stories."

He looked up at her, his dark eyes wide. "You and me are friends?"

She nodded. "Yes, we are, and friends tell the truth to each other."

"Okay, I'll tell you, just 'cause we're friends, but you can't tell no one else about it, okay?"

She could see how serious he was, so she nodded. "Okay."

"Come on," he said, and motioned her to follow him as he headed back to the front hallway area by the main entrance. He stopped at the boys' restroom. "In here," he said, pressing one hand against the newly painted door.

She hesitated. "Anthony, that's the boys' room."

He nodded. "Yeah, but there ain't no one around, and I gotta show you." He pushed the door back. "Come on."

She followed him into the room, freshly painted with pale-blue walls, floors tiled to look like hopscotch games, and a series of round mirrors over thigh-high sinks. Anthony went across the room, passed the stalls with doors done in different primary colors, then stopped by the far wall. He pointed to something in the corner, something blocked from sight by the stalls.

"I heard 'em through there," he said and disappeared from sight.

She hurried over to where he'd been, then looked around the side of the stalls just in time to see him hunkered down, pulling at a large grate, maybe three feet by three feet, painted the same shade of blue as the walls. He tugged at it and she could see that there was only one screw in the upper left-hand corner holding it to the wall so it could swing up and out of the way. It exposed a metal ventilation duct, and after Anthony wedged the wire barrier back against the corner of the wall, he dropped to his hands and knees. Before she knew what he was going to do, he'd scooted into the opening, then looked back out and up at her. "See, it's big in here. You could even fit."

"What are you doing?"

He turned and was out of sight immediately, but his voice echoed back to her. "Showing you how I heard."

She crouched down and looked into the opening. Anthony was deep in the shadows, maybe ten feet from her, looking back at her. "You can hear people talking through here?"

"Naw, you gotta go into it," he said.

"Well, I don't want to go in there, and you shouldn't either."

"Come on. I told you I'd show you," he said and crawled off into the duct.

Brittany dropped to her knees and cautiously crawled into the vent. "Anthony?" she called, and her voice echoed all around her.

"Pull the screen down." His voice came out of the shadows and she could tell he was getting farther ahead of her.

She turned, got hold of the edge and eased the screen back down, then turned to the shadows in front of her. Anthony's voice came back to her. "Hurry and be real quiet. They can hear you, too."

She felt like Alice in Wonderland falling down the rabbit hole, but she was following a little boy, not a rabbit. She caught a flash of movement ahead of her, then he was gone. She went faster, found a bend in the ducting, turned the corner and almost ran into Anthony's rear end. He'd stopped just past the turn where light filtered into the shadows. He held one finger to his lips, then pointed in front of him to another grate where the light came from.

"There," he whispered as he put one hand on her shoulder. "That's the skinny one."

She looked out and realized they were in the wall by the front reception lobby. She could smell the scent of pine from the huge Christmas tree that partially blocked her view out the vent. But she recognized Rita standing by the reception desk, a purse in one hand and what looked like a clipboard in the other. It seemed she wasn't the only one putting in extra hours.

Brittany was startled when Rita spoke, and the sound carried so clearly that it was almost as if she was right next to her. "Of course, I took care of it," she said to someone Brittany couldn't see. "But, I'll double-check. And no word on Miss Lewis and her quest for the perfect wardrobe to do justice to her new office."

The other person laughed and it was a laugh Brittany knew so well. With the strange acoustics in the vent, it seemed as if Matt was laughing right beside her, and the sound practically overwhelmed her.

Chapter Eleven

"Don't worry about her," Brittany heard Matt say. "Let Miss Lewis do whatever she wants."

Right then he came into view, and Brittany automatically moved back a bit, but couldn't take her eyes off him. An off-white silk shirt was taut across his wide shoulders, and snug-fitting brown slacks defined strong legs and lean hips. She'd almost forgotten how big he was, and in a lighter color that she'd never seen him wear before, he was even more imposing. She wished she could forget how just the sight of him made her heart start to hammer. "Don't waste your time worrying about her. Let her do her thing. Her father thinks she's working hard, doing a great job and turning her life around."

"You're kidding."

"No, I'm not. I've been thinking that maybe Daddy could get her into acting, then she'd get paid for all of this lying and pretending."

Brittany hated this, and would have turned to get away from their words, but Anthony's hand on her shoulder tightened when Rita spoke again. "Speaking of money, the boy helping the artist in the new center, Miss Smythe, he's too young to be on the payroll. Can't do it. What do you want to do, maybe enroll him in the center?"

"See, I told you," Anthony hissed right by her ear.

She hushed him quickly. Being caught by the guard in the car with Matt was bad enough, but to be found in the air ducts eavesdropping would be even worse. It was also becoming harder to stomach what people were saying about her.

"I'll think about it and get back to you," Matt said.

"Did you get things straightened out with Dunlop?"

"I hope so. It's been eating up all my time today."

"Are you on your way home now?"

"In a bit. First I have some unfinished business with Miss Smythe. I haven't had time today because of the mess with the papers and—"

"No, don't bring that up again. The next time you sign anything, I'll read it out loud to you first. Okay?"

"Deal," he said with a soft chuckle.

"I just got the boys out of here so I could get my Christmas shopping done without them being around. Now I'm leaving. If you need anything else tonight, forget you know my phone number, okay?"

Matt laughed, an easy sound. "It's forgotten."

"Good night, boss," she said and hurried toward the front of the building.

Matt turned and strode out of sight in the opposite direction. "Shoot," Brittany muttered as she turned and touched Anthony on the shoulder. "I have to get back. I don't want him to see me in here."

"No problem. Come on," he said and scooted around her, heading back the way they'd just come.

She felt as if she'd been thrown into a bad B movie, Brittany thought as she made her way through the air ducts. Normally she would have found this all very funny but at that moment, there wasn't much humor in her. Matt was coming, and she was in the air ducts off the boys' room. It was beyond ridiculous.

She hurried around the corner, toward the light from the restroom. Anthony got there first, twisted the screen back up, but as he got out, there was the sound of a door slamming close by. Footsteps echoed on the hard tile. Anthony looked back at her in the duct, then held one finger to his lips and quietly eased the screen down, effectively trapping her in the shadows.

The next thing she knew, Matt's voice was everywhere, and so close she almost felt the vibration in the air around her. "Hey there, kid. I didn't see you at first."

All she could see were Anthony's feet and legs a few feet away on the other side of the grate. "I was just hanging," the boy said.

Brittany pressed against the side of the duct to stay out of sight.

"I was looking for Miss Smythe."

"In here?"

Matt laughed at that. "No, not in here. I was just looking around the place while I waited for her. Do you know where she is?"

"Hanging."

"Where?"

"Around."

"Can you give me some idea where 'around' is?"

"Around."

She heard Matt exhale. "Do you have a guess where she'd be?"

"Maybe."

She heard Matt coming closer, and she caught a flash of movement beyond Anthony, then Matt's boots and the bottom half of his dark-brown slacks were all she could see of the man.

"Listen, I'm not the enemy here, kid."

"My name's Anthony, and you're trying to put me in that day-care thing, aren't you?"

"What are you talking about?"

"You told that lady you'd think on it, and that mean you're gonna do it, and you'll just lie to me. I ain't no dummy. I know what you're up to."

Brittany stared hard at the fancy boots and worn tenni shoes. "What are you talking about?" Matt asked.

"You're one of them 'do' guys."

"What guys?"

"The guys that let people think they do good, but they're out to do you in."

"Let me tell you something, if I say something, I mean it. I don't do anything for show."

"Yeah, sure, dude," Anthony muttered.

"The name's Matt, not dude. And you think you're tough, don't you?"

Brittany fought a surge of protectiveness for the boy and forced herself to stay very still. "I take care of myself. Es ther, well, she's just…just there. I don't care what she doe to me. It don't matter."

"Doesn't it?"

"No. Never did, never will."

"Now *you're* lying," Matt said, his voice droppin, lower.

Brittany could see Anthony's tennis shoes shuffle a bi "You don't know nothing," the boy muttered.

"I know more than you do, that's for sure. I used to be like you, a kid who thought I was so damn tough I coul handle anything. I did what I wanted, and I didn't mucl care what anyone did to me. My old man beat me up, m mother cried a lot and didn't do anything, and I did what wanted to do. I didn't care, until I did something that was so bad that they locked me up.''

Brittany was horrified. He'd been telling the truth about the joyride in the car? About his parents? God, that protectiveness she'd felt for Anthony was spilling over to the child Matt had been.

"You've been in jail?" Anthony asked.

"It's called 'youth authority' where I came from. I was locked up for three years. A long, long time, with other kids who thought they were the biggest, toughest, baddest guys ever.''

You shouldn't eavesdrop. Her own words haunted her.

"You're kidding," the boy said.

"I wish I was, but I'm not. I'm not proud of it, but I can tell you that if you keep going the way you are, you'll end up like I did.''

Anthony snorted. "Oh, come on, you're rich. You might've messed up, but you got this great job and even Esther's scared of you.''

Matt hunkered down in front of the boy and Brittany could see his hands pressed to his thighs. "I figured out what I had to do before it was too late for me," he said. "That's all. But I almost threw away any chance of having what I've got now. Listen, Anthony, you trust yourself. Don't trust anyone else. You're all you've got, and you can make the difference, and you keep your word. I said I'd pay you. I will. I said you aren't going to day care, and you aren't.''

Anthony shifted again, his feet scuffing at the tile floor. "You mean that?"

"I told you, I say what I mean."

"Okay," Anthony whispered.

Brittany had thought that Matt was a bit of a hero after the way he dealt with Esther, but this man talking to this boy was hitting her on a level she couldn't even fathom. He'd said that if he went to war, he'd like her to fight for him. Well, she'd just simply like to have him as friend. She felt her eyes burn, and was startled when he stood and spoke in a normal tone.

"So? Where's Miss Smythe?"

"I told you, Matt, she's hanging somewhere around here. Do you want me to go look with you?"

"I'd appreciate that," Matt said.

"Okay," Anthony said, then the leather boots and the tennis shoes walked away and out of sight.

Brittany sagged back against the cold metal wall and took a shaky breath. A friend. A real friend. Had she ever had one? She had to search her memories, but knew that she'd never really had anyone in her life who qualified. Not any more than she had anyone in her life—besides her father— who she really loved. She shuddered as another thought exploded in her. If things were different, if life hadn't taken the turns it had, she could have Matt for a friend, and she could love him. Really love him.

Brittany heard the door slam at the same time a single word came to her. *Impossible.* There was no way she could let herself love him, let herself fall into that trap. No way at all. He'd never love her, not when he knew she was Brittany Lewis. She swallowed hard and realized that every other time she'd thought she was in love had been an illusion. Matt was reality. And that reality was almost too painful. She pressed a hand to her stomach and exhaled a shaky breath before reaching for the grating in front of her. The reality was, she'd never known love.

That last realization seemed stark and sad. But even sadder was the thought that she probably never would. She lifted the screen and crawled out into the bathroom. She stood there, taking breaths, but nothing settled her inside.

"B.J.?" she heard someone calling. Then they called again, farther away, and she headed for the door.

"THERE SHE IS," Anthony called, as Matt followed the boy out of the back hallway into the main area of the center.

B.J. was there, sitting cross-legged on the floor, under the tree, holding a cup and staring at the wall where she'd obviously been working. In jeans and a short sweater, her hair pulled back in a high ponytail, she almost looked like a high-school student—until she looked up at him, and all the pull that she had on him was there in full force. He stopped where he was, giving himself some distance.

"I found her." Anthony went toward her and dropped down on the floor, sitting by her side under the spread of the fake branches of the tree. The boy looked up at him. "I told you she was hanging."

Matt came into the open space. "So she is," he murmured.

"You were looking for me?" B.J. asked without moving or looking at him.

"Yeah, Matt wanted to talk to you, and he was looking for you in the boys' bathroom," Anthony said, that grin on his face a bit shocking after the sober kid Matt had first encountered in the bathroom.

Matt went closer. "I was checking out the work they've been doing." He motioned to the platforms in the branches over them, at the wooden bars that contained the napping areas now. "I see they put in the rails to keep kids from pitching to the floor while they sleep."

He halfway expected B.J. to say something about the cynic in him, but she didn't. She smoothed the flats of both hands on her thighs, and then touched her tongue to her lips. "They got that done this morning," was all she said.

Matt went closer, thankful that B.J. stayed seated. "So,

this is hanging?'' he asked, aware that he could catch the scent of her in the air, that touch of light perfume, a freshness about her that was very appealing.

''I guess so,'' she murmured looking up at him with those green eyes. ''How about you? Did you get your problem fixed? The signature?''

He'd been right to keep his distance today while he sorted out the mistakes he'd made with the production papers. There was no way he could have done what he'd had to do with B.J. anywhere close by. ''I think so.''

''Did it mess up the production?''

''It doesn't seem so.''

''You got off easy, didn't you?''

If she meant spending a whole day fighting the urge to chuck work and go and find her, no, he didn't get off easily. But he knew what she meant and she was right. ''I guess so.''

''You messed up?'' Anthony asked.

He looked at the kid, that grin firmly in place. The boy was enjoying this, and he wondered if he'd done the right thing telling him a bit about his own misspent youth. ''We all do, kid,'' he murmured.

''Anthony, the name's Anthony.''

He nodded. ''I remember. Anthony.''

''Tell her that you ain't gonna send me to the day-care thing or that you ain't gonna fire me, neither.''

Matt crouched in front of the boy. Damn it, he felt as though he were looking at a version of himself from years ago. ''Why?''

The dark-brown eyes narrowed on him, the smile slipping. ''Cuz she listens to you, that's why. And if you say, 'No way he goes up there,' then she'll listen to you.'' He leaned toward Matt. ''You're the man, Matt, the boss,'' he said in a hissing whisper. "You say what's so. So, go ahead and tell her."

"Yeah, Matt," B.J. said. "Just tell me."

He looked at her, taken aback by the deep humor in her green eyes. She was suddenly enjoying this, too, and damn it, so was he. Teasing, connecting. He felt like a thirsty man getting a cold drink. "Okay, this is the way it is. The kid...er...Anthony, is not going to day care. Understood, Miss Smythe?"

"Yes, sir," she said, with a mock salute.

"And he's going to get a raise. Fifty cents more an hour just for him." He looked back at the boy. "How's that?"

"Just for me?" Anthony asked and when Matt nodded, he said, "Way, way cool."

There was a banging on the back security door and Matt stood. "Are you expecting a delivery or something?"

Anthony scrambled to his feet. "Oh, shoot, I bet it's Esther." But he didn't head for the door. "You mean that about more money?"

"I told you that—"

"I know, you don't lie. Okay, that's good. Real good."

The banging came again. "I gotta go," he said, then started to leave.

"See you Monday?" Matt asked before the kid could take off.

"Sure, Monday," he said, then looked at B.J. "What time? We got Christmas vacation next week."

"What time does Esther come to work?"

"Noon."

"Perfect. Come then. We've got a lot of work to do."

"Great," he said, then looked at Matt. "Thanks," he mumbled before he turned and ran when the knocking came again. He jerked open the door, and before he could step out and close the door behind him, Matt heard Esther's voice.

"Whadda I tell you? Be waiting for me. I don't have time to go hunt you down. You're just a—" The door clicked shut and the words were gone.

Matt shook his head, then looked down at B.J., who was about to stand up. "Don't. It'll only make things worse."

She rested her hands, palms up, on her knees and stared at the floor. "How could Child Protection Services place him with her? Okay, she's sort of related, but for God's sake..." She took a slightly unsteady breath. "He seems to accept the fact that she hates him. That's even worse."

He hunkered down again, right in front of B.J., but he didn't touch her. He stared at her bent head. "Listen, this bothers me as much as it bothers you."

She looked at him then, lifting her head, her green eyes meeting his and they were overly bright. "Why should any kid just be tolerated?" She swallowed hard, and he could see the emotion in her. "God, he's a terrific boy. He should be loved and cared for and cherished."

Matt took in the lift of her chin, the way her lips trembled slightly, the shadow of emotion in her eyes. *She* should be loved and cared for and cherished. Loved. Loved and cherished, and loved again. He felt slightly lightheaded as that thought sank in, as well as the fact that he wished he was the man who would love and cherish her forever. It stunned him, and he stood abruptly, turning from her to look blindly at the wall that held her work.

"He's a tough kid," he said for lack of anything else to say at that moment.

"He's not that tough. He's a kid. And he's not getting any childhood." He heard her inhale and it made his body tense. "I just hope that he ends up doing well and not getting in trouble."

"It's his choice."

"And how good are nine-year-olds at making choices?" she asked. "I was horrible at it back then, and I'm still not that great. What chance does he have?"

He turned and was shaken to see her face buried in her hands. The nape of her neck looked so vulnerable, as vulnerable as she seemed right then. "The same chance most kids like him have." The words sounded cold even as he said them.

She slowly lowered her hands to her knees again and she sat up straighter. He could see her taking breaths and easing them out. Her eyes were closed. He went back toward her, watching her, seeing the rise of her high breasts under the short sweater, the way each breath lifted the knit material exposing just a fraction of an inch of her midriff. Her fingers slightly curled.

There was silence, except for her regular breaths, and he moved closer still. He was a foot from her, right in front of her, and she kept it up. Breathe in, breathe out. Breasts lifting, skin being exposed with the rhythm. The world was revolving around each movement of her body, the soft parting of her lips, the curls that had escaped from the confines of the ponytail. The world revolved around her. His world.

He crouched in front of her, then touched her, his fingers barely making contact with her chin. He felt her breath catch, then her eyes opened, the deep green seemingly capable of pulling him in, letting him lose himself completely in their depths.

"What are you doing?" he asked.

"Yoga, something to…to…help."

"Is it?"

"What?"

"Helping?"

She exhaled heavily. "No. It's not."

He drew back and sank down on the floor in front of her, crossing his legs and leaning forward. "Maybe we can figure out something to help him. You and me."

She blinked at that and he could see that her lashes were damp. "He won't take charity."

"Of course not."

He saw her fingers curling slowly into fists on her knees. "So what can we do?"

He covered her hand with his. "First of all, you have to look at it logically, not emotionally."

She looked down at his hand resting on hers, but she didn't draw away. "He's a human being, Matt. He's not a stock merger or an error on some papers that you signed by mistake."

"Of course not, but if you get emotional, you won't think clearly."

"You sound like my father," she murmured.

"Well, I'm not your father," he heard himself say. She took a shaky breath and a surge of pure protectiveness almost suffocated him. "But I'll help."

Maybe if he hadn't felt her start to tremble, or maybe if she hadn't looked up right then, her eyes bright with unshed tears, or maybe if her hand hadn't turned in his and their fingers hadn't intertwined, he could have said some platitude, stood and walked away. But he couldn't. He felt her fingers tangling with his, that trembling in her body, saw those eyes, and he acted impulsively. He leaned toward her, his free hand slipping around the nape of her neck, and he drew her to him.

Her forehead pressed to his chest and she took a shuddering breath. "God, I've never felt so helpless," she whispered.

Any dream he'd had didn't compare to this reality. To her softness, her heat, the feel of her under his hands, and he drew her even closer. He eased his legs out straight, and she was on his lap, her face now buried in his neck.

And he held her, just held her, slowly stroking her back, whispering against her hair. "Hey, it's going to be okay. It really is. We'll make it right somehow."

She shifted, and for a moment he thought she was going to move back and break the contact. But she tilted her head back, until she was looking up at him. "What did you...you want to talk to me about?" she asked.

He drank in her delicate features, the way her lips parted softly, and he whispered, "Obviously more than I thought," and his lips found hers.

Brittany had never felt so safe in the arms of another person. Even though she'd been engaged three times, things had never felt right with anyone else. Never. But at that moment, she felt grounded and so safe that it brought more burning to her eyes. She scrambled closer to Matt, shifting until her legs were around his hips, and his lips were playing havoc with any and all sanity she might have had the moment before the kiss began.

His taste and his scent were everywhere, and she could literally feel his heart beat against her breasts. She was closer to him that she'd ever been with anyone, and the sense of being complete was growing in her. His mouth ravished hers, his breath mingling with hers, and she felt his response to her, as real as the response that was exploding in her, shattering all reason. She wanted Matt. She needed Matt. She was tangled with him, her fingers sinking in his hair, the feel of his hardness against her.

Together they fell back and sideways, onto the carpet, ending up with her legs still around him, both of them on their sides, facing each other. His hands explored her, tugging at her sweater, shifting the soft knit fabric high enough to find her breasts barely protected by her lace bra. Then the bra was gone, and she felt skin against skin, fire against fire, and her nipple hardened instantly between his thumb and forefinger. His lips trailed along her throat, finding a sensitive spot by her ear, and she arched toward his touch.

She wanted more, wanted to feel him too, and she tugged at the silk of his shirt, worked her hands under the fine material and found his chest. She felt the muscles, touched his nipples, and felt them harden under her touch. He took a shuddering breath as her hand spanned his stomach, and the tips of her fingers worked their way under his waistband. She'd never lost control this way, never wanted a man the way she wanted Matt, and had never before exposed herself emotionally, as she was now.

She answered kiss for kiss, touch for touch, pressing to him, feeling his barely confined desire in his slacks. She fumbled with his belt buckle, swearing softly when she couldn't get it undone, then his hand was on hers, manipulating the buckle and she held her breath when she felt him. The cotton of his shorts was all that separated them, and she hated it, pushing her fingers awkwardly under the elastic waistband.

She touched him, felt his hardness against her skin, and felt him shudder from the contact. "Oh, yes," he moaned, and his hand found hers, holding it there, the world starting to tremble for her.

Then, suddenly, that world came to a screeching halt.

Chapter Twelve

Brittany heard a door slam at the same time someone yelled from the back hallway. "Anyone in here?"

Matt jerked back, his fingers touching her lips as unsteadily as she felt, and she couldn't hush her ragged breathing. He looked down at her, then twisted to one side, getting to his feet in one swift motion. She watched him pull his slacks back up, leaving the belt loose, then tug his shirt completely free of the slacks, the silk tail of the garment falling low enough to hide the evidence of what he'd been doing.

"Yes, who's there?" Matt called as he raked his fingers through his hair.

"Security," someone called back.

Matt hesitated, stooped, gave Brittany a quick, fierce kiss and whispered, "Stay here."

Then he strode off toward the back hallway and around the corner. She could hear him talking, but it barely broke through her horror at what she'd almost let happen. What she'd almost fallen into—willingly. More than willingly.

"What's going on?" Matt was asking as Brittany tugged her bra into place, ignoring the tenderness in her nipples, then grabbed her sweater and fumbled putting it back on. Her fingers barely worked on the buttons as a man spoke up.

"Oh, Mr. Terrel, I was checking the doors and I saw the light. I figured I'd better check things out," another male voice said.

"Good work, but we're fine. Just taking a look at the work on the refurbishing down here."

Brittany managed to get her sweater on, and pushed herself to her feet.

"You need anything?" the other man was asking.

A brain, she thought, some courage, some character. She was shocked to find that her pants were undone, and she hadn't even been aware of them being unbuttoned.

"No, just lock the door on your way out, okay?"

"Yes, sir."

There was the sound of the door closing, then a click, and she heard Matt coming back.

As he rounded the corner, Brittany got to her feet, her clothes relatively straight. Matt stopped when he saw her. "Sorry about that," he murmured.

His hair was vaguely spiked, and the silk of his shirt hugged his broad shoulders. Why did he have to look so good, even in disarray? And why did she have to be standing there like an idiot, just staring at him?

"It…it's for the best," she said, turning from him, not sure what to do, but knowing that she had to get out of there. She was short of breath still. "I don't know why I let that…" She sensed Matt coming closer, then felt the air stir with his movement. "I'm sorry, too."

He was right behind her, and his hands touched her shoulders. Light, but compelling, and she felt his touch along her back. "I'm not sorry about that," he whispered as his lips touched the back of her neck.

She gasped and moved forward, away from the way he seemed almost to be seeping into her soul. This was wrong, so wrong. She'd promised her father she'd be rational and sensible, and Matt thought he was with a woman of honor, a woman who was everything he knew Brittany Lewis wasn't.

She turned, the air seeming very cool all of a sudden, as if the air conditioning had been kicked into overdrive. Matt wasn't moving, but his eyes held her as surely as if he still had hold of her. "All I'm sorry about is rushing things."

"Yes, rushing," she said quickly, unable to come up with anything other than that to keep him at a distance. She couldn't tell him she hadn't wanted what had just happened. She wasn't a good liar at the best of times, and now would be an impossible time to pull one off. "It's...it's too soon," she said, brushing nervously at her jeans, hiding her shaking hands from Matt.

"Okay, I understand," he said, staying where he was. "I understand."

She wished she did. She wished she understood how just looking at him made her heart leap in her chest. And why she ached to touch him again. She pushed her hands behind her back and clenched them into fists so tightly that her nails bit into her palms. The pain was a good distraction as Matt started to tuck in his shirt with sharp, hard strokes, but he never looked away from her. "I...I need to get going," she said.

"So do I," he said.

He motioned around. "Need to clean up some?"

"No, I...I'll be back later. I just need to go and...and pick up some supplies."

He came closer to her. "I'll give you a ride."

"No." The word stood between them, hard and cold. "No, thank you," she said, trying to soften it. "I'm fine. You go. It's getting late."

He hesitated, and she wasn't sure if he was going to leave or not. "I don't know about you being here alone like this."

"I'm fine. Security's around. No problems." Especially if he wasn't around. "I'll be okay."

"Are you sure?"

"Positive," she said, feeling that the assurance was a lie, but she wasn't going to figure out why. Not now. "What did you want to see me for?"

"Oh, yes." He looked around, then crossed to the hallway at the front. He crouched down, reached for his briefcase and took out some papers. He handed the papers to her. "Insurance papers you left in my car last night."

She hadn't even thought about them. "Thanks," she murmured, taking them, but not looking at them. "Good night."

His eyes narrowed, and she was almost certain he was going to touch her again, but thankfully, when that touch came, it was a mere tap on her chin. "You be careful, B. J. Smythe," he uttered, then turned and left.

She watched him go and her legs lost all ability to support her. She sank down onto the carpet, leaned back against the wall behind her and just tried to breathe. That was all she could do right then. Breathe. She'd worry about everything else later. Much later.

December 21

BRITTANY HAD BARELY SLEPT that night, a restlessness that wouldn't ease, keeping her up late and getting her up early. She stayed away from LynTech on Sunday and didn't go back until Monday. Anthony showed up right at noon, his navy sweatshirt and torn jeans looking as if he'd slept in them. He got right to work and didn't speak much unless he had to. Matt was nowhere to be seen.

"I gotta go soon," Anthony said at least fifteen minutes before six.

"How come you're leaving early?" she asked as she

dipped a brush in some solvent. She eyed the part of the mural she was working on, getting just the right skin tones to suggest the face of Amy's daughter, Taylor. "Got Christmas shopping to do?"

Wrong thing to say. Anthony was behind her and his voice sounded horribly flat. "No, Esther's leaving early and I have to get back to the hotel when she's ready."

She put the brush back in the solvent and grabbed a rag. "I'll walk with you."

"Naw, you don't have to. I ain't no—"

"I know you're not a baby. I'd like to walk with you. I'm going to get something to eat and I could use the company partway." She looked at him. "Will you let me walk with you?"

He nodded. "If you want."

"I want," she said, and crossed to her purse. She took out some money, pushed her purse behind a stack of cleaning things, then turned to Anthony. "Ready?"

"Yeah, let's go."

"Where are you two off to?"

Brittany looked at the entry, and Matt was there. Damn the man, he didn't show all day, then he popped up without any warning. Although she didn't think any warning would get her ready for that first sight of him. He never wore a jacket, even when it had been raining and tonight was no exception. He was dressed in an off-white shirt, open at the throat, exposing tanned skin. He wore it with snug slacks that looked as if they could be suede. And the boots.

"B.J.'s walking me to the hotel, then she's going to eat," Anthony offered before Brittany could say anything.

"What a coincidence. I need to eat before getting back to work, too."

"I'm just going to get a quick bite."

"Me, too."

"I mean, like fast food or something."

"Sounds good," he murmured, a smile playing at the corners of his wide mouth. She was as trapped now as she'd been in the air shaft last night. And by the same man. "What sounds good to you?"

"Tofu."

He was really grinning now. "They have fast-food tofu?"

Why did his smile have to be so damned appealing? "Actually, yes, they do."

"I've never heard of it, but I'm open to anything. Come on and I'll drive the two of you where you're going."

They were wasting time. Anthony had to get back to the hotel, but she wasn't going to get in a car with Matt again. "We're walking. You can drive," she said, then looked at Anthony. "Let's go."

She started leaving with Anthony, and Matt was right there when they went out into the reception area. "Why not drive?"

She talked as they walked toward the front doors. "We're going to walk."

"Okay, lead the way," he murmured.

Matt fell in step by Anthony when they got out onto the street and continued with them to the hotel. "So, Anthony's going home and we're going to get someone to kill a tofu for us?"

"Tofu is from soy and soy isn't killed to feed the masses. It's harvested," she murmured.

Christmas music filtered into the street from speakers on the light posts, and mingled with the din of the traffic. Anthony started to almost skip and Brittany hurried to keep up. He was obviously afraid of making Esther angry. Brittany would have given anything if he didn't have to go with the woman. Matt walked without speaking until they approached the front of the hotel, a multi-storied building that soared into the night sky.

"Bye," Anthony said to both of them and broke into a dead run for the entrance.

He was gone so quickly Brittany didn't even get a chance to tell him good-bye. Then it was just her and Matt on the street, and she started walking again, quickly.

"Hey," Matt said. "Can we take it a bit slower?"

She eased up her speed and felt Matt's arm brush hers. The night was cold and clear. The scent of pine filtered into the air, and the music seemed to be following them. They reached a row of shops that were all adorned with Christmas themes.

"Do you do this often?" Matt asked.

"Walk? I've been doing it all my life. How about you?"

"The restaurant. Have you been to it before?"

"A couple of times. I found it by accident when I was looking for a place to get solvent. The receptionist thought there was an art-supply place down here next to a candy shop, but I never found it. But I did find Earth's Treats, and their food is really good."

"Tofu on a stick?"

"No, but there's tofu ice cream and tofu hot dogs and—"

"Never mind. I get the idea."

She glanced at him. "You can go back and get in your car and get a big juicy steak if you want. I promise not to get upset if you leave."

She cast him a look and found him watching her intently. "No, I don't think so," he said. "Not even for a steak."

She stopped and looked at him. "Feel free."

Matt looked at B.J. and wondered where his freedom had gone. He wasn't free to walk away from her, not any more than he was free to do what he wanted right then, kiss her in the middle of the street. With his luck lately, a cop would catch him and jail him. So he said, "Let's go," turned from her, started off down the street again and she was right beside him. He wasn't going anywhere without her tonight. Tomorrow was something different, but tonight he was staying right where he was. With her.

He heard *Jingle Bells* playing on the outdoor speakers and started humming the tune under his breath. He'd never been much on Christmas or any holiday, but suddenly he felt festive for some reason.

"I just meant that tofu isn't for everyone," B.J. said at his side. "Believe me, I don't go around trying to convert anyone."

She could convert him to just about anything at that moment. "That's a relief," he said.

She started walking faster, and he adjusted his stride to keep up. Most women couldn't match his stride, but she was forcing him to adjust to match hers. That tickled him on some level, and he kept right by her as she walked.

"There it is," she said, pointing to a hole-in-the-wall place just up the block.

From what he could see, it was little more than a storefront, with twinkling Christmas lights framing the windows on either side of the door. A wooden sign over the entrance, framed by lights too, read, Earth's Treats.

There were no more than ten small wooden tables arranged on a stone floor in the place. The walls were murals of nature, and a counter at the far end fronted an opening to the kitchen in the back. He had to admit that there was a good fragrance of food in the air. Nothing he recognized, but it smelled good enough to make him remember he'd skipped lunch and was very hungry.

A young girl by the cash register wore a brilliant red and green tie-dyed T-shirt, an obvious homage to Christmas. Another homage to the season was a pair of reindeer antlers topped with bells she was wearing on her short blond hair. They tinkled as she glanced in their direction, and she smiled.

"Merry Christmas. Eat in or taking out tonight, folks?"

Brittany crossed to the order counter and spoke up before Matt could stop her. "Take-out, please."

He wouldn't have minded just eating right there, in the tiny place, with Christmas carols playing, a girl with antlers and B.J. and her tofu. But he wasn't going to push it.

The girl pointed to a menu on the wall behind her. "Our specials tonight are mock turkey loaf, spinach lasagna, sweet potato pie, carob brownies, fried tempe with marinara sauce, and our ever-popular tofu adventure." She smiled even more. "Now, that's my personal favorite."

Matt scanned the menu, searching for something that sounded like anything he'd ever heard of.

"Are you sure you want to do this?" B.J. asked as if she'd read his mind.

He looked at her and knew that he'd do whatever it took to keep this contact going. He glanced at the menu again. "Is there anything like a hamburger?"

"Yes, sir," the girl said. "We've got great veggie burgers with all the trimmings."

"Trimmings?" he asked cautiously.

"Tomatoes, lettuce, onions, mayo. Well, unless you're vegan and we can substitute dairy-free dressing, if you'd like. And we've got tofu cheese and—"

"Real mayonnaise, real cheese and no onions."

"Okay," the girl said, and rang it up on the register. Then she looked at B.J. "And you?"

"Tofu adventure, extra soy sauce, extra noodles and no snow peas."

"Sounds great," the girl said, rang it in, then turned and went through the half door into the back of the place.

Matt glanced at B.J. who was nervously smoothing the worn wood of the counter with the flats of her hands.

B.J. looked at him, then smiled, but didn't say anything.

Then her smile deepened and so did his pleasure basking in it. He wished he knew how to keep her smiling all the time.

The bells sounded and the girl was back, going to the cash register to total the order. "Do you have wine?" Matt asked.

"Of course we do. Wonderful wine made from organic grapes and naturally fermented without chemicals from the—"

"You don't need to sell me on it. Just add it to the total, anything in red."

She rang in the extra item, then smiled at Matt and gave him the total. He paid for it, then asked, "How long will it be?"

"Not long," she said, then went back through the doors.

Matt turned to B.J. and motioned to a table by the window. "Do you want to sit while we wait?"

There was tension there, coming from nowhere, and he didn't understand it. He knew what had happened last night between them had been explosive, had shaken him to the core. It had to have been the same for her, and it had obviously made her a bit uneasy. "I told you, it's fast food. They won't be long." She reached in the pocket of her jeans and took out some bills. "I'll pay my half," she said.

"No, you won't. My treat."

He was thankful that she didn't fight him, but instead pushed the money back in her pocket. "Thanks."

He leaned one arm on the counter and watched her. "So what's tofu adventure, or do I want to know?"

"It's a stir-fry with chunks of marinated tofu, an assortment of vegetables, mushrooms, baby corn, snow peas—"

"That you didn't want?"

"I don't like them," she said. "It's got this great soy sauce on it, and sort of hot spices. Nothing major, but enough to get your attention."

The girl was there with a wine bottle and showed it to Matt. It had a homemade label that said it was a burgundy, no year, and he didn't recognize the vineyard. "How's this?" she asked.

"Fine, just fine," Matt said.

She went back into the kitchen area, and Matt looked at B.J., but she'd moved closer to the windows and was looking out at the street. He saw her shoulders move with a sigh, and he remembered her breath on his skin, remembered it all too well. "So, we've got wine. I'm not sure how good it's going to be, though. Any wine with a homemade label becomes suspect," he said.

"The packaging doesn't mean a thing," she said without turning back to him.

"Tell that to someone in marketing," he countered, staying by the cash register and looking across the space at her. "You see the label first, and that's what sells you on a product."

"It's what's in the bottle that counts."

"Absolutely. But what if the label told you it was white wine, a dry white wine, and you opened it and got a red wine that was really fruity? Wouldn't that shake any confidence you had in the product and wouldn't that mean you'd be leery of buying that wine again?"

"But if the wine was just plain excellent wine, wouldn't that make a difference?"

He had no idea how this whole discussion had started, but it fascinated him. A woman with a brain, who could point and counterpoint with him. Yes, he liked that. One more thing about B.J. that was more than intriguing.

"You've got a point there. But remember, there are a lot of excellent wines out there. Possibly things would hinge on the cost of the wine. And was the quality worth the aggravation?"

"And if it was, would you ignore the faulty packaging?"

Was she thinking about Anthony? Was that why she looked so bothered all of sudden? He didn't want to see her like this. "If you're thinking about the kid—?"

She turned then, but didn't come closer. "Anthony, his name's Anthony."

"If you're worried about Anthony, I told you, we'll do something."

"Like what?"

He hated not having answers, especially for this woman. "I'm not sure. I need to check with an attorney when I get the time."

"You're an attorney."

"Business law. Nothing like child rights or custody law."

"Do you know someone you could talk to?"

He had a whole staff who'd know someone. "Yes, I do. And I'll get in touch with someone tomorrow."

The jingle bells sounded and the girl was back with two bags. She smiled at Matt. "Here you go, sir."

He took the bags, then turned to B.J., but she was already opening the door. "Thanks," he said to the girl and went after B.J.

B.J. slipped outside into the cold air, and Matt fell in step with her, carrying the food. He looked at her, just watched her for a minute, the way she lifted her chin slightly as she walked, the way she hugged her arms around herself, and when she spoke, it startled him.

"I've never been around people like Esther," she said in little more than a whisper.

"Well, I have," he said.

Her huge eyes looked up at him, the impact not lost on him even with the shadows her lashes cast. "You mentioned that before…about your childhood. Was it that bad?"

After years of never mentioning his background as a kid to anyone, he'd told a nine-year-old a bit and now he was about to tell B.J. "It was my childhood, like it or not. And it wasn't good. No."

"Your mother was like Esther?"

He looked away from her and kept walking. "Not really. My mother was a weak woman, trapped in her life, very unhappy, but didn't do anything about it when my father did his thing."

"Which was?"

Matt stared at the people ahead of them. "Whatever a raging alcoholic could think of doing to anyone within arm's reach."

"He beat you?" she asked, and he knew she was watching him.

"He batted me around on a regular basis," he found himself admitting. Words he seldom even thought, much less said.

"Oh, God, I don't understand how a parent could hurt a child."

He didn't want pity, not from this woman. "It happens. I survived."

"Are your parents dead?"

"No, last I heard they were living back east somewhere."

"You don't see them?"

"No, they aren't part of my life anymore. They haven't been since I was old enough to get the hell out of the house and be on my own."

"How old were you then?"

"Seventeen. I was gone from the house for a while, and when I came back, I couldn't live there. So, I left. I haven't been back. Don't want to and won't. I didn't have anyone to rescue me, so I rescued myself. And it worked out just fine.''

"So, you don't have any family?''

"I don't want any. I'm fine on my own.''

"Forever?''

He looked at her, and stopped in the middle of the street in front of her. "Nothing's forever," he said and wondered why that sounded so…cynical.

"Do you always tell the truth?'' she asked.

He nodded. "I try to.''

She started walking again and spoke softly. "Do you think what I'm doing is good work?''

He hadn't expected that question. "Yes, I do.''

"Am I talented?''

"Yes.''

"Intelligent?''

"Absolutely.''

She slanted him a look as she kept walking. "Am I worth what you're paying me?''

"I wouldn't pay you if you weren't.''

"Do you consider me a hard worker?''

"You work as hard as anyone I've ever known, including Zane.''

"Thank you,'' she said softly and walked faster as they passed the hotel where Esther worked.

"What was that all about?'' he asked.

She shrugged. "I just wondered what you really thought of me.''

He shifted the bags to one hand, and reached out to touch her with his other hand. She stopped, then slowly turned to him. He couldn't tell her here what he *really* thought of her. Not in public, because he really wanted to show her.

So he settled for a simple truth. "You're a very special person, B. J. Smythe. And I'm very glad we met.''

Chapter Thirteen

Brittany looked up at Matt and hated his words. B. J. Smythe was special and he was glad they'd met. That cut her to the core. She turned from him, walking as quickly as she could away from the man and the words. But he was still there beside her. "Are you ever going to tell me what B.J. stands for?"

"Anything you want it to," she said without looking at him.

"No clues? No hints?"

It was there for Brittany, her opening, her chance to stop the insanity of her deception. All she had to do was say, "The B is for Brittany and the J is for Jayne, and end it with Lewis, instead of Smythe." But she could hardly form the words, much less say them.

Brittany felt an overwhelming sadness. Matt had told her she was worthwhile, a good worker, talented, intelligent. She had it all, but she still couldn't say the truth. She couldn't make herself admit what she'd been doing.

The cold night air cut through her lightweight clothes and the sky was clouding again. Anthony had told her that he sometimes slept on the balcony of their apartment when Esther wasn't in a good mood, but she suspected that Esther locked him outside. She just hoped that tonight wasn't one of those nights.

"Do…do you suppose that Anthony is okay?" she finally asked as they neared LynTech. "It's so cold and it looks like it's going to rain again."

"It's winter, even here in Houston. Nothing like New York or Maine, but cold enough."

"Anthony sleeps outside sometimes."

"I used to, pretended I was camping out to get out of the house for a while."

"Even in winter?"

"No, not then. But I was raised in upstate New York so that wasn't an option for me. I went to the cellar."

"You'll get in touch with the attorney first thing tomorrow, won't you?" She stumbled slightly, not sure if it was the uneven sidewalk or her feet not working just right. But the result was Matt reached out and put his arm around her shoulders.

"Steady there," he murmured and kept walking.

She let herself put her arm around his waist, and kept walking. He felt steady and sure, solid as a rock. And so right. She kept herself from getting even closer as they approached LynTech. At the front Matt let go of her to push the entry door with his free hand. But the door didn't open.

He shook his head and looked up at her. "Locked tight."

"We can get in through the parking garage and go in the back door to the center," she said, hurrying to keep up with him.

"Do you have a security key for the center?" he asked without missing a step.

"No, no," she said, catching up to him.

"Then it's up the elevator to the executive level, and we'll have to take the regular elevator back down."

The garage door was up and they hurried into the parking

garage. They crossed to the executive elevator, Matt pressed in a code and the doors opened. They got in, and as the doors closed, Brittany held to the railing and felt the car starting up. Neither of them spoke until they were almost to the top, then Matt said, "Maybe we should just eat now. The food's going to get cold."

"When I get to the center."

"Okay," he murmured as the elevator stopped. The doors slid open, and they stepped out into a dark office that had been her father's. She'd spent a lot of time in here when she was young, but now it looked so different. All of her father's furniture had been replaced, and what looked like toys were lying on the coffee table in the conference area.

She followed Matt through various doors until they had slipped into the corridor.

She headed to the elevators, but Matt was there with the food in his hand before she could hit the Down button. He stopped, and she met his gaze, and she knew it was time to run like hell. "Here," she said, "you take the wine. I don't want any." She pushed it toward him, managed to hit the food bag with the wine bag and, as if in slow motion, she saw both bags fly to one side.

There was a crashing sound, as the wine bag hit the metal frame on the elevator doors and a gurgling sound as the food bag settled on top of it. Both bags were almost upside down, with brown liquid oozing out of one, and red wine seeping out of the other, mingling on the short-pile beige carpeting.

"Oh, shoot," she gasped, dropping to her haunches to reach for the nearest bag, but when she grabbed the paper, it tore, and food went everywhere.

"We killed wine and tofu in one fell swoop," Matt said, above her.

She looked up at him, at a deadly smile on his lips, and she felt lost.

Everything dissolved for her at that point. It was ridiculous, everything was ridiculous. The mess of food, the lies, being locked out, then being here alone. She wanted to run, yet she wanted to stay forever. Nothing made sense, and she wasn't aware that she was crying until Matt dropped to his haunches in front of her and touched her cheek.

"Tears? What's this all about?" he whispered.

"I don't know," she choked. "This mess…it's…a mess…and I don't know anything anymore."

"Maintenance will clean up the mess." His finger brushed at her tears. "And we'll live without organic wine."

"Stop," she mumbled, and stood, hurrying away from the oozing mess by her feet and reached for the elevator call button. She hit it hard just before Matt grabbed her by her upper arm.

"Where are you going?" Matt asked.

She turned, and he was inches from her. Inches. All she had to do was reach out and touch him. To feel that connection. To be a part of someone. To be grounded. But she couldn't. And that made the tears fall again. "Away." She'd painted herself into a corner with her charade and her lies, and the worst part of all was, she loved this man.

But she couldn't. If she let herself, she would. She could. She did. "Just…just away."

He framed her face with both hands, his thumbs brushing at the tears. "Did I ever tell you that you aren't boring? That you can add that to your list of virtues?" His voice lowered. "And that I want you, more than I've ever wanted anyone in my life?"

His words exploded in her, and the next thing Brittany

knew she was in his arms, holding to him for dear life, sobbing. And she knew she wanted him, too.

Matt broke all of his rules with B.J., one by one. And now, the minute she came into his arms, there were no more rules intact. They were gone, crumbled, and as he held her close, he didn't look back. All he wanted was her. That had been the truth. And he wasn't turning back.

She lifted her face to his, and he didn't hesitate to capture her lips with his. Tasting her, exploring her, and in a burst of passion that left him spinning, he scooped her up in his arms. She snuggled into him, trembling, her head buried in his chest, and he carried her down the hall to his office.

He kicked the door, and it swung back to expose shadows in the outer room. He crossed to his private office, and slipped inside with B.J. in his arms. Shadows were everywhere as he crossed the main room and eased back the door to the side room. He'd kept the room for the times he didn't make it home at night, a small space with a daybed, a half bathroom, even a scaled-down kitchen area.

He carried B.J. to the bed, the soft whisper of raindrops hitting the windows, and the lights of the night filtering into the room. Together they tumbled onto the daybed, held each other, knew there would be no going back. He barely dared breathe until he felt her shift, felt her fingers at the buttons of his shirt, and the moment her touch was on his bare chest, his world rocked out of control. There was need and desire, a hunger that he never knew existed. It was everywhere, consuming him, and it all centered on B.J.

He touched her and discovered her. He felt her and caressed her, and he knew if he lived to be a thousand, he'd never get enough of her. Her hands were on him, his shirt gone and he couldn't remember it coming off. Kisses were wild, the urgency stunning and he tugged at the fine material of her sweater. He thought he heard buttons pop, but he didn't stop to find out. He slipped the fabric off her, then tasted her breasts through the delicate lace of her bra.

But skin against skin was all he really wanted, and he discarded the bra, tossing it somewhere behind him in the shadows. He had a flashing image of her, high breasts straining toward him, nipples hard nubs, and his body ached for completion. He knew he'd told her there was no forever, but that's just how long he wanted this to last.

She was touching him, her silky skin on his, her hands awkwardly making trails of fire along his chest, her lips following suit, almost uncertainly, then she was tugging at his pants. He moved back, just long enough to slip out of his pants, then his briefs, kicking both articles to one side before going back to her. Clothes were gone, her jeans and panties were gone, and he lay with her, his body alongside hers, their heat mingling.

Her hand pressed to his stomach, and he touched it, bringing it lower until her touch found him. "Oh, yes," he moaned, and he felt her jerk slightly away. He wanted to catch her, hold her to him, the way he'd tried to before, but before he could do that, she touched him again. She made that vital contact, then gradually circled him with her fingers. One movement, and his moan became almost animal.

"Oh, I'm sorry," she gasped. "I...I hurt you."

Hurt him? He would have laughed if he could have. She pleasured him in a way that was beyond real to him. "No. No," he whispered, cupping her hip with his hand, drawing her closer to his need.

Then his hand slipped between them, spanning her stomach, then lower and he felt her sharp intake of breath when he found her center. He gently pressed his palm to her, then he entered her with his finger, one, then two, and when he moved, her reaction was a soft gasp, then her hips lifted to him, and there were small whimpering sounds as he moved in and out.

His need for her was almost desperate, and he shifted to get closer, his hands pressed on the comforter by her shoulders. He looked down at her in the shadows and saw the wild tumble of curls, her lips parted, her nostrils flaring with rapid breaths. And he knew he had to be careful, he had to do this right. Not rush things. Not scare her.

Even as he wondered how he'd ever control himself with her, she moved under him, opening to him, lifting her legs around his hips. And he felt her, he tested her and she arched, circling his neck with her arms, and whispering, "Please...please."

He entered her, filling her, and the sensation was overwhelming, more than he thought he could bear and still live. Then slowly, ever so slowly, he moved and her hips came to meet his, matching his motion, and he lost himself in her.

The rain beat on the windows as together, thrust for thrust, they matched each other perfectly, her hips rising to his, the ecstasy building in a rapid tumble of pleasure, higher and higher. He inhaled her, he had her, and in one pure moment he knew that he'd found a home he hadn't even known he'd been looking for all of his life.

B.J. It was her. And he fell into a place of perfect satisfaction, holding her carefully, her legs around him, his arms at her waist and hips. He kissed her lightly on her forehead, tasting her slightly salty skin, feeling his heart beating against his chest, and she buried her face in his shoulder.

Her sigh made her body tremble, and he rubbed her back with his hand, kissing her curls, and it was then that he realized what had eluded him. Something that had been there, but he'd been lost in the jumble of emotions. He knew from her actions that she hadn't been with many men, the hesitancy, the awkward touches, the way she trembled. And that made what they'd just done all the more special.

He held her closer. He'd expected that anyone as beautiful and as desirable as she was would have been more knowing and experienced.

She trembled again, snuggling closer to him, and he knew that she'd touched his soul. She'd become a part of it, and he was falling in love with her. He took a breath, the idea of love as overwhelming to him at that moment as having her had been moments earlier. And the thought sank into his being, as he slowly let sleep claim him.

WHILE RAIN BEAT DOWN outside, Brittany was in a warm, safe place. She was in a tumble of pillows, linen and Matt, and she wished she could stay there forever. Her body tangled with his, the pleasures he'd given her lingering in every atom of her being. Love. It seemed so simple now. The thing she'd run after all of her life had come up and surprised her when she least expected it.

She felt Matt stir, his arm tightening around her waist, and she closed her eyes tightly. She could pretend for a few more minutes that everything was perfect. That Matt wanted her here, that he wanted Brittany Lewis and all that that entailed. She could pretend that there were no truths that had to be said, and she could hide from the visions she had of that moment when she would admit the truth to Matt.

She pushed that thought away as Matt's hand moved on her, trailing up to her breasts, and she gasped softly.

"I didn't think you were asleep," he whispered to her through the shadows as he found her nipple.

The feelings were still so strong. She'd thought they'd be sated, but they weren't. If anything the need was stronger, more urgent now. She had to tell him. She'd known that all along. But as he shifted, gently turning her on the tangled comforter until they were face-to-face, the words wouldn't come. Her breasts pressed to his chest, his heart beat against hers. Her hips were against his, and she felt his need, hard and firm against her stomach.

Any words she'd managed to formulate fled when his mouth claimed hers, and as she felt him over her, his weight on her, she knew that there would be time for words later. First, she'd love him. She had a flashing thought that this might be all she had, and a choking sadness overwhelmed her. But the passion immediately burned it away. White-hot urgency obliterated it, and she gave herself to Matt once again.

He was over her, then entering her, and as they became one, she let go of everything. She let go of reality, of space and time, and lost herself in Matt and what they had together. Later, later, she told herself, as she surged higher and higher, then the world was light. It shimmered in shards of ecstasy and everything was perfect.

MATT FELT BRITTANY SIGH softly, turn from him and curl in a ball with her back to him. He watched her in the filtered light that came from a moon trying to break through the heavy rain clouds, the curve of her naked shoulders, their movement with each breath. He'd tried to give her time, tried to pace himself, but with B.J., waiting was practically impossible.

She sighed again, her back pushing closer to him, and he felt a response immediately. Not touching her right then was every bit as hard. He wanted her again and again. And he never wanted it to stop. He closed his eyes for a long moment to let that thought sink in. He'd never wanted anyone "forever," and that was another first with B.J. He didn't see an end to this, and more amazingly, he didn't want it to end.

That shook him, both with pleasure and with uncertainty. He'd never looked past the present with any woman, and he hadn't intended to with B.J., but it was a fact. He eased back, slipping carefully off the daybed to stand over her. He looked down at her, his eyes traveling over every curve and swelling, and he knew that he wanted this to just be the start.

For a man used to making instant decisions, to going ahead with logic and reason, his uncertainty was stunning. He had to think. He reached down and, with slightly unsteady hands, brushed back the hair that clung to her face, then tugged the mussed comforter up over her. Think. This was going so fast. B.J. was like a whirlwind in his life, rushing in, spinning it out of control.

He raked his fingers through his hair. No, he had control. He wanted this. He wanted her. He turned, found his clothing and quickly got dressed. The he went back into his office, crossed to the desk, grabbed a sheet of paper and scrawled a note for B.J. He placed the note by her on the bed, grabbed his boots and left. He headed out into the corridor and flinched when the office door accidentally slammed behind him.

BRITTANY WOKE abruptly, something startling her out of her deep sleep, and she didn't know what it was. But she knew that she was alone. There was nothing there, no connection, just something light covering her, darkness around her, no sound of rain, and emptiness. She turned, her legs tangled in the bedding, and pushed herself up. She didn't have a clue what time it was, beyond the fact that it was dark outside the rain-streaked windows.

Gradually, her eyes adjusted, and she could see the shadowy outlines around her. She scooted to the edge of the daybed and stood, feeling something brush her foot. It was a piece of paper.

She reached for the paper, and in the faint lights from the outside she could make out a dark scrawl. "Gone to make arrangements to bury the tofu and wine. We need to talk. I'll be back." There was no signature.

Her heart lurched. Yes, they had to talk. It was more than time for the truth. But even as she admitted that to herself, panic set in. He'd just touched and made love to her, but she couldn't forget the distaste in him when he talked about Brittany Lewis. Disgust. Dislike. He never would have touched Brittany Lewis the way he had B. J. Smythe.

But she had to face him. She had to tell him and that thought made her shake. She looked into the shadows, found where her clothing had been tossed to one side and, with awkward hands, got dressed. She had to tell him. She looked at the note then reached for it and went out into the main office.

She needed just a bit of time, time to find the words and brace herself for the moment when the truth came out. She went to the desk, found a pen and under Matt's writing, she penned, "I'll be back." She hesitated, then signed it with a single B. She stared at it, then quickly, before Matt returned, put the note back where he had left it for her. She hurried out of his office into the empty hallway and saw the light on the nearest elevator flash as the car went down. She didn't know if it was Matt or not, but she wasn't going to wait around to find out.

The mess of food and wine was still there, and she avoided even looking at it too closely as she went past it to the other elevator. She got in, then hit the button for the lobby.

The doors shut completely and the car started down, forcing her to stare at the stranger in the reflection. The person looking back at her had wildly curling hair falling around her shoulders, slightly swollen lips, and she was hugging herself as if to keep from falling apart.

She closed her eyes and didn't open them until the car stopped, literally holding her breath until she was sure no one was there. She stepped out into the lobby and headed for the doors to the new center. Locked. She fumbled in her pocket for the key, found it, then unlocked the door and went inside.

She meant to get her purse, to take a few minutes to gather herself before going back upstairs, but as soon as the door shut, she started shaking again. She moved quickly into the room, found the lights that had been installed in the tree play center and turned them on. They looked like a thousand fireflies flitting around the branches where the platforms were, and she sank down by the wall facing the tree.

Hugging herself, she sat there, trying to breathe, trying to get control. Trying to figure out what she could ever say to Matt to make him understand.

Chapter Fourteen

Matt walked back into his office, crossed to the side room and found nothing but the mussed bed and the note. He stared at it, startled at his disappointment that she wasn't here waiting for him. He'd just gone to Zane's office to find the extension for the maintenance crew for the clean-up of the wine and food. He'd been gone maybe ten minutes, and she had left. He looked down at the note. She'd be back. But he didn't want to wait. He had an idea where she'd gone, as he turned and headed out of the office.

He hurried back out into the hallway and crossed to the elevators. She had to be down in the center. He remembered she'd left her purse there with his briefcase and there was no other place for her to be at this time of night. He got in the elevator, hit the button for the lobby and felt the car start its descent. Damn it, he was running after a woman, he thought, then grinned at his reflection in the closed doors. He was running as hard as he could and as fast as he could.

He glanced at the floor numbers, then the light for the lobby lit up and the car stopped. The doors opened and he headed for the center. But suddenly something caught his eye in the lobby area. He looked toward the front of the building, at the twinkle of lights from the Christmas decorations and couldn't see anything moving. Then he heard something. A sliding sound, soft, but there.

He hesitated when he heard a faint thud. B.J.? Security? He turned to look back and heard another sound, paper rustling. He still didn't see anything moving, but the sounds were real and they came from the left, out of the shadows that were around the reception desk. He went toward it, stepped into the lobby, glanced at the desk, then crossed to it quietly. He stopped by the side, heard the rustling again and pressed both hands flat on the top to lean forward and peer at the space behind it.

It wasn't B.J., Security or even rats, but a nine-year-old boy on the floor, methodically going through the bottom drawer of the desk. Anthony. Matt watched him take something out of the drawer, stuff it in the pocket of his sweatshirt, then carefully slide the drawer shut. He started to reach for the next drawer, stopped, sat motionless with his hand on the handle, then slowly looked up.

Their eyes met, and Matt could sense the kid was trying to think of something to say that would get him out of this mess. Matt knew what it felt like to get caught red-handed, as Anthony just had.

"What're you doing here?" the boy asked, still sitting on the floor, obviously thinking a good offense was the best defense.

"What are *you* doing here?" Matt countered.

"Hanging," he muttered.

"Stealing?" he asked.

Anthony stood then, but he wasn't backing down. He never looked away from Matt. "It's just candy."

"What?"

Anthony reached into the pocket of his sweatshirt and held out his hand to Matt. There were three pieces of hard candy in his palm. "See, just candy. And she won't miss it."

"You broke in here to take candy?"

"Nah, I was in, and I remembered the candy."

"You were in? How did you get in?"

He started shifting back and forth, the way he had when Matt had found him in the restroom. "I just did."

He and B.J. couldn't get in, but this kid had gotten in? It didn't make sense. "Did B.J. let you in?"

"No. I ain't seen her here."

"Then how in the hell did you get in?"

"Just did," he repeated.

"Not a good answer," Matt said, standing straighter. "I'd suggest that you tell me the truth—now."

The boy lifted his chin. "Or what? You gonna hit me?"

Matt shook his head. "Just tell me how you got in."

"Then you'll hit me," he muttered.

"I don't hit people, especially kids. I just want you to tell me the truth."

He looked past Matt at the door, and Matt knew the boy was weighing his options. He could run like hell for the door and maybe make it. But then again, maybe he wouldn't. Matt moved a bit to block his path.

"Okay, okay, but if I tell you, you can't get mad and you can't call the cops, *and* you can't fire me."

Now he was making the rules? Matt could live with them, at least for now. "Okay, I give you my word. Now tell me the truth."

"I'll show you," he said, then moved. Matt expected him to go back toward the center, but instead, he went toward the Christmas tree. He stopped, looked over his shoulder at Matt, then dropped to his haunches by the wall. Matt went after him in time to see that the grating over the air vent was loose and Anthony was tugging it open.

"What in the—?"

"You said you wouldn't get mad," Anthony said as he dropped to his hands and knees and disappeared through the opening. Then he was there again, looking out and up at Matt. "This is it."

Matt dropped to the floor and looked into the hole that was maybe three feet by three feet, an old air-ducting system. "You came in through here?"

Anthony was watching him. "Yeah, sure. It goes all over the place, at least down here." He moved back a bit. "Come on. You can fit if you get down real low."

"Get out of there."

He moved farther from the opening. "You wanted me to show you, and I'm showing you, so come on."

In the next instant Anthony was out of sight. He could hear him moving, but there was no way he could see the boy now. Today had gone from the sublime to the ridiculous, from making love with B.J. to chasing a nine-year-old into air vents. He slipped into the tubing and knew he was too old to be doing this, and too big.

He felt his shoulders and head brushing the metal around him as he went after Anthony. He'd never felt claustrophobic, but by the time he rounded a corner and saw some light, he'd had enough. Anthony was by the light and he called out to him. "Stop right there."

"It's farther," the boy said.

"Well, I'm not going any farther. Can we get out here?"

Anthony turned, and there was the sound of squeaking metal on metal. When Matt got to where Anthony had been, the boy had the grating up and out of the way and he was halfway out of the tunnel. Matt hurried after him, easing through the opening and realized he was in the boys' room at the center. He crawled out, got to his feet and took several breaths as he swiped at his clothes. "So, that's what you were doing in here the other day?"

"Yeah, just hanging."

"Okay, it gets you in here. Where do you get out?"

"I was gonna show you," he muttered, "but you chickened out."

Matt frowned at him. "Just tell me."

"You keep going, down a ways, way back, past some storeroom, and you end up at the back, and you can get out there into the alley by the parking thing."

"You got in through an outside vent cover?"

"Yeah." He eyed Matt. "And you said you wouldn't be mad."

"I'm not mad at you," he muttered as he tucked his shirt back into his slacks. The security team was another thing all together. "Now I know how you got in, I want to know why. We left you at the other building to go home with Esther. You came all the way back down here for candy?"

"Naw, Esther wasn't there. She must've got mad waiting cuz I was late." He shrugged. "Then I got hungry."

"Esther left you down here, so you decided to stay here for the night?"

"Yeah."

"You've done it before?"

"Some."

He thought of the food that he and B.J. had wasted earlier while this kid was starving. "When did you last eat?"

He shrugged again and headed for the door. "I don't know," he tossed over his shoulder. "Better put the screen back down."

Matt slipped the screen back in place, then went after Anthony and found him in the main room of the center. Small lights laced the strange tree, and he went with Anthony out into the room. The two of them stopped, the boy obviously seeing what he was seeing, and just as shocked as he was by the sight. B.J. was there, sitting on the floor, staring at the two of them.

Brittany thought perhaps she was having delusions from not eating. Matt was there with Anthony, the two of them looking down at her. "What's going on?" she asked as she scrambled to her feet, aching just looking at the man.

"I found him in the lobby helping himself to a dinner of candy. He brought me back through air ducts that the Count of Monte Cristo would have loved to use."

They came in through the air-ducting? "You were in the walls again?" she asked Anthony.

"He asked how I got inside and I showed him, just like you."

Matt looked at her. "You, too?"

She nodded. "Yes. But I don't understand what's happening. Why's he here at all?"

"It seems Esther didn't wait for him, so he came back, got in and settled in for the night."

"It was raining," Anthony said. "I was just hanging until it stopped."

And she was worried about herself, about what Matt would do or say, while the child was on his own in the middle of the night worried about getting in out of the rain. She put her arm around the boy's shoulders, felt him stiffen slightly, but he didn't move away. "I'm glad you could get in," she said. "Now, we have to figure out what you're going to do for the rest of the night." She looked at Matt. "How about your place?"

"That might be touchy, taking him out of here. I don't want anyone to get any ideas about abduction."

Matt was right. Esther would love to have a chance to sue someone and get money. "Oh, yes, I see. How about that room off of your..." Her words trailed off and she bit her lip at the memory of the mussed bed and what had happened in there. "No, that won't do."

"Zane has a room off his office that might work." Matt looked at Anthony. "You're hungry and we can find you some food, okay?"

"Sure, anything's fine."

"There's a cafeteria on the fourth floor. There has to be some food there." He looked at B.J., then back at the boy. "Why don't we take him up there and see what we can find?"

She looked from the boy to the man and knew that no matter how horrible this was for Anthony, it had given her a reprieve. They couldn't talk now. Not tonight. And she couldn't be here until they could. "Why don't you two do this? A guy thing? I think that might work out better."

Matt narrowed his eyes, and she could almost see him wanting to argue, but he didn't. He was putting the boy first, and that touched her even more. "Okay, that sounds fine."

She let go of Anthony to grab her purse, then she looked at Matt again. "I'll call a cab and...we'll talk in the morning?"

"Yes, absolutely. And I'll get in touch with the attorney, too. As soon as I can tomorrow."

She wanted to hug him, just hold on to him for a moment, but she knew that was out of the question. Instead, she looked at Anthony. "You do what Matt says and you'll be okay. You hear? You can trust him." She looked at Matt. "You go on ahead and get him some food. I'll call my cab."

"Okay," he said, then put a hand on Anthony's shoulders. "Come on, Anthony, we've got a date with junk food."

They headed for the doors, opened the barriers, then stepped out. The doors closed behind them, and Brittany fumbled in her purse for her phone, called the cab company and agreed to meet the driver outside. She put her purse down on a table that held her paint supplies and waited. For five minutes she stayed there until she was certain Anthony and Matt were gone, then she crossed to the doors and left.

She went through the quiet lobby, crossed to the front doors and exited. As soon as the doors clicked behind her, Brittany realized she had left her purse inside. And her cell phone. She stared through the glass at the empty space. Then she felt in the pocket of her jeans. She still had the twenty dollars she'd put in there earlier. She'd get her purse tomorrow.

She stood under the overhang of the doorway to keep out of the steadily falling rain. For the first time since being at LynTech, Brittany knew exactly what was going to happen and what she was going to do. Matt would make sure that Anthony was taken care of and protected. She knew that with as much certainty as she knew she'd do anything to help the boy, too. And with as much certainty as she knew that tomorrow Matt would know she was Brittany Lewis.

That last thought scared her to death, but there could be no more lies. Not now. Not after tonight.

MATT BOUGHT FOOD for Anthony from vending machines in the lobby of the locked-up cafeteria, then took him to the room off Zane's office. The boy stepped inside and looked around at the mattress on the floor, the baby toys in a pile to one side and the television fastened to the wall just out of reach of little hands.

"They got babies here?" the boy asked.

"A little boy," Matt said, putting the food and the cans of pop on the mattress to one side. He motioned to Anthony. "You can sleep here, watch TV, eat. And you'll be okay."

Anthony went to the mattress, then turned and fell backwards onto it and looked up at the ceiling. "Esther's gonna be real mad."

"Don't worry about Esther. I'll take care of her."

He looked at Matt. "And you never lie, do you?"

He crossed to the boy and crouched down by the bed. "You know, I told you something once that wasn't true, at least, not exactly true."

He sat up, his face in a frown. "What you mean?"

He crouched in front of the boy. "Anthony, I told you not to trust anyone, just trust yourself. You remember?"

The boy nodded.

"That's not exactly true. You can trust B.J., and you can trust me, okay?"

Anthony stared hard at Matt, and the image of himself when he was a boy came to Matt. He'd learned so well never to trust anyone. No one. But suddenly he knew that trust was everything. And he wanted Anthony to know that. Not trusting people was a lonely way to live.

"If you say so," Anthony said in a low voice.

"I say so." It was a start. The same way he himself was learning to trust. "You settle in, turn on the TV or whatever and I'll be right back. I left my briefcase downstairs." He'd totally forgotten it, and he knew that sleep wouldn't be an option tonight. He'd work, get through the night, and wait until tomorrow.

"Okay," Anthony said.

Matt left and headed back down to the center. He found the doors unlocked and went inside, but B.J. wasn't there. He spotted his briefcase, grabbed it, then saw her purse still on the table by the paint supplies. He crossed to it, then called out, "B.J.? Are you still here?"

There was no answer so he took the purse and the briefcase back upstairs. He put the briefcase and purse on Zane's desk, then went into the side room. Anthony was there, shoes off, sitting on the mattress, papers from the packaged food all around him, a can of pop in one hand, the remote for the TV in the other. Matt took one look at the TV, at cars being blown up, and he was certain he saw a body, or part of one, flying through the air.

He crossed, took the remote out of Anthony's hands and hit the channel buttons. After a few flicks, he found cartoons and looked down at the boy. "Now that's better, don't you think?"

He shrugged. "Fine by me."

"Good. I don't have anything for you to wear to sleep, but why don't you take off your sweatshirt?" He looked at the food wrappers. "I don't have a toothbrush for you, either. You're roughing it tonight, okay?"

Anthony tugged off his shirt, then leaned back, supporting himself on his elbows as he looked up at Matt. "When do I gotta get out?" he asked.

"No time limit. No one's working in this office right now, so sleep as long as you want."

"I gotta get down there for when Esther comes looking for me. She wants the money, you know?"

"Yes, I know, and I told you, let me worry about Esther." He hunkered down in front of the boy. "If I can work it out, would you like to live someplace other than Esther's?"

His eyes narrowed. "Where?"

"I have to think about it." He needed to talk to B.J., to see what ideas she had, and to the attorney to see if he could even do it. "Maybe a better foster home, or a good boarding school?"

Anthony frowned. "It don't matter," he said and fell all the way back on the sleeping pad. He looked up past Matt at the television, and Matt knew he'd said the wrong thing. He just didn't know what he should have said.

He straightened, said, ''I'll be in the office out there for a while, then down at my office. You know where that is?''

''Nope.''

''It's just down the hall to the right, but I'll put a note on it so you know which one it is. Okay?''

''What's the note gonna say?''

''Boss?''

Anthony grinned at him. ''Sounds good to me.''

December 22

''Boss? Boss?''

Matt woke with a start, not sure when he'd fallen asleep or how long he'd slept for. Or why Rita was standing over him holding a hand-lettered sign that said ''Boss'' on it, the one he'd stuck to the outer door last night.

He pushed himself up in the daybed, ignoring the muss of linen and the empty spot by him, then twisted and sat on the edge of the mattress. He hadn't undressed, but remembered lying down just for a minute after making sure Anthony had finally fallen asleep.

''What time is it?'' he asked, scrubbing his hands over his face to try and get rid of the lingering webs of sleep.

''Eight-fifteen,'' the woman said. ''What's going on?''

He looked up at her as he raked his fingers through his hair. ''I must have fallen asleep.''

''I'd say so,'' she said and held up the sign. ''Boss. You've been working all night?''

He stood, and she moved back a bit as he took the sign and balled it up into a crumpled mess. ''A reminder,'' he said and looked down at his unbuttoned shirt, mussed beyond repair at the moment. ''Do I have any clothes here at all?'' he asked her, tossing the ruined paper onto the bed.

She crossed to a small closet in the room, opened it and

returned with a plain black polo shirt in her hands. "This, but no pants. No shoes."

He took the shirt from her. "This will do for now." He stripped off his shirt, tugged the polo shirt on and again raked his fingers through his hair.

"You've got meetings this morning with Davis and Evans, and I got back the check on Gallagher."

He crossed to the bathroom and went in, leaving the door ajar as he checked out his appearance. He looked like a mile of bad road, from the beginnings of a beard to his hair spiked at odd angles on his head. He reached for the brush, took care of his hair, then reached for his electric razor as he turned to go back into the side room. All the while he was talking. "Change the meetings to...whenever you can next week. And what about Gallagher?"

"Married young, divorced young, one kid—you know, Mr. Mom sort of situation, worked out of his home, took them with him when he traveled, which was enough to require a tag-along tutor and nanny for his son. Lives mostly in Vermont, out in the wilds somewhere, alone, never remarried. No felony convictions, not even littering, and his son is in college, Ivy League, big bucks. A straight shooter from what anyone will say in the business world. The guy's worth—"

"Never mind."

"Why did you want that?"

So, George had been wrong? "It's not important." He kept shaving as he moved out into the office with Rita following him. "Get me an appointment with Ron Heally, A.S.A.P."

"Heally's not corporate law, he's family law."

"I know." He reached for the phone, dialed the number to the new center and a man answered. "Yeah?"

"Is Miss Smythe there, the artist doing the wall murals?"

"Is the artist around?" he called, without covering the mouthpiece. Then he spoke to Matt. "No, not here."

"Anything else?" Rita asked as he put the phone back on the hook.

"Yes, there's a kid in Zane's office, actually in the nap room that Lindsey made for Walker. He's probably still asleep. The boy from the day-care center, the one who helps out down there? Anthony?"

"Oh, sure, the one you called the hoodlum, I believe?"

He ignored that. He found his cell phone and pushed it in his pocket. "Come on. I'm going out that way. I'll show you."

He went out of the office and down toward Zane's. "When he wakes up," he was saying as they walked, "tell him he's not to go with Esther, no matter what. That he's to wait for me or go down and work with B.J, but he's not to go with Esther. He'll know what I'm talking about," he said as they went into Zane's office complex. He went across to the private office, quietly crossed to the nap room and looked inside. Anthony was still asleep, sprawled on the pad, his face buried under one of the pillows. The food wrappers were everywhere and the TV was still on.

He eased the door partly shut, then turned to Rita. "I don't know how long he'll sleep. He was up most of the night." He turned, spotted B.J.'s purse still on Zane's desk and picked it up, then looked back at Rita. "Maybe you can stay in here and work for a while? He needs to know where I am and that I'll be back. And you took the sign down."

"Where are you going?" she asked.

"I need to find someone, but I'll be back soon," he said over his shoulder as he headed back out into the hallway. "Call if there are any problems with anything." He crossed to the elevators, hit the button and the doors opened immediately. He got in, reaching for the Lobby button and turned to find Rita had followed him out into the corridor. "Don't forget Heally," he said.

She nodded. "Oh, boss?"

"What?" he asked as the doors started to close.

"Nice purse."

Matt looked down at B.J.'s purse and burst out laughing. By the time the elevator stopped at the main level, nerves had killed the humor. He went to the center, found it swarming with workmen, but no B.J. After looking around, then out in the parking garage, he went back through the center, ready to head back upstairs. But as he reached the elevators, he glanced ahead at the lobby area.

As if his need had made her materialize, there was B.J., walking in through the doors. Her hair was pulled back from her face, but he remembered the curls, loose and wild, lying on his skin. Denim overalls worn with a long-sleeved white shirt just allowed the suggestion of the curves he knew were there. She came closer, not looking up, not seeing him, and he stayed still, just watching her.

He was vaguely aware of an elevator door opening near him, then Rita was there at his side. "Boss?"

He glanced to his right at Rita who had Anthony with her, holding him by the hand while he rubbed his eyes with his other hand. "He said he wanted to find you," she said, then looked past him and her eyes widened slightly. "Oh, my God, Brittany Lewis is back."

He turned and at the same time heard someone calling out, "Miss Lewis, Miss Lewis!" and someone else saying, "Your car, Miss Lewis!"

Brittany Lewis? He looked around, but all he could see was B.J. A man was going toward her from the reception desk, the security guard from the town houses, calling her Miss Lewis. The kid from the parking garage was hurrying toward her from the front doors, saying something about her car, calling her Miss Lewis. Then Rita was talking by his side. "Do you want to get the hell out of town and let me deal with her?"

"Who?"

"Brittany Lewis," she said, pointing right at B.J.

Chapter Fifteen

The world moved in slow motion for Matt, actions taking an eternity to happen. B.J. was turning in the middle of the lobby, looking to her right and behind her, then she was smiling at the guard. They shook hands, laughed slightly, the man looked very pleased. Then the guard left as the parking lot attendant touched her arm and she turned to him. He spoke to her seriously, nodding emphatically, then she took something out of her pocket. Folded papers. Handing them to him and the attendant starting to leave, but calling over his shoulder, "Your Porsche will be good as new."

Then Anthony was running toward her. "B.J.?" he called out and she turned to him. "B.J.!"

B.J. Brittany Lewis.

"If you want to get out of here right now," Rita was saying, "I'll run interference for you, boss."

B.J., no, Brittany, smiled at the boy, listened to him talking about the night before, and Matt felt his world crashing all around him. A man who faced anything head-on and damn the consequences found himself backing up slightly, motioning to Rita. "Come here," he said, moving away from the elevators, turning his back to the boy and the woman in the lobby. "*She's* Brittany Lewis?"

"In all her glory," Rita said. "Although her fashion taste sucks. Unless she's going to do the office in rustic casual."

He felt sick, his stomach knotted so tightly that he could barely stand it. "Rita, I have no desire to meet her now or ever. Get that appointment with Heally for today, and cancel what meetings you can. I'll talk to you in a bit."

"Okay, boss," she said.

He started walking toward the back of the building, never looking back, and didn't stop until he was out in the parking garage. He heard the door slam behind him, and he stopped in the cavernous structure, closed his eyes and she was there. She was the center of the universe, that smile for Anthony, the way her lashes shadowed the green of her eyes, the way she'd touched him in the night. Brittany Lewis. The lie ran through him like an electric shock, leaving him almost unable to move, unable to absorb a sickening sense of betrayal that spiked through his being.

Trust? He'd been so close.... He cut that off, opened his eyes and ran a hand over his face. So close. He hated the idea of what she'd done, the way she'd made a fool out of everyone, especially him.

He'd known she was a spoiled brat, but he never dreamed anyone would go as far as she had to entertain herself with the "common person." And damn it, he was as common as hell. Letting himself fall right into her games. He needed to get away to think. But he couldn't. He couldn't go anywhere, not with Anthony's future depending on him, and the running of LynTech squarely on his shoulders.

His gut knotted and he had a sneaking suspicion that he might just be sick right there and then. He moved abruptly, crossing to the executive elevator. He put in his code, got in the car and as he hit the button for the executive level, he realized he was still holding the purse. He stared at it in his hands, then opened the snap and saw her wallet.

He hesitated, then took out the slim leather holder, opened it and there was a driver's license, a Texas license, with a name on it—Brittany Jayne Lewis, and her picture right beside it. He stared at the small photo, and wondered how features that, even in a photo like this, were so breathtakingly beautiful could cause him so much pain?

He closed the wallet, shoving it back in the purse, and hid from the fact that he'd thought he loved her for one brief, insane moment in time. That made the sickness churn in him, and when the elevator stopped, he got out, strode through Zane's offices and out into the corridor. A security guard was walking toward him, and he stopped him, glancing at his name badge. "Chambers?"

The man looked at Matt, then recognized him. "Yes, sir, Mr. Terrel?"

He held the purse out to him. "Take this down to the new day-care center and give it to that artist, Miss... Smythe."

"Yes, sir," the man said and took the purse.

Matt kept going to his own offices, went in, and almost ran into Rita who was going out. "Oh, boss, good," she said, stopping in front of him. "I got Heally to agree to an eleven o'clock here," she said. "Gallagher called and he's heading in for the reception and asked for more information on the demographics for the West Coast. I'm going down to marketing to get it and fax it to him. I see you escaped from Miss Lewis in one piece?"

"I escaped," he said, but doubted he was in one piece.

"Good, I'd hate to have to break in someone new," she said with a smile, then hurried out.

He went into his office and had barely closed the door when the phone rang. He crossed to get it. "Terrel."

"Matt, it's me, B.J. How are you?"

Her voice drew at every atom in his being, sending a

strange ache through him. ''Busy,'' he said, hating the edge in his tone, but unable to soften it.

''Can you talk for a minute if I come up?''

He winced, the idea of talking to her face-to-face was unthinkable at that moment. ''No, I'm snowed under. I've got an eleven o'clock with a family law attorney about Anthony.''

''Do you need me there for the meeting?''

As much as he hated to admit it, he still needed her. But that was his problem to deal with alone, when he could. ''No, that's not necessary,'' he said, closing his eyes so tightly that colors exploded behind his lids. ''I need to get going.''

She was silent for a moment. ''Can we talk later?''

''Later,'' he said and hung up, that ache in him getting worse and he hung up.

BRITTANY PUT DOWN the phone, not at all sure what had just happened. Matt, the man she'd made love with, the man who had shown genuine caring about Anthony, wasn't the Matt she'd just talked to. She exhaled, then turned and looked out the door of Amy's office in the center to see Anthony rolling out the drop cloths for her so she could get to work.

The boy hadn't stopped talking since he'd found her in the lobby. ''Matt's real neat,'' he'd said over and over again. ''He's cool.'' Talking about spending the night in the building, junk food, watching TV, and not being afraid of Esther. She watched as he smoothed the canvas, then plunked down in the middle of it, sitting cross-legged, staring at the wall.

Matt had helped Anthony. He'd been there after she left. She remembered that Matt had crawled through the ventilation system. She wouldn't have thought he'd fit, and smiled at the memory. The smile felt good, but not nearly as good as being in Matt's arms, and loving him. That word sank into her. *Love.* It filled her, flowing through her, and all she wanted to do was see Matt. Just see him.

She wished she'd seen him with Anthony earlier, but the kid from the garage had been there saying her car was almost done, but that needed the insurance papers signed. And the guard from the town house had been there, thanking her for telling him to come in to see about hiring back on. He was hired and starting work at the reception tomorrow night. She hadn't seen Matt.

"B.J.?"

Anthony was there. "What?"

"Did you talk to Matt?"

"Yes, but he's really busy."

He smiled at B.J., just like the smile she was putting on his figure in the mural. That had been something she'd made up at the time, what she thought he'd look like when he was really happy. "He can fix just about anything. He's real smart, and you know, when he was a kid, he got in lots of trouble, but he fixed that, too. Now he's rich and cool and he can do anything."

She went toward Anthony. "I have to agree," she said. "He's pretty terrific."

"You like him, right?"

Her smile faltered a bit. "Well, yes, I do."

"Good," he said.

"Why did you ask?"

He shrugged. "Just wondering," he said, then took an unnerving change of direction in the conversation. "What's B.J. stand for?"

She motioned him into Amy's office, closed the door, then turned to face him. "Can I tell you something that you won't tell anyone else, not even Matt until I say that it's okay?''

He studied her with his head cocked to one side. ''Your real name's ugly, huh?''

She laughed. ''No, it's pretty, at least I always thought so, unless my dad was mad at me and then he used both my names and that meant trouble.''

''Your dad's mean?'' he asked, his smile completely gone.

''No, no, not at all.'' She crouched down in front of him. ''He's terrific. Just great.''

''Like Matt?''

That startled her, but she had to admit that Matt and her father were a lot alike. Dedicated in business, but smart and caring, as well. ''I think so. Yes, they're a lot alike, actually.''

''That's cool.''

''Yes, it is, very cool,'' she said.

''So, what's your name?''

''Brittany Jayne Lewis.''

She watched him stare at her, then his eyes widened and his mouth formed an O shape. ''You? That person that Matt's been talking about?'' He frowned at her. ''No, that's not so, is it? Your name's Smith something.''

''That's my mother's maiden name, the name she had before she got married.''

''Well, Matt hates Brittany whoever, but he likes you. That don't make sense.''

''It doesn't make sense,'' she said, correcting him automatically, but as she said the words, she felt her heart tighten a bit. ''I need to explain to you, Anthony.'' She sank down onto the floor. ''Sit down and let's talk. But you have to promise that Matt won't know any of this until I can tell him personally. Deal?''

He dropped onto the carpet, echoing her pose. "Okay. Deal. Now, what's going on?"

"DAMN, YOU'RE GOOD," Matt told Ron Heally.

The two men were in Matt's office for the second meeting of the day. The slender, red-haired man almost blushed at the praise as he tugged nervously at the cuffs of the jacket to a navy pinstripe suit. "No, I'm just doing what can be done," he said as he stood to face Matt across the desk. "You understand that this is really going to cost you?"

"I told you, I expected that. The woman can have what she wants, as long as she leaves the kid alone. She hits him, and she's been making him sleep outside on a little balcony at their apartment, when she even lets him come home with her."

Heally grimaced. "What figure are you thinking of?"

"Start at ten and go from there," Matt said.

"Ten thousand? She'll go for that like a donkey to strawberries," Heally said as he put some papers back in his briefcase and closed the lid. "So, who approaches her? You or me?"

Matt sat back in the swivel chair, clasping his hands on his stomach. "I want to do it. She'll be showing up here to get the kid in a bit. I'll take care of her, just tell me what's in place, and what power I have."

"Legally, you have no power until the courts say you do. But she doesn't have to know that. And as soon as I can get it on the docket, we can get you as his guardian." He looked at Matt. "You've got it clear what that means, don't you? The kid's a stranger to you, basically."

Matt knew Anthony. Matt had been Anthony in his childhood. "I know what I'm getting into, believe me."

Heally stretched out his hand to Matt. "With the holidays,

anything's going to have to be set in place after the new year.''

"I know," he said as he stood and held out his hand to Heally. "Thanks for making this happen."

"Don't thank me just yet. You're the one who has to deal with the woman."

"I know." The men shook hands. "Get the papers to Rita as soon as you can, and I'll let you know how much she goes for," Matt said.

"Good. Good." Heally picked up his briefcase. "One more thing?"

"What's that?"

"Who's this B.J. person that the boy was talking about when he came up here at noon?"

Matt shrugged, blocking the thoughts as best he could. He might have to face Esther, but the idea of facing B.J. again was much harder to think about. "She's Robert Lewis's daughter."

"What? I was under the impression that she works here."

"She does, painting murals in the new day-care center."

"Well, if she's involved with Anthony's situation, you've got some big guns behind you."

"She's involved when it suits her purpose," he said, bitterness rising in his throat.

"Like getting engaged when she's bored?" Heally asked with a rueful smile and a shake of his head.

"Exactly," Matt said. "But I'm doing this with Anthony, and she won't be involved."

"Too bad, what with her being Lewis's daughter and a woman. The court always smiles on a woman involved in a custody suit."

"Trust me, Esther isn't going to fight any of this. Not after I get through with her."

"Well, good luck," Heally said.

Matt went around the desk to show the man to the door. "Thanks again," he said.

Heally had barely got out the door when Anthony ran past him. "Matt, Esther's gonna be here soon," he said, barely looking at the attorney.

Heally nodded to Matt then left, and Matt turned his attention to Anthony. "I know. I'm taking care of her. Mr. Heally got everything straight, and now I just have to talk to Esther."

"Cool," Anthony said, trying to look cool, but the fear was just below the surface. He was used to things not working out, used to being shunted aside and disposed of. He was so much like Matt as a kid, trying to be cool, trying to be an adult long before his time.

"Let's go down and meet Esther." Matt glanced at the wall clock. Almost six. "She'll be here soon enough, and if she isn't, we'll go find her. She won't be in your life after today."

Anthony looked up at Matt. "You telling me the truth?"

"Absolutely."

He hesitated. "We'd better go on down. B.J.'s there all alone."

"She's still here?"

"Yeah. She's still here. She's working. She says that the party tomorrow night is real important and that you're going to get people to like LynTech and it'll be a good company again."

"Oh, she did, did she?"

"Isn't that true?"

"I guess so." He saw the way Anthony was shifting from foot to foot, a clear sign that something was on his mind. "Is there something you want to tell me?"

The boy looked away from Matt, staring at the floor, then

he huge dark eyes met Matt's gaze. "Just you and B.J., you both, you're okay."

Matt held his hand out to Anthony. "So are you," he said. "Let's do this."

The boy hesitated, then put his hand in Matt's. Matt felt the smaller fingers curl around his, and he knew he was doing the right thing for Anthony. He'd worry about the rest of his life after he had this settled, and Anthony would be part of that life.

THE NOISE OF THE WORKMEN had been reverberating in the rooms of the center most of the day, but now, around six, it was just Brittany working alone. Anthony had gone up to find Matt. She hoped he'd bring Matt back down with him. Brittany had realized sometime during the day that her need to see Matt was like a hunger. And it was getting worse the longer she went without him being close to her.

She made some fine touches on the face of Anthony in the mural, then looked intently at the skin tones. It looked right to her, and his expression was perfect. That smile. She loved it. If Matt could get the answers she hoped for, the smile would be around a lot more in the future. Maybe she could talk to her father about it, too. He had connections. It was too bad he probably wouldn't make it home for Christmas. She'd love to talk to him about it.

"B.J.?" Anthony said as he came into the center.

She turned, and Matt was there. The sight of him, back in a black shirt, quite literally took her breath away. She watched him coming in behind the boy, a giant of a man, a tender man. A caring man. She loved him. She smiled, but the expression faltered slightly when he came closer and she saw his eyes. Narrowed. Almost shuttered. And no answering smile anywhere.

She'd been so excited to see him again, yet so uneasy.

The uneasiness rushed up at her as he came even closer. This was all wrong. That closeness, that vulnerability that had existed last night, was gone. He didn't come closer. He didn't make any effort to touch her. He stood, with Anthony in front of him, his hands on the boy's shoulders. "Is Esther here yet?" he asked, his voice deep and slightly rough.

She shook her head and crouched to put her brush in the solvent, staring at the clear liquid swirling with the tan color of the skin tones. "No, not yet."

"Then we'll wait," Matt said.

She left the brush in the can and stood, taking a rag out of the pocket of her overalls. She dared to look at Matt again, and almost flinched at the way he was looking at her. She knew something was so wrong, and her heart lurched when she thought of Anthony. "You...you want to tell me why you're waiting to talk to Esther?"

"I talked to my attorney, Heally. He seems to think we can help Anthony." His hands moved on the boy's shoulders, and a part of her ached to be that close to him. "We'll see if he's right in a few minutes."

His tone cut off any more questions, but she knew that Matt wasn't the sort to worry about some woman like Esther, who was no better than trash. No, it was more than that. Matt, the man who said he'd never settle down, that he couldn't imagine being in one city long enough to put down roots—her heart sank. He'd never mentioned love. Not once. That was her doing. She knew what was wrong. There was no forever for Matt. And now he regretted even being with her, probably thinking that she'd be making demands about forever. Being Brittany Lewis wouldn't be the problem. Wanting more than she'd had for one night with him would be.

"Anthony!"

The yell made her jump, and she saw Anthony's face fil

with shock and fear before she spun around in the direction of the scream. Esther. The woman was coming up the back hallway. Coming fast, her face dark. "There you are, you little—"

She stopped when she saw Matt and Brittany. The woman was almost comical, the way she instantly rearranged her expression and slowed her stride. "Mr. Terrel. I was worried about the boy."

Brittany darted a look at Matt and saw that he had his hand on Anthony's shoulder, keeping him beside him. The first time he'd faced the woman, Matt had been all seductive smiles and cajoling. This time his look was even colder than it had been moments ago. "You were worried about him?" Matt asked as he stepped forward and eased Anthony partially behind him.

"He disappeared all night, and I was worried sick."

"You left him down here in the middle of the night all by himself in the cold and rain. I can see why you'd be worried. That's neglect."

The woman looked from Matt to Anthony, then to Brittany, and her expression hardened perceptibly. "He's been lying to you two, hasn't he? The kid's a liar. He makes up stories. You can pay him now, because he won't be back. You can't trust him at all."

"He's not going with you," Matt said.

Her face darkened again and she went closer. "I don't know who you think you are, but you can't just take a kid."

"Yes, I can," Matt said with remarkable control.

Brittany was starting to shake from nerves, and Anthony was holding on to Matt's arm for dear life. Then Esther moved closer, and before Brittany realized what was going to happen, the world went crazy. Esther lunged toward Anthony, striking him in the shoulder, screaming at him, words that echoed around the center, then Matt had her by the wrist, twisting her arm up and back, and she was screaming at him now. But he didn't stop. He pushed her back, away from Anthony, putting his body between the two of them, and Brittany saw his other hand balled into a tight fist.

"You let me go, you jerk, or I'm calling the cops!" Esther screamed up at him.

"Let's do that," Matt said. "They'd like to know what you've done with Anthony, locking him out of your apartment, making him sleep outside all night. Hitting him. Abandoning him down here by himself. Letting that excuse for a man you live with knock him around when he felt like it. Why don't we call the cops and let them iron this whole thing out?"

Esther twisted hard to try and get free, but Matt wasn't letting go. "You don't know what you're talking about. He's a liar. He's always been a liar." She glared at Anthony who was peeking out from behind Matt. "I'll teach you when we get home," she ground out. "After me taking you in when no one else wanted you! You pay me back with all this!"

"You're not going to teach him anything. You're going to go and leave him here with me. In the morning, you'll get papers that release you from any obligation for Anthony."

"You can't do this!" she ground out, pulling against his restraint on her arm.

Matt kept talking as if she hadn't said a thing. "What you've done, your treatment of Anthony, borders on the criminal. But if you walk away, and sign those papers tomorrow, no one has to know about anything you did. And there'll be a check with the papers. My advice to you is to give the attorney Anthony's things when he comes, take the check and forget you ever knew Anthony or me."

She stared at him, then exhaled. "You guys with money, you always get what you want?"

He spoke in a low voice. "If I had what I wanted with you, you'd be in jail. Count your lucky stars you aren't being arrested right now."

She jerked back and this time Matt let her go. She rubbed at her wrist. "You bastard," she muttered. "You can all go to—"

"You can go," Matt said through clenched teeth. "Now."

Still rubbing hard at her wrist, Esther evidently realized that there was no way she could win this at all. "How much?"

"How much what?" Matt asked.

"Money? The check?"

"Ten thousand dollars, *if* you sign the papers and disappear."

She blinked at Matt, then backed up. "You'll get them papers signed and you're welcome to him. He's nothing but trouble. You'll find out," she said and turned from the three of them to head off to the back of the building again.

Matt went after her, and there was the sound of talking, but Brittany couldn't understand it. All she knew was she'd thought Matt was a hero before, now he was more than a hero. And she loved him so much she ached from it. Anthony was by her side, his arm going around her waist and she hugged him to her. "Matt promised," he whispered. "He promised."

"Yes, he did," she said, holding him, unnerved to feel him trembling.

Chapter Sixteen

Matt was there, coming back into the open space, passing the fake tree. "Is she gone?" Brittany asked.

He nodded, then crouched down in front of Anthony. "It's over," he said and brushed the boy's hair. "Are you okay?"

Anthony turned to look at Matt, but he stayed by Brittany. "She's awful, awful mad," he said in a small voice.

"It doesn't matter. She won't be back. In the morning the attorney's going to get your things, and that's it. We'll go from there, okay?"

Anthony hesitated, then he went to Matt and hugged the man around the neck. Matt hugged him back, then looked at Brittany over the boy's head. "I'm taking him to the loft for now."

She wanted just to hug Matt, too, after what he'd done. But she simply nodded. "Okay."

Matt held Anthony back from him. "Ready to go? Dinner, TV and I've a cat you need to meet."

"A cat?" the boy asked. "Any dogs?"

"No, no dogs. Just this huge orange cat."

"Sounds cool," Anthony said, then with one arm around Matt's neck, he looked up at Brittany. "You coming, too?"

She looked from Anthony to Matt, waiting, hoping he'd

ask her, but there was no invitation. Maybe that was best. He could be with Anthony and reassure him. "I...I have to clean up here."

"I'll help."

"No, you go with Matt and get settled in. I'll finish up here."

Anthony looked at Matt. "B.J. should come, shouldn't she?"

Matt stood up, one arm around Anthony's shoulders as he looked at Brittany with those eyes narrowed and unreadable. "She has things to do, and so do we," he said. Simple words, but they made Brittany feel cold all over. He didn't want her anywhere around. He looked at the boy. "Ready?"

"Are we coming back here?" Anthony asked.

"No, we aren't," Matt said.

"What about tomorrow?"

"No one's working. They're getting ready for the reception."

"But what about all this stuff?" he asked, motioning to the barely started mural.

"Even if you worked all night and all day tomorrow, it wouldn't get finished." He looked at Brittany. "And that's not going to happen."

Anthony looked from Brittany to Matt. "You two talk, I forgot something." He ran for the front doors. "I'll be right back," he called over his shoulder, then he was gone.

The door swung shut behind him, and it was just her and Matt, facing each other, space between them, and the words that she'd practiced over and over again were caught in her throat.

"What's going on?" Matt asked, not coming any closer. "What's he up to?"

"I think he's very perceptive," she murmured.

"What did you tell him?" he asked abruptly.

"About what?"

"About you and me?"

"Nothing," she said, her face on fire. "I'd never tell him anything like that. Although, I think he suspects something."

"What does he suspect?" Matt asked in a low voice.

That I'm madly in love with you, that I never even knew what love was until now, she thought, but bit her lip hard. "That we...that you and I..."

"What?" he asked, and this time he came closer. "You and me. What about us?" he asked in a voice barely above a rough whisper.

He brought heat with him, that scent that was all his, a scent that seemed to seep into her soul. She couldn't look away from him, but she couldn't reach out and touch him, either. There was a barrier there, something that was between them, something from Matt. And the words of truth on her lips never came. "I don't know," she said truthfully.

He was closer still, then he touched her, his hand on her face, his fingers cupping her chin, keeping her head tilted so she had to look up at him. "Don't you?"

Matt stared down at B.J., not knowing who he hated more, her for being so damned desirable and giving such a false illusion of truth and vulnerability, or himself for still wanting her so much that he could barely focus on reality. Her skin was silk, her lips lusciously full and softly parted. Her fragrance permeated the air between and around them. God, he had tried to leave, to keep his distance, but he was failing as miserably at that as he was at remembering why he shouldn't be here.

"Mr. Terrel!" someone called out to him, shattering whatever insanity had been claiming him. He stared hard at B.J., at those green eyes that looked overly bright, then drew back, breaking the contact and falling into a world that felt bleak to him.

He turned and saw the security guard holding Anthony by the scruff of his jacket. "I found this kid out in the lobby rummaging through the desk drawers. He says he's with you."

Matt took a breath that helped to settle him, and refocus him. "Sorry to say, he is," he said as he went toward the boy and away from B.J.

"Okay, as long as things are okay with you." The guard touched the bill of his cap. "I got to get back to work. Have a good evening."

Matt looked down at Anthony. "The candies again?"

Anthony shrugged, not at all embarrassed at being caught red-handed. "I was hungry."

"That's what was so important that you had to leave?"

"Man, they're good. All creamy and some got chocolate on them."

"From now on, if you're hungry, ask me about food. Don't go and rip off some poor receptionist for her candies, okay?"

"Sure. Okay." He moved past Matt toward B.J. "So, you two talked?" he asked.

She shook her head as Matt went toward them. "Not really," she said in a low voice, then reached out and hugged Anthony tightly.

Matt kept walking, not looking at the embrace and called over his shoulder as he headed into the back hallway, "Come on, kid, we've got things to do, and food to find."

He heard the two of them whispering, then Anthony was running to catch up and was by him. "Okay, let's go," he said and took his hand again. He liked that. It made him feel connected at a time when B.J. was making him feel so unconnected.

They went out the security door and headed for his car. When they got to it, Anthony let go of him and touched the chrome handle. "This is yours?" he asked.

"For now."

Anthony let out a low whistle. "That's a cool car," he said. "I bet it goes fast."

"Fast enough," Matt murmured as he deactivated the security. "Get in."

Anthony opened the door and scrambled in as Matt went around and got behind the wheel. "Seat belts," Matt said as he sat there for a moment, just breathing, gripping the leather-covered steering wheel.

Anthony settled in the seat, then spoke to Matt. "So, do you like B.J. or not?"

Matt stared at the boy. "What's that all about?"

"Well, I was figuring, she likes you, I can tell, and you like her, I can tell, and I like both of you—"

"Whoa," Matt said. "Stop right there. This isn't a package deal, kid. B.J.'s got her life. I've got mine, and I'm trying to fix yours. That's as far as it goes. That's the first thing we need to concentrate on. That and feeding you and getting you some clothes for the party."

The boy looked at him intently, and Matt braced himself for the next volley of surprise questions that seemed to come out of his mouth on a regular basis. But instead he sat back in the leather seat and Matt could see that his feet didn't even touch the floor. "Clothes? What sort of clothes are we talking about here?"

Matt turned the car on and put it into gear. "Maybe a tuxedo."

"Oh, no way, man, no way!"

Matt smiled, and it felt good to finally be able to smile. "Okay, let's forget clothes for now and concentrate on food. What do you like?"

"What's tofu?"

The smile was gone. "What?"

"B.J. said that it's really good and that it's good for you."

Matt had to ease his grip on the steering wheel when his fingers clenched so tightly that he was sure he'd snap the wheel. "I've never had it," he said, then asked again, "What do you like to eat?"

"Pizza's cool, and hamburgers and stuff like that."

"A man after my own heart," he murmured and drove up the ramp and out onto the early-evening street.

"Do you like Christmas?" Anthony asked.

Matt remembered B.J.'s comments about his attitude about Christmas. "Not that much usually," he admitted. "When I was a kid, we didn't have much of a Christmas, and I never got in the habit of making much out of it."

"Yeah, me too," Anthony said in a low voice.

Matt looked at the boy and thought of B.J.'s words about the magic of Christmas, how that's what it was all about for her. He didn't know if that was a lie, too, but it hit him right then. Anthony had never known magic. Not many people did, and when they did, it didn't last. He was proof of that. "You know what, I think this year will be a good time to make something out of Christmas."

The boy looked at him. "You mean it?"

"Sure, why not? Both of us need it, don't we?"

"I got money, at least, you said you'd pay me. I can buy stuff."

"Yes, you can," he said and changed his plans. He turned the car at the next intersection, and headed toward the mall. He thought he'd seen the sign for a huge toy store. That's where they'd go. "Do you like trains?" he asked Anthony.

"I don't know. I never had one."

"Me neither," he said.

"Honest?"

"Honest. But we're going to change that," he said, and was thankful for something to think about besides those last moments with B.J.

December 23

"WELCOME TO LYNTECH," a gentleman in tie and tails said to Brittany as she stepped into the lobby just after eight that evening. "Reception is on the sixteenth floor, and sit-down dining is on the fifteenth floor." He took the embossed invitation that Amy had given her, then smiled. "Please, enjoy your visit to LynTech, the vision of the future, and a very Merry Christmas."

Brittany tried to smile, but her face felt tight. That sense of disconnection that had started when Matt had left with Anthony the night before was only deepening. She was used to this sort of gala, had been through a lot of them over the years. But right now, she felt awkward and strange.

She moved to one side near the Christmas tree when more people came in behind her, and she slipped off the fine lace shawl she was wearing over a shimmering silver sheath, letting an attendant take it to a makeshift cloakroom by the reception desk. She stood there for a long time, then turned and almost ran into Amy. "Oh, I'm so sorry," she gasped.

In an ice-blue, cocktail-length dress that had a diaphanous skirt and a slender bodice below an off-the-shoulder cowled collar, Amy looked almost ethereal. "My, oh my," she whispered, looking Brittany up and down. "You are stunning."

Brittany almost said that the dress was old and dated, but bit her lip. That sounded so...spoiled. And she *was* spoiled. She'd realized that over and over again since working here. What she took for granted was something that others only dreamed of. They saw a person like her as having everything. She almost laughed at that thought. She had so little right now. "I'm glad you like it," she said. "So, what do we do now?"

"The investors are being taken in small groups, and they'll be going through the center. I guess it's up to you and me to sell the program as a real asset to the company, something that makes the company more desirable for investors." She grimaced. "I hate this part of things, I really do."

Brittany had watched her father wine and dine people to benefit LynTech forever. "Tell them the truth," she said, echoing what her father always said. "But remember to smile."

Amy giggled softly. "Got it. I can do that. Truth. Smile. Okay. Are you coming in?"

All she wanted to do was find Matt and Anthony, see if they were here. Just see them. But she nodded, said "Lead the way," and started across the lobby to the back corridor with Amy.

But before she got to the open doors to the center, framed with gold Christmas wreaths and twinkling lights, Anthony was there, running toward her, calling out to her. "B.J.!"

She stopped and watched him in wonder. He'd had a haircut and was wearing a real tuxedo, with polished leather shoes and even a bow tie. "Oh my goodness," she said as he stopped in front of her. "Who are you? Do I know you?"

He grinned at her. "Ah, come on, you know it's me." He brushed a hand over the front of his outfit. "This is real weird, I know, but Matt said if I came I had to look like this, and this guy came, a tailor guy, and he got this for me. Matt, too. He's got a suit like this, too."

"Well, you look very, very handsome," she said.

"You look real cool, too." He looked at Amy beside her,

then grabbed Brittany's hand and pulled her down so he could whisper in her ear. "Is your dad named Mr. Lewis and he's sort of nice with white hair and he calls kids lads?"

"That sounds like him, but how do you know?"

He glanced nervously at Amy, then got even closer and whispered, "I know people aren't supposed to know about you being Brittany Lewis and all, but there's this guy upstairs talking to another guy that Rita was showing around, and he was asking her about you, about Brittany Lewis, and about seeing your office and finding you, and he says he's your dad."

The last time she'd talked to her dad, he was to be spending Christmas in Paris. But he was here? "Are you sure you heard right?"

"Yeah, and he was going to your office, at least that place they think you're supposed to be in."

Amy tapped her on the shoulder. "Listen, I need to get inside. Come on in as soon as you can." She smiled at Anthony. "Looking good," she said, then hurried down the corridor.

Brittany straightened, looked at Amy leaving, then back at Anthony. "Thanks for telling me," she said and started for the elevators, with Anthony right on her heels.

"Where're you going, B.J.?"

"To find my dad," she said and hit the Up button. She had a sudden need to find him. Maybe he could help her make sense out of her life.

The elevator doors slid open, a group of well-dressed people stepped out, then Brittany got in with Anthony shadowing her. "Then that's really your dad, huh? The one who made you get a job?"

"Well, he suggested it," she said as she hit the button for the floor her office was on. "And I didn't think he'd be here for Christmas. He told me he was too busy."

"He's mad at you or something?"

"Not right now," she sighed. But she wouldn't bank on that being the truth in a few minutes.

The elevator stopped, and when she got out, Anthony fell in step beside her, walking with her down the corridor toward her "office." The door was ajar, and she reached for it, pushing back the barrier, then stepped inside and her father was there by the desk.

There was another man there with him, in a tuxedo, with thick gray-streaked hair, tanned skin, and a full gray mustache. But all she saw was her dad. She hurried over to him. "You didn't tell me that you'd be here," she said, walking into his open arms and holding on to him for dear life.

"I got an offer I couldn't refuse and thought I'd surprise you." He held her back. "I guess this is a bit more of a surprise than I thought."

"Oh, Dad, I'm so glad you're here. So glad." She took a shaky breath. She felt very much like that little girl who used to awaken in the side room off her father's office, and then had gone searching for him through the building, thrilled when she finally found him. "I thought you didn't want to come back to LynTech?"

He smiled at her, brushing one hand across her flushed cheek. "I should have come sooner, I think, and I wanted to talk to Mr. Gallagher, too." He motioned to the man beside him. "Quint, this is my daughter, Brittany. Brittany, Quint Gallagher."

The other man held out his hand to her. "I've heard a lot about you," he said in a deep, rough voice touched by what might have been a Texas twang. As if he read her mind, he added with a crooked smile, "Not to worry, your dad only tells people the good things."

She looked back at her dad. "I can't believe you came after all."

''Well, I was talking to Matt and he actually asked me to be here for the reception. So, you owe him.'' He glanced behind her and nodded. ''And so do I. I need to thank you for that, Matt, and for what you've done for my daughter.''

She'd heard of the world stopping, of everything screeching to a halt in one horrible moment. And now she knew it was possible. Everything stopped. It was as if someone had hit a Pause button, and only she could move, think and feel. She turned and Matt was there.

Matt, staring at her. He knew. He knew. How long? God, she could feel something draining out of her, something leaving her oddly numb. It couldn't be life. That was far too dramatic for being caught in a lie with this man. But it felt that way. It left, and she was empty.

Then movement started and Matt was coming toward her in a full tuxedo, dark as night, with a silver-gray shirt and pearl studs. Matt, as huge as a mountain, his hair slicked back from his face. And his eyes. God, his eyes. Yes, he knew.

She tried to take a breath, to think, to form words, but he was talking, saying something to her, and she had to literally watch his lips move to figure out what he was saying.

''...and they're very impressed with the work. It's going to be perfect.'' His eyes were narrowed, and so unemotional. He seemed to be praising her...but he wasn't. But only she knew that as he said, ''She's very inventive, and has a great imagination.''

Her father looked from Matt to her, frowning slightly, as if he knew things weren't right, but was at a loss to know why, when the man was saying all the right things in such cold, clipped words. ''I knew Brittany would do well, once she got here,'' he said. ''Although I never figured that she'd end up on the creative end of the business.''

''Oh, she's very creative,'' Matt murmured.

Anthony chimed in. "She's done real good."

Her father looked at the boy who stood between her and Matt. "Thank you. I'm proud of her."

"She's cool," the boy said, then looked at Matt. "And she's real nice. Matt is, too. They got rid of Esther and everything."

"Esther?" her father said, looking at Matt questioningly.

Matt touched Anthony on the shoulder. "It's a long story, but Anthony's staying with me for a while."

Her dad smiled. "A boy should have a man around. I always wished that Brittany had had a mother around." His smile faltered. "It just never worked out."

"A lot of things don't work out the way we think they will." Matt tapped Anthony on his shoulder. "Are you coming or are you going to stay here with Miss Lewis and her father?"

The boy looked from one to the other and said, "Why don't all of us go and do stuff together?"

Matt never even glanced in Brittany's direction. "Sorry, she's got things to do here, and I've got to go. You hang where you want, and we'll meet up in the office later," he said, then looked at her father. "Sir, it was good to see you again, and Quint, we'll finish up later."

Gallagher nodded, taking the hand Matt offered in a brisk handshake. "Absolutely," he drawled.

Then Matt turned and left. Before Brittany even thought about it, she said, "Dad, I'll be right back," and went after him. She stepped out into the corridor and saw him striding away from her, and she half ran to catch up.

"Matt?"

He stopped by the elevators, turned to her and she was only vaguely aware of Anthony coming up behind her. "What?"

"Can...can we go someplace where we can talk?"

Matt shook his head, knowing that he couldn't be any closer to this woman and survive. He'd thought he could shut her out, go a whole day without seeing her, without looking into green eyes filled with lies or hearing that husky voice. But he'd been wrong. As long as she was anywhere around, he wasn't going to be able to keep himself together. "I don't have time for this."

"It's not what you think," she said quickly.

It was probably exactly what he thought. "Listen, you've had your fun. You've done your thing. You win the bet. Now run along and go back to Paris or wherever the hell you came from and have your laugh, then go hunting for another man."

Her expression tightened as she spoke. "I've got work to do here. I'm not going anywhere."

Matt felt sick right then, and when she came a few steps closer, he forced himself not to move. How could she look so hurt? So vulnerable? She played games. She did what she wanted, selfishly destroying people in the process. Oddly he felt sympathy for all those fiancés who must have fallen under her spell the way he had. "Well, I am," he muttered.

Anthony stepped between the two of them, looking from Matt to her, then back to Matt again. "You two stop."

Matt looked down at the boy, and he ached for the pain he saw there. "You're right, none of us need this."

"I want you two not to be mad at each other. You and B.J. are the only people I even like, and you hate each other."

He only wished he could hate her. If he had that luxury, he knew he could walk away and forget. But he didn't, and he wouldn't. "This isn't about you, buddy, not at all. It's about…" He looked right at B.J. "She'll explain it to you."

"She did and it's nothing, and you two can't go doing

stuff like this. You just let her tell you what happened, and it'll be okay."

Her face was stained with high color, and perversely it only made her look more delicate and desirable. "I don't have time for a story," he said hoarsely, then turned from her and walked to the elevators, hitting the Down button with so much force the light in it flickered for a moment before coming on. The doors opened and he stepped into a car, thankful it was empty. As he turned to reach for the button for the next floor down, B.J. was there, grabbing at the door to keep it open. Anthony ducked under her arm. "You're making B.J. sad and it's wrong and you're mean, and I…I…"

"Calm down. I'm not making her sad," he said, unable to look away from B.J. "She's mad, because she's the one who usually calls the shots. She's always the one who decides to run like hell when she gets bored, or wants a change of scenery…or a new challenge. Well, too bad. She's not doing it this time. I am."

She didn't say a thing as he stared at her, and a pain came to him that he'd never felt before. Betrayal was bitter on his tongue, and he was thankful when she slowly drew her hand back. The doors silently slid shut, sparing him the sight of her any longer.

Chapter Seventeen

"I'm Brittany Lewis and I'm sorry," Brittany whispered to the closed doors as the impact of what she'd done settled deeply into her soul. "I'm so sorry." She'd destroyed her own life with her cavalier charade and she ached from what she'd done to herself.

"B.J.?"

Anthony. She swallowed hard and swiped at her burning eyes. "I…I thought…" She tried to clear the lump in her throat. "Oh, shoot," she finally breathed.

"You and Matt, you talk to him, you tell him what you told me, and he'll believe you. I know he will."

She looked down into his brown eyes and the ache deepened. It wasn't just her she'd hurt. Not by a long shot. "I don't think—"

"No," he said abruptly. "No, you gotta talk to Matt. You and him. You two talk."

"Anthony, he won't talk to me," she said, her voice tight.

"He's gotta listen to you."

She crouched down in front of him, taking him by his hands and was unnerved to feel him trembling slightly. "Anthony, sweetheart, I'm so sorry. This is all my doing. It's all my fault. But Matt's mad and he's got every right to be mad. I thought I could do this, pretend that I wasn't who I was, then I thought I'd do a good job and he'd see how well I worked and how...I tried." She had to clear her throat when tears started burning behind her eyes. "I was wrong, so wrong, and I have to figure out what to do, but it won't affect you. I promise you that. Matt will still be there for you, and I'll be there for you, too. Always. I promise."

Anthony was very still. "You're lying and he's lying and you both are gonna just go and leave me."

"No, I promise I'm not going to go anywhere."

"You're lying, just like Matt thinks," he muttered, then twisted free of her hold and bolted down the hallway.

"Anthony!" she called as she ran after him. But he got to the stairwell door, opened it and without looking back, ducked out of view as the door slammed behind him. She got to the door, pushed it back, and went into the stairwell. "Anthony!" Her voice echoed back at her, but there was no other sound. "Anthony!"

She heard a door close in the distance, then nothing at all. "Oh, damn, damn," she breathed, and pressed back against the cold metal of the closed door. She'd tried, really tried. And she'd done it all wrong again. One more time. But this time, it was the last time. This time she'd lost everything.

One hour later

MATT STOOD IN HIS OFFICE looking at George, his neighbor from the loft, George in a full tuxedo with his long hair pulled sleekly back from his clean-shaven face. The only hint of the hippie within was the tie, a purple and blue tie-dyed bow tie at the man's throat. "I'd say you have more than a few shares in the company," Matt said to him.

The man looked a bit sheepish. "Sorry. I don't think of myself as a major investor."

He'd thought the man was an overaged, overgrown hippie, and here he was, with enough shares to be a force to reckon with on any vote. He was learning the hard way that people could be totally different than they appeared. "Well, you are."

"And I'm worried about Gallagher," George said.

Rita slipped into the office, almost unrecognizable from the efficient assistant who worked with him. She looked elegant, transformed in a deep-red sheath with the flash of diamonds at her ears. She crossed to him, glanced at George with a smile and murmured, "I'm sorry to interrupt," then looked at Matt. "I really need to talk to you, boss."

He nodded, then looked at George. "Gallagher is in the board room. Why don't you go and talk to him yourself?"

George rubbed his hands together. "A great idea. Great. I'll get back to you," he said and left.

Matt looked at Rita. "Okay, what is it?"

"Anthony, the boy, he told me to tell you that he's leaving and that he'll do okay, and you can keep the train."

Matt had thought nothing could be as awful as seeing B.J. again, but this felt like a fist in his gut. "Where is he?"

"He's down in the center, last I saw, in that back storage room putting stuff in a backpack. He was looking for food to take. What's going on?"

"That's what I'm going to find out," he said, already on his way to the door.

BRITTANY RUSHED through the people in the main room of the center, barely noticing Amy by the murals speaking to two formally dressed men. She didn't stop until she got into the back hall and to the last door before the security exit. It was partially open, and she pushed it back, the door striking the wall with the force. "Anthony!"

She stopped dead just inside the entrance of the room piled high with boxes and supplies. Matt was there, near the back wall, a backpack in his hands, and he turned as she burst into the room.

"Matt, what are you doing here?"

"The same as you, I guess. Anthony's leaving."

Her stomach knotted. "He's gone?"

"No, I don't think so, not yet." He held up the backpack. "He's been packing. He must have gone to get more food before taking off." He dropped the backpack on boxes to one side, and raked his fingers distractedly through his hair. He narrowed his eyes on her as if he couldn't bear to look at the world right then, let alone her. "Rita found me and told me that he'd said he was leaving and that he was down here. When did you see him last?"

Her heart sank. "Earlier, after you left. He was upset, and he ran off and I couldn't catch up with him."

"What?" He came closer, but didn't touch her. "Why did he run?"

"Because we were fighting and he was upset, and I told him it didn't matter what you thought of me, that you'd never walk away from him...and I wouldn't either." She turned from Matt, unable to look at him. "He said I was lying and he ran off. I thought he'd cool off and either go and find you or come back to see me."

"Damn it," Matt ground out and it made her flinch. "What an unholy mess this is, because you—"

"Me?" She spun around. "Me? It's you who wouldn't listen to me, or even let me explain anything."

"You're the one who lied all this time, who pretended to be some starving artist with principles who cared about an abused kid and who let me—" He cut off his own words, then shook his head and motioned sharply with both hands. "Your lies, your doing."

"And you being a pig-headed, opinionated, self-righteous jerk doesn't have a thing to do with any of this?"

"Forget it," he muttered. "I'm out of here."

But even as he said the words, the door behind them slammed shut with a resounding crack.

She turned and crossed to the door. She grabbed the knob, twisted it and tugged on it, but the door didn't open. It was either stuck or locked. She twisted the handle back and forth, muttering, "Oh, no, not now, not now," then Matt was right behind her.

She felt him brush against her back, and she twisted out of his way as he grabbed the knob himself. "What in the hell?" he muttered, pulling so hard that she saw the whole door shake. "It's locked."

"Then unlock it," she said.

"It's locked from the outside."

"How could it be?" she said, grabbing for the doorknob, but Matt reached it at the same time. His hand closed over hers, and she jerked back. The impact of his touch was searing, and she quickly put distance between them, moving back to give them some buffer of space.

He cast her a hard look, then turned and, balling his hand into a fist, he hit the door so hard that it shook. "Hello!" he yelled, then waited, staring at the door. "Hello!" Nothing happened.

"This is crazy," she said, backing up even more until she felt the cutting edge of some boxes at her back. "How can it just lock?"

"It can't," Matt muttered, turning from her. "Hell, I've got people waiting."

"My dad's going to wonder what happened to me," she murmured. "He came all this way."

"Don't worry, Daddy will forgive you for anything." He moved to one side and sat down on a stack of boxes. He looked at her, the harshness of the overhead lights exposing deeply etched lines bracketing his mouth. "I suspect that he already has forgiven you worse things than just standing him up."

She hugged her arms around herself. "You think he just goes, 'Oh, it's Brittany messing up again,' and it's okay?"

"Isn't that the way it is?"

She turned, crossing to a table stacked with office supplies and stared hard at bundles of crayons and pencils on top. "No, it's not. Whether you believe it or not, he's very demanding and he expects a lot from me. He always has."

"Poor Brittany."

She turned, looked at him, wondered where the heat had gone. It was freezing in the room. "No, it's more like 'Prove yourself, Brittany,' and me always trying to."

He crossed his arms on his chest. "I don't get it. You really care what he thinks?"

"Of course I care."

"Why?"

"I love him. He's my father."

"I don't care what my father thinks of me."

"If you love someone, you care. Period. I love him. I care. Is that simple enough for you?"

He studied her for a long moment. "Yes, it's simple enough for me. But that begs another question."

"And I'm sure you're going to ask it," she muttered as she moved back to the door and grabbed the cold knob again. It didn't give.

"If you care so much, how could you mess up your life so spectacularly?"

She jiggled the door futilely, but it was something to do so she could talk without having to think too much. "I was trying to find the right road. I kept going down the wrong road," she admitted as she rattled the door. Then she stopped and turned. "Any more questions?"

"The four fiancés were...wrong roads?"

"Three." Her face was on fire.

"What couldn't you figure out about them?"

She closed her eyes. "You wouldn't understand."

"Try me." He motioned around the store room. "I'm not going anywhere."

"No," she said, not about to expose herself any more to him. Not to this man. The man she'd made love with, the one she loved, was different than this Matt. She turned back to the door and pressed one hand against the cold wood.

She was startled when Matt spoke from right behind her. "No? Just like that?"

She closed her eyes tightly, hating that sense of heat at her back. It only made her feel more isolated and unanchored. "Can't you take no for an answer?"

"Usually," he whispered. "But not this time."

"Why?"

"I think I deserve to know what sort of company I'm in." She felt the air stir behind her. "So, tell me," he said, even closer now.

She kept her eyes closed. "I always wanted what my mother and father had, that sort of heart-stopping, earth-shaking, forever love. I kept thinking if I looked, I'd find it, somehow." She exhaled and opened her eyes, but didn't turn. "I always thought I would."

"You never found it?" he asked, his voice almost echoing in her now.

She laughed at that, but it was a miserable sound, more like a sob. "Just once," she whispered.

"Which one was he, number one, two...three? Which one?"

She took a breath, then made herself turn. Matt was right there, not more than a foot from her, and he seemed to fill the world around her. She noticed everything, from the way his hair swept back from his temples to a small scar that cut through his left eyebrow to the slight crookedness in his nose. So much to store away for later when there would be no Matt in her life.

"We…we need to get out of here and find Anthony," she breathed, her voice tight and low.

"We aren't going anywhere until someone lets us out."

She hated this, and would have moved away from him, except she'd definitely have to touch him in the process. She couldn't touch him again. Then moving was totally out of the question when Matt leaned toward her, his hands pressed to the door on either side of her.

"Matt, please."

"Who was he?" he persisted.

She looked at him, and breathing became almost impossible for her. "You didn't want explanations before. Why now?"

He leaned even closer, his voice growing lower and edged with roughness. "Because Anthony isn't the only one you're driving mad. Why didn't you just walk in here and say who you were and let it go at that?"

"I was going to. But…you ran into me."

"You ran into me."

"And you said things about me, about Brittany Lewis and you were so damn sure that I was a parasite and a brat and just riding on my father's coattails. You didn't know me then, and you don't know me now."

He was very still for a moment, then he moved back and that sense of being surrounded by him shattered. And she felt totally alone again. "I guess that's my point," he murmured as he turned from her and crossed to the boxes. "Never knowing you."

She bit her lip to stop the trembling there. He had "known" her in ways no man ever had, but he didn't even realize it. "You said I was talented and smart and…I forget all of the things on the list."

"So you win the damn bet—but the apology isn't going to happen," he ground out.

"I don't care about the bet." That seemed a lifetime ago. "As long as I was B.J., I was okay."

"It was all about you," he murmured as he undid his tie and tugged it free of his collar. "All about you."

It was all about him, every breath she took, every move she made. All about him. "Forget it," she breathed. "Just forget it." She turned from him, leaning toward the door, pressing her forehead against the smooth wood and closing her burning eyes as tightly as she could. She just wished she could imagine a life without him.

"Don't you get it? I can't forget it. If I could forget it, I'd be sleeping at night and not thinking about how to avoid running into you, and how to stay clear of that scent you wear, and how not to want to touch you." He was right behind her, not touching her, just being there as he whispered. "I can't."

She took a sharp breath, then spun around. "I'm sorry," she said. "I'm sorry. I'm sorry. I don't know what else to say. I regret it, I hate it, I wish I'd never started it. Tell me what to say and I'll say it," she sobbed.

There was silence, with only her own ragged breathing sounding in her own ears, until another voice startled her. "Tell him what you told me."

Anthony was speaking, and he was so close she could have sworn that he was right by Matt. "Anthony?"

"Just tell him," the boy said, and she looked to her right,

between stacked boxes, and saw the grate. Then she saw Anthony, close to it, watching them from the shadows.

Matt crouched in front of the grate. "Get out of there," he said.

"Can't. They fixed it so it don't open anymore," Anthony said, but didn't sound too bothered by that.

B.J. was by Matt, crouching beside him. "Anthony, what are you doing?"

He looked at Matt, then at B.J. "You tell Matt what you told me, that you really like him, and he's better than anyone, ever and that you don't hate him, and he's special and that…"

"No, Anthony," she said quickly. "Don't."

"You locked the door, didn't you?" Matt asked the boy.

"You two gotta talk. And you both wouldn't do it, and I thought you should, so I—"

"Anthony, you don't understand," Matt said.

"I understand. I really understand good. You liked her a lot, you really liked B.J., but then when her name wasn't B.J., she suddenly wasn't B.J., and she wasn't who you liked at all…just because she wasn't B.J. But she is B.J., and that's the truth."

Matt listened to the garbled ranting of the child, and whatever sanity had been eluding him since that moment in the lobby when he'd found out who Brittany Lewis really was came flooding back to him. From the mouths of babes. Raw, straight truth. He didn't know Brittany Lewis, but he did know B.J. He didn't like Brittany Lewis from what he'd heard about her, but he loved B.J. He loved B.J.'s eyes, B.J.'s chin and B.J.'s lips, that way she had of making life seem…magical. He'd fallen in love with B.J.

He turned, and B.J. was inches from him, those green eyes bright with the remnants of tears, and the truth was there. He loved her. Why had his feelings ever seemed confusing and crazy? Why had he been so damn self-righteous about her lying? It was so simple. He must have started to reach out to her, because she jerked back all of a sudden and stood. He stood too, and she pressed back against the stacked boxes behind her, as if to put as much distance as she could between them.

He loved her, but that was only half of his life. She held the other half in her hands. The hardest thing he'd ever done was not to touch her then, to keep his hands at his sides when she said, "Oh, Matt, I'm sorry."

"No, I'm sorry. I'm more sorry than you'll ever know. You're bright and talented and hard-working and kind and caring and beautiful, and Anthony's right. You're B.J. and I'm everything you said I am. A pig-headed, opinionated, self-righteous jerk."

"I'm sorry, I shouldn't have said that."

He moved then, cupping her chin with one hand, and ignoring the way she tried to move back from the contact. "Just tell me who the man is that you found that love with, the heart-stopping, earth-shaking, forever love?"

She twisted to one side, freeing herself, but he blocked any escape for her. The boxes were behind her, he was in front of her, and big enough to prevent her from doing anything. But all he wished he could do was make her tell him the truth. "Just tell me," he said.

She closed her eyes, then swiped at them, and looked right at him. "Okay, you asked. It's you. It's always been you, and I'm still Brittany Lewis, no matter what."

"I don't care if your real name's Brittany Lewis or Mother Goose. It won't change the fact that I love you."

She stared at him for what seemed an eternity, then she started to shake. "You...you love me?"

"Yes, and I'll call you whatever you want me to call you, as long as you love me."

The next thing he knew, she was in his arms, and they were both holding on for dear life. He thought he heard Anthony say a soft, "Yes!" but all he could really focus on was B.J. Holding on to her, feeling as if he'd just found a place in the world that was made just for him.

Then they were kissing and laughing and Anthony was there, with them, in their hug, all three of them holding on to each other. Matt closed his eyes tightly, almost afraid that this was a dream, that he'd wake up with Joey on his chest, licking him and purring.

But he knew it was real when B.J. kissed him quickly and smiled at him. "So, it's true?" he said, one arm around B.J., and one around Anthony.

"What's true?" she asked.

"There really is a love that's heart-stopping, earth-shaking and forever?"

"Absolutely forever," B.J. whispered.

Anthony smiled up at both of them. "Cool. Way cool."

December 30

"ARE YOU SURE about this?"

"Absolutely."

"I mean, you've got twenty-four hours, a lot of time to change your mind."

"That's not going to happen."

"You aren't going to disappear on me?"

"Never."

"If you want to wait, I'll understand."

"I won't understand. Tomorrow, an hour before midnight, here, you and me, Anthony, the justice of the peace. That's it. Unless you want a wedding at the chateau in France, with five hundred people you hardly know, six months from now?"

Brittany laughed softly in the shadows as she raised herself on one elbow and looked down at Matt. ''No, no, no,'' she murmured. ''Been there, done that, and it was all wrong. Very, very wrong. This is right.'' She looked at Matt, naked beside her as raindrops softly beat against the high windows. The only light in the bedroom of the refurbished warehouse loft was the shimmering glow that came from the streets below, slightly blurring his image. But that didn't stop the way her breath caught in her chest when she gazed at him. ''Tomorrow, just the four of us, you, me, Anthony and Dad...and the justice of the peace. Next year we'll have a party, a big party, if you want to. With Zane and Lindsey, and anyone else you can think to ask. Maybe even George. He likes a good party.''

He chuckled softly, and as his hand touched her bare skin, she trembled. ''Yes, George deserves a good party. If he and your father hadn't started talking about trains over dinner, your father never would have remembered that train he used to have, and George wouldn't have gone with your dad and Anthony to your house to find it. And, we wouldn't be here now.'' His hand found her breast, cupping it and she gasped softly. ''But we don't have much time.''

''They said they're going to stay there for the night.''

''Ah,'' he said. ''Yes, they did, but it's not good luck for the bride and groom to see each other after midnight, and I don't want to do anything to jinx this wedding. So, I figure that only gives us four hours.''

He pulled her back down to him, and she laughed softly against his skin. ''So, you believe in luck?''

''Maybe, definitely in magic.''

''The cynic is dead?''

''The cynic is happily in bed with the woman he loves, and isn't about to waste any of the next four hours. Then it's New Year's Eve, the wedding and the start of a life I could have never even imagined. You, Brittany Jayne Lewis, a nine-year-old hoodlum—'' She frowned and he amended that with, ''Okay, okay, I said that affectionately. A nine-year-old...wise child who thinks that life is just starting for him, too.''

''That's if Esther stays gone, and the courts let him stay with us.''

''I've been told they look favorably on an intact family unit, a man, a woman, a child.''

''Family unit, that sounds lovely, doesn't it? You and me and Anthony?''

''And your father. Robert really took to the kid, didn't he?''

''You weren't the only one who was a bit of a hoodlum when you were younger.''

His fingers brushed at her curls, then cupped the nape of her neck. ''No, don't tell me—Robert the criminal?''

''Well, he never went to jail, or took a car for a joyride when he was a kid, but in his misspent youth, he told me he threw a chair through a plate-glass window and got caught.''

Matt really laughed at that. ''Oh, he and Anthony definitely have a lot in common. Really incorrigible, both of them.''

''They understand each other, and I think Dad kind of likes the idea of a grandchild he can actually talk to.''

''And play trains with?''

''You got it.'' She spread her hand on his chest, splaying her fingers over his heart, and felt the beat, steady and sure. Just like the man himself. ''Four hours, huh?''

''Yes, and we shouldn't waste any of it.'' His touch was like fire on her as his hands skimmed along her arm, then found the swell of her hip. ''Not a minute of it,'' he whispered and suddenly she was on top of him, looking down at him again, straddling his hips. She could barely make out a smile when she felt his arousal against her. "We've wasted too damn much time," he murmured.

"Absolutely." She bent to kiss him, to taste him again, and when their lips met, passion was there with a speed that shook her.

There was no leisurely coming together, no waste of any time. Matt shifted her, slowly lowering her onto him, and he entered her, filling her. Sensations possessed her, exquisite pleasures that only grew with each movement between them. Movements that drew her higher and higher, until she flew into a place where there was no loneliness, no doubt, no hesitation. Just the two of them. Then the ending came, but it was just the beginning, too.

She tumbled into the linens with Matt, finding herself in his arms, the shards of pleasure slowly diminishing, but nothing diminished the joy in her. "Heart-stopping," she whispered against his skin.

His lips touched her forehead. "Definitely earth-shaking."

"Absolutely forever," she said, snuggling even closer to him.

"Love," he breathed. "And, as Anthony says, that's cool, way cool."

* * * * *

Look for

MILLIONAIRE'S CHRISTMAS MIRACLE,

as Mary Anne Wilson's

JUST FOR KIDS

continues in November 2001,
from Harlequin American Romance.

There's a baby on the way!

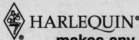

*H*ugh Blake, soon to become stepfather to the Maitland clan, has produced three high-performing offspring of his own. But at the rate they're going, they're never going to make him a grandpa!

There's *Suzanne*, a work-obsessed CEO whose Christmas spirit could use a little topping up....

And *Thomas*, a lawyer whose ability to hold on to the woman he loves is evaporating by the minute....

And *Diane*, a teacher so dedicated to her teenage students she hasn't noticed she's put her own life on hold.

But there's a Christmas wake-up call in store for the Blake siblings. Love *and* Christmas miracles are in store for all three!

Maitland Maternity Christmas

A collection from three of Harlequin's favorite authors

Muriel Jensen
Judy Christenberry
&Tina Leonard

Look for it in November 2001.